WHEN *Cardinals* APPEAR

KATIE EAGAN SCHENCK

Faery Whisper Press
Pasadena, MD

ISBN-979-8-9884803-6-5

Cover design by: Teresa at BookBrush

Printed in the United States of America.

Dedication

In loving memory of my grandmother, Marie McRorie.

Contents

Chapter One   1

Chapter Two   44

Chapter Three   76

Chapter Four   112

Chapter Five   152

Chapter Six   181

Chapter Seven   209

Chapter Eight   243

Chapter Nine   278

Chapter Ten   323

Chapter Eleven   361

Chapter Twelve   388

Chapter Thirteen   412

Chapter Fourteen   439

Chapter Fifteen   459

Epilogue   477

About the Author   486

Also By Katie Eagan Schenck   488

Acknowledgements   490

Chapter One

WHOEVER SAID YOU CAN'T go home again clearly never faced the arduous task of closing out their late mother's estate. I felt that in my bones as I entered my childhood home and shut the door behind me before collapsing against it with a groan.

There were no direct flights from Seattle, where I'd just completed my master's, to Baltimore. After braving two layovers, crowded airports, and what felt like the longest drive ever with a talkative taxi driver, I breathed a sigh of relief at the quiet stillness of the house. Returning to Cedar Haven was not my choice, but a part of me was glad to be home.

I left my suitcases by the door then shrugged out of my wool coat. Moonlight filtered in through the windows, but otherwise, the house was dark. Flicking on a light switch, I turned toward the living room. Little had changed since I'd left six months ago.

Well, that wasn't completely true. The hospital bed was gone and with it the IV pole that had supplied my mother with the sweet elixir of pain relief. Also missing was the annoying, repetitive beeping that kept time with her heartbeat. I shook my head. What I would have given to hear that obnoxious beep again. The noise and her labored breathing had at least provided proof that she still lived.

I squeezed my eyes shut, fighting to suppress the ache in my chest. It had been a hell of a year. When I took off the spring semester last year to help my mom after her diagnosis, I never thought I would be planning her funeral six months later.

I crossed the room to my mother's worn-out red couch, which contrasted nicely with the soft-pink cherry blossoms she and I had sponge painted on the wall behind it, a memory I would always treasure. The day of my parents' divorce, she insisted we needed to liven up the place. My father never would have let her paint something so "girly," as he would say, on the walls of a common area. In defiance, she'd roped me into helping her, and we'd spent a Sunday afternoon dripping paint all over the hardwood and laughing at ourselves.

The ache in my chest spread. She'd found a way to make a dark day bright but only after she'd extracted a promise from me. The promise was one I risked breaking by my mere presence in our house, in my hometown. But it was her fault I'd returned, so I supposed she couldn't hold it against me if my fulfillment of that promise was delayed.

Sinking down into the lumpy cushions, I let my eyes sweep the room. The flat-screen television my older brother, Steven, had insisted on installing hung on the opposite wall, gathering dust. Had he stopped by at all to check on the house? If he had, it didn't surprise me to find he hadn't done much cleaning. When we were growing up, he used to pay me part of his allowance to clean his room.

With a sigh, I pushed off the couch and headed to the kitchen. Picture frames dotted the walls, right where Mom had left them. Family portraits from before the divorce hung by the stairs, and framed collages of school pictures were on full display in the hall. As I moved deeper into the house, my annoyance grew as I realized how little Steven had bothered to do in my absence. A groan rumbled in my throat. Only then did it dawn on me what a monumental task I was undertaking as the personal representative of the estate.

My phone vibrated in my pocket—James had texted to make sure I arrived safely. *Should I text him back?* I hesitated before pushing the call button, needing to hear a familiar voice after a day surrounded by strangers.

James answered on the first ring. "Hey, honey. How was your trip?"

"Long and exhausting, but I'm here." I turned on the light in the kitchen. The oval oak table was covered with faded crayon marks, and the six cushioned chairs surrounding it featured a faded flower pattern.

"Is it weird to be back there?"

I rolled out one of the chairs and plopped down. "Yes and no. The quiet is almost unnatural, but it still *feels* like home." Mom's kitchen had always been simple, homey. A calendar from the year before was pegged to the wall beside a useless old phone, disconnected years ago. Mom insisted on keeping the misplaced relic in honor of bygone times.

"I get that. I wish I could have come with you."

"It's fine. You needed to get settled before you start your new job on Monday." I ground my teeth and winced at the ache in my jaw. It served me right for lying. He could have joined me. The "new job" was only a transfer from Seattle to Los Angeles, and they'd offered him a flexible start date in light of the move. He simply chose the earliest one.

The front door opened, and an unmistakable male voice bellowed, "Hello?"

"Listen, can I call you later? Steven's here, and we've got some things to discuss."

"Well, I've got a call with Germany at four tomorrow morning, so I need to get to bed soon."

"Okay." My heart sank, but there was no point in pressing the issue. Despite it being only six o'clock on the West Coast, I knew that any pushback would lead to an argument. "Call me when you get home."

"I'll do my best. Bye, babe. Love you."

"I love—" My phone beeped three times in my ear, indicating he'd already disconnected. I slammed my phone down onto the table. Once again, James failed to recognize how much I needed him. I didn't know why I expected anything different. I was used to it.

"Lanie?" Steven called. "Where are you?"

"In the kitchen."

I stood as Steven barreled in, dropped his briefcase, and engulfed me in a bear hug. "Man, am I glad to see you! How's it going, little sis?"

I extricated myself as delicately as possible from his vise grip, bristling at the nickname. "Don't call me that."

"I can't help it if you're both shorter and younger." Steven gave an impish grin. "Why didn't you call me from the airport? I could've given you a ride."

His hazel eyes, lighter than mine, held a note of suspicion, and I forced myself to focus on the changes in his appearance to hide my annoyance. We shared the same dirty-blond hair, though his was closely trimmed on the sides and longer on top. The one thing that hadn't changed was his height. He stood a good foot taller than me, something he inherited from our father, hence my annoying nickname.

"I'm sorry. I wasn't sure when you typically got off work." Although that wasn't technically the truth, I hoped to avoid trying to explain my desire to have a few minutes alone in Mom's house because I feared it would sound like I didn't want to see him.

"I'm the boss, so I can take off whenever I need to." He arched an eyebrow. "Dad was home, though, and he's retired. You could've asked him."

I nodded. My father and I had argued a lot recently, and the last thing I needed was a never-ending drive alone with him on which he could interrogate me about my life choices.

"Was the ceremony nice?" Steven asked.

The tension in my shoulders relaxed at the subject change. "It was okay. I didn't know any of the other graduates. But some of my friends came, and James."

"I'm sorry I couldn't be there. Setting up the office has taken all of my time and money."

"No worries." I turned away to hide my face. I understood why he and Dad hadn't come, but that didn't make it hurt any less. It might have helped alleviate some of the pain from Mom's absence to have the rest of my family there. But I didn't say that. Graduation was over a month ago, and I didn't want to argue. Besides, I hadn't come home for Christmas, so I supposed we were even.

I stepped over to the refrigerator and peered inside. It had recently been stocked with the bare necessities: milk, eggs, cheese, and coffee creamer. I smiled. While Steven hadn't bothered with the upkeep of the house, at least he'd had the forethought to buy some supplies.

After closing the refrigerator door, I turned back to him. "Have you opened yet?"

"Oh yeah. We took on a few small clients in November and had a grand opening right after New Year's." His face broke into a broad grin. "It was the biggest party Cedar Haven has seen in years."

"I'll bet." I struggled to keep the sarcasm out of my voice. My hometown wasn't exactly known for being party central. I checked the cabinets next. Mom's everyday plates were neatly stacked, and glasses shimmered in the kitchen light. From the looks of things, he hadn't started packing. I stifled a groan. Looked like I would have my work cut out for me in preparing the house for sale. Perhaps not starting my new job until May was a good thing. I was really out of my element and had no idea how long it would take to finalize the sale of the house and the rest of Mom's estate.

"I suppose congratulations are in order. How does it feel to have a master's degree?"

"Not much different, to be honest. I'm sure that'll change once I start teaching." I closed the cabinet door and faced him, leaning against the granite counter.

"Speaking of." Steven cleared his throat, and my stomach clenched. "Are you sure you want to live all the way out in California? Can't you find something here?"

I glared at him. "Been talking to Dad?"

Steven widened his eyes in faux innocence. "Why would you assume that?"

"Because he's been hounding me about moving home since I left." I rubbed my temples with my forefingers, hoping to stop the headache that was forming behind my eyes. "And as I'm sure he told you, I'm not coming back. James helped me find the perfect job. It's an entire school dedicated to children with special needs. We're going to find a place together."

"Okay, but your family is here." Steven crossed his arms over his chest. He resembled Dad when he did that. His forbidding posture and furrowed brow was totally a Max McAllister stance.

"Can we not talk about this right now?" *Or ever.* "I just got here." If I was being honest, I struggled with my own reasoning sometimes, which meant I would have an even harder time trying to articulate it to my family, who loved everything about Cedar Haven. My main aversion to moving home revolved around Mom's dreams for me to have a better life and the promise I'd made to her. But the house and the town also held too many memories. They were painful reminders of all I'd lost and people I would rather forget. If I stayed, the ghosts of my past would haunt me, and I wasn't sure I could live with that.

Steven's face softened. "I'm sorry. It's just... You know, Dad and I would love to have you home." He picked up his briefcase then opened it on the kitchen table. "Anyway, I wanted to drop off the paperwork for the house and Mom's will. You should be familiar with it, as it's the same stuff I emailed you a few months ago."

Oh no. My mouth went dry.

"There's also a docket sheet that includes court dates for probate," Steven continued, oblivious to my growing discomfort. "You'll need to attend those." He set out a separate stack. "I've already spoken to John over at Peak Realty, and he gave me the documentation for the house. We'll need to have it assessed, both for value and any necessary repairs."

Keeping my eyes on the documents, I tucked my hair behind my ears, my stomach squeezing. While I'd received his emails, I hadn't actually looked at anything he sent.

"I wish I understood why Mom made me executor," I said, trying to quell the growing panic. "You're the lawyer, after all. It makes more sense for you to handle her estate."

"I'm sure she had her reasons." Though his expression remained impassive, I detected a slight bitterness in his tone. He put a hand on my shoulder and gave me an awkward pat. "Like I said, this should all be familiar to you. All you need to do is sign." When I shifted my weight to my other foot, he finally seemed to notice my change in demeanor. "You did read the emails I sent, right?"

"Well..." I hedged.

His head fell back as he stared at the ceiling. "Seriously, Lanie? I sent everything to you back in August."

"I was busy with school."

"Your semester ended before Christmas." He shot me a pointed look. "Which means you've had almost a month without classes."

"I-I was packing." Even I could hear how flimsy the excuses sounded. I stared at the floor, avoiding his gaze. The truth was, every time I'd tried to open the attachments and review the information he'd sent, I'd become overwhelmed with grief, and I'd shut down my computer. I couldn't deal. Avoidance had become my new modus operandi.

With a sigh, he pinched the bridge of his nose. "I should have known something was up when you didn't ask any follow-up questions after confirming receipt of my emails. It's bad enough we postponed this while you were finishing grad school, but now you've given us a deadline of May." He shook his head. "Or really April to give you time to get back to the West Coast to settle in before your new job starts."

"I'm here now." My hands on my hips, I lifted my chin. "How long could it possibly take?" I hoped I sounded more confident than I felt. If the state of the house was any indication, it would take a lot of time and effort.

"There are court deadlines we need to meet." After riffling through the stacks on the table, he thrust a document at me. "This is the calendar of court dates. I set all of this up under the apparently incorrect assumption you were on top of things."

My chest tightened as I scanned the paper. He was right, but I sure as hell wasn't going to tell him that. "What about the house?" I waved a hand at the unpacked kitchen. "You didn't need me to clean or pack up all of Mom's stuff."

"I was a little preoccupied with setting up my law practice." Steven glowered at me, and I resisted the urge to shrink away from him. "And for your information, I cleared my calendar for Friday so we could start sorting Mom's things and prep the house for sale."

"Oh." My defiance deflated, and I hung my head. "I'm sorry."

"It is what it is." He glanced at his watch. "Listen, it's late, and I know you're tired. Why don't you get settled, and you can look these over this evening. We can meet at my office tomorrow morning around ten to go over it all. How does that sound?"

I blew out a breath. Some time alone was exactly what I needed. After traveling all day, I could use some downtime, though I had no idea how I would get through all that paperwork in a single night.

Steven gave me a quick hug before he left. As I stared at the documents, a sinking feeling hit my belly.

I'll feel better once I've unpacked and grabbed a bite to eat. I went to the front hall and gathered my suitcases before climbing the stairs to my old room. It was exactly as I had left it, with posters covering the walls, a netted hammock full of stuffed animals hanging in one corner, and my bookcases overflowing with all my favorite stories, including every book Jane Austen had ever written. Mom had planned to turn my room into a craft haven once I went off to college, but between my summer visits and then Mom's cancer diagnosis, things had changed.

Really, my insistence that Mom not overexert herself had put a pin in most of her plans. Melody McAllister was always a force to be reckoned with. Even as the cancer weakened her physically, mentally, she remained strong and determined. Maybe stubborn was a better descriptor. I smiled and shook my head, remembering how exasperated some of the nurses were when Mom insisted on doing things for herself despite how difficult those tasks were for her. But my smile faded as quickly as it had appeared. At the end of the day, all the determination in the world hadn't been enough to save Mom.

I set my suitcases on the bed and unpacked my clothes. Leaving grad school had been rather anticlimactic. Graduation wasn't the same without Mom there. It was a quieter affair than I'd expected. After taking the spring semester off to care for Mom, I'd had to catch up on my studies. My friends had all graduated in May, which meant very few people came to celebrate.

Mom had always been so proud of her children's accomplishments, and I could almost picture her in the crowd, cheering louder than anyone else.

Tears pricked behind my eyelids, and I blinked them back. I didn't have time to fall apart. First things first, I needed to fulfill my duties and settle Mom's estate. Maybe once I returned to the West Coast, I'd finally find time to grieve.

After setting up my toiletries in the bathroom, I yawned and stretched. The thought of sifting through legal documents drained what little energy I had left, but I needed to make up for the time I'd lost avoiding the task. If I didn't take care of it that night, Steven would kill me.

I went downstairs and grabbed one of the stacks and a snack before climbing upstairs to my room. As I read through the boring legalese, my eyelids drooped, and I lay back on the pillow to rest for a moment.

The sunlight streaming through the curtains woke me, and I blinked bleary eyes at my surroundings. *Where am I?* Instead of seeing the pristine walls of my Seattle bedroom, I found myself staring at demotivational posters my brother had given me as a joke when I was a teen. Each one depicted an inspirational scene such as a guy climbing a mountain at sunrise or a bear catching a fish, but underneath was a cynical quote or emoji. I loved them.

Rubbing my eyes, I tried to remember how I got there. Had I slept through the night?

Mom! I scrambled out of bed, sending papers flying, and rushed to the living room, only to find it empty and silent. The reality of what I'd lost crashed over me again, and I stumbled to the couch. *That* was why I couldn't stay there. If the promise to my mother wasn't enough to drive me away, the painful reminders alone would spur me to go. Even if I moved clear across town, I would never be able to move far enough away for the memories to dissipate. Seattle hadn't been far enough. California wouldn't be far enough, either, but at least it was a fresh start.

When I regained my composure, I returned to my room and gathered the papers I'd scattered in my panic. I took them to the kitchen, where the other stack still sat on the table, mocking me. I swore it grew overnight. The microwave clock said it was seven in the morning, which meant I had only three hours to sort through everything before I needed to leave to meet Steven at his office.

"Before I dive into this mess, I need coffee!" I set a mug in the Keurig, added a dark-roast pod, and pressed the start button. The air filled with the delicious aroma of roasted hazelnut. An unopened box of cherry toaster pastries was in the cabinet. Fortified with food and caffeine, I prepared to breach Paper Mountain.

After what seemed like hours, I finally finished signing the real estate forms and took a break to sip my lukewarm coffee. The kitchen had a large window on the back wall, which overlooked the small yard. Mom had kept bird feeders on the deck, and they had sat empty since she died. All the birds must have moved on to more plentiful homes.

As I gazed out at the quiet wintry morning, a spot of red caught my eye. I stood and walked toward the window, fascinated by such a bright color against the barren, snow-covered landscape. A little cardinal flitted around the railing of the deck. It was the only wildlife out that early, as even the squirrels seemed to be hibernating in their warm dens.

The cardinal stopped moving, and its small black eyes met mine. We gazed at each other for some time. Its vibrant red feathers reflected the first rays of the sun. Without thinking, I lifted my hand to open the window, startling the bird, and it flew away.

I shook my head and returned to the table. While I couldn't explain it, my steps were a little lighter, and I drank the rest of my coffee before rinsing the mug in the sink. I hadn't reviewed the will yet, but I'd run out of time. *Oh well.* If I didn't get through everything before I needed to leave, I would just go through it with Steven at his office. The important thing was getting the house on the market. Until it sold, we couldn't finalize the rest of the estate.

After one more glance out the window to see if the cardinal had returned, I went upstairs. I chose a dark-blue sweater and a pair of slacks—a respectable outfit for visiting a lawyer's office, even if said lawyer was my brother.

With great care, I put everything Steven had left into the respective folders, slid the folders into a bag, bundled up for the cold, and walked out to Mom's old car. As I approached, I wondered if it had been driven at all since I left for school. I climbed behind the wheel, dropped the bag in the passenger seat, and started the engine. The morning air was frigid, and my damp hair formed icicles as I waited for the car to warm. I cranked up the heat, knowing it probably wouldn't put a dent in the cold before I reached Steven's office.

I backed down the driveway and onto the small cul-de-sac that held my childhood home. Most people were heading to work, and I waved at a couple of neighbors. Old Cassandra Winters was out in her bathrobe and slippers, grabbing the paper. My heart rate kicked up its rhythm, and I swallowed then shook my head with a scoff. As children, Steven and I were convinced Ms. Winters was a witch. Mom often sent us over with baked goods, and her house always had an overpowering scent of sage. Ms. Winters had two cats, one gray and one black, who enjoyed swirling around our legs in an almost menacing manner, as if the cats wanted to trip us.

As I pulled onto Main Street, I saw the same quaint little shops and restaurants that had been there since I was young. Collins Hardware Store sat on the corner of Main Street and Chesapeake Way, though it looked like it had recently received a fresh coat of paint. Betty's Boutique Salon was already hopping with elderly women coming in for their weekly shampoos and sets. I sighed. When was Cedar Haven going to join the twenty-first century?

My car suddenly jolted and made a popping sound. *What the—?* I pulled over on the shoulder and got out. The driver's-side tire was flat. A quick glance behind me confirmed I had driven over a pothole.

Great. Just what I needed on my first day back in town. I reached into the car and grabbed my cell phone.

"Hey, Lanie, are you on your way?"

"I was," I hissed. "But I just hit a pothole, and I've got a flat."

Steven sighed. "All right. I'll call over to Sanders's Tire and Auto and get someone out there to help you. Shouldn't take long."

"Can't you come get me?" I pleaded, cursing myself for never learning how to change a tire.

"Sorry, sis. I'm swamped this morning." When I didn't respond, he hurried on. "But I can take you out for lunch to make up for it."

My stomach knotted. The last thing I wanted was a possible run-in with the owner of the auto shop, but I wasn't sure how I could avoid it. "Okay. Well, thanks for calling them for me."

"No problem. I'll see you soon."

"Bye." I mumbled and shoved my phone into my pocket. Mr. Sanders was a nice enough man, but having him fix my tire would be awkward. His son, Nate, and I were high school sweethearts, but we hadn't spoken since our awful breakup.

In retrospect, pledging to stay in a relationship before going away to college on the other side of the country had been a stupid move, but I was smitten with Nate and convinced we could survive the distance. Unfortunately, the distance was only one aspect of the odds against us. Between classes, new people, and the time zone difference, we barely made it through my first semester. When I came home for Christmas that year, we had a huge fight and broke up.

I couldn't recall what had caused the fight, but it didn't really matter. I was devastated. Since then, Nate and I had an unspoken agreement to avoid each other at all costs. When I came home last spring to care for my mom, I'd tried to be cordial the few times I saw him. But Nate wouldn't even look at me, which made no sense. He'd been the one to end things, after all, not the other way around.

The last time I saw him was at Mom's funeral, but he hadn't stuck around after the service. I caught only a glimpse of him as I followed the casket out of the church.

Knowing I had no other choice, I resigned myself to my fate and climbed back into the car. At least in a town so small, I shouldn't have a long wait. I figured it would be as good a time as any to look over the paperwork I hadn't gotten through.

I'd barely begun to review Mom's last will and testament when a loud rap on my window startled me. I looked up, and my stomach plummeted as I met a familiar set of dark-brown eyes. It was Nate, not his father, who'd come to rescue me. I tried not to notice the short length of the black hair I'd once loved to run my fingers through. Or the way his once-soft features had given way to a chiseled jawline.

His eyes widened, and his mouth dropped open. A plethora of emotions crossed his face before his full lips pressed in a grim line and his dark eyebrows knitted together. Was he really that upset to see me or just shocked that I was here? *Well, here goes nothing.*

I steeled myself for what I expected to be a most unhappy reunion. But hey, at least he couldn't avoid me. I opened the door and climbed out.

"Hey, Nate," I squeaked with an internal cringe. "It's, uh, been a while. How've you been?"

"Fine," Nate responded gruffly. He walked around the car, assessing the damage.

"How's your family?" Jeez, couldn't he throw me a bone? I was *trying* to be nice.

"Great. Do you have the spare?"

"Uh, sure, it should be in the trunk." So, he was going to be all business. Well, fine, then. Two could play that game. I walked around and opened the trunk for him before taking a step back and crossing my arms.

He pulled out the spare and inspected it. "It's flat too."

Ugh, seriously? My face warmed despite the bitter cold. It hadn't occurred to me to check anything in the car. Of course, I hadn't expected to end up with a flat tire either. The day was off to a spectacular start.

I struggled to maintain a cool and detached tone. "Sorry, this is my mom's old car. I'm not sure how much it's been used since I returned to Seattle in July... after she passed."

Nate finally raised his eyes to meet mine, and my attempt at indifference wavered when I saw how much they had softened with sympathy. A part of me preferred his gruff attitude. I hated pity.

He inclined his head toward the tow truck. "The truck's unlocked. Go get warm. I'll pull your car onto the bed and then take you to the shop."

I hesitated, thinking I should thank him or something. For what, I wasn't sure. Basic human kindness, perhaps? But Nate had already started moving the truck bed to an incline to load the car. Without another word, I grabbed my bags and climbed into the passenger seat of the tow truck.

The cab was nice and toasty, which was a godsend after being out in the frigid air.

I glanced out the back window to watch Nate's progress and couldn't help admiring how much he had grown into himself in the last six years. He appeared to have bulked up quite a bit, though it was hard to tell through his thick winter coat. As he bent down to attach the chain to the car, his hands worked quickly, the chain rattling as he moved. Did he do this often? I hadn't expected him to have taken a job with his father, as he'd always talked about becoming a veterinarian. Then again, he might not have had much choice in the matter. His father had hinted on more than one occasion that he wanted Nate to take over the business.

He came over to the controls and pulled the car up the incline. Then he raised the bed onto the truck. After securing all four tires with straps, he climbed into the cab beside me, and put the truck in gear.

The pregnant silence between us made the once-comforting warm air stifling. Should I try to talk to him again? It might relieve some of the tension, but Nate hadn't said much since his arrival. Perhaps since he was no longer focused on getting the car onto his truck, he would be a little more amenable.

"How long have you been working for your father?"

"I don't work *for* my father." His expression darkened.

Um, okay, then. That had seemed like a safe and innocent question but whatever. I gave up trying to be civil and leaned back against the seat, crossing my arms.

He glanced at me. "My dad retired. I own the business now."

"Oh, wow. That's great! When did that happen?" I latched onto anything to alleviate the awkwardness.

"About a month after your mom…" He cleared his throat. "He had a heart attack."

"I'm so sorry. I hadn't heard." I reached out to him, but the look on his face told me he wouldn't welcome my touch, so I dropped my hand. "Is he okay?"

"He's better." Nate shifted in his seat. "But between the heart attack and your mother's passing"—his voice cracked on the last word—"I guess he realized life's too short and decided it was time to retire."

I bit my lip and turned away, blinking back a surge of tears. The news was hardly surprising. Mom's death had shaken the whole town, not to mention my entire life. All my plans for moving to California directly after graduation had been obliterated the moment I'd learned she had cancer. I'd never intended to return after she died, but her inexplicable decision to name me executor had further altered my course.

Squeezing my eyes shut, I swallowed a sob, but a rogue tear still managed to slip through my herculean efforts not to cry. I swiped my hand over my face to dash it away but not before Nate saw.

"I'm sorry," he murmured. "She was a good woman."

I whipped my head around, raising my eyebrows. Nate and Mom had never gotten along. In fact, Mom was thrilled when I came home crying about the breakup. Ha, what an understatement. If I'd let her, Mom probably would have thrown a party.

Some of Mom's animosity was perhaps my fault. At one point, I had considered postponing college. At the very least, I proposed starting locally at the community college before heading off to my dream school, when Nate could join me. But Mom put her foot down, threatening not to pay for any of it if I didn't go. She didn't want me to wait for "some guy," as she so eloquently put it, to pursue my dreams. I knew she was still bitter about the divorce, but her angry objections to Nate always felt misplaced. He'd never done anything to warrant her dislike, but I'd always assumed he just reminded her too much of my dad. Or our relationship reminded her too much of theirs. My parents were also high school sweethearts, and Mom never quite forgave herself for graduating high school and jumping into marriage.

She said she wanted a better life for me, and she made me promise to move as far away from Cedar Haven as possible and never to settle. That was what she felt she had done. She'd given up some of her dreams when she married my father. They were so young, and it was natural that she worried I was making the same mistake. In the end, she won. She convinced me to go to Seattle, but I defied her in one way. I stubbornly stood by my commitment to Nate. And we saw how that worked out.

As if he'd sensed my thoughts, his cheeks reddened. "Your mother and I…" He cleared his throat. "We made our peace."

"You did?" I couldn't believe my ears. They talked? When? While I was away? I stared at him, the questions burning in my throat, but Nate simply nodded and didn't elaborate.

"Well, that's something, I guess," I said. "With everything that happened, I never would've expected you to forgive her."

Nate frowned but kept his eyes on the road. "I never held any ill will toward your mother."

"Just toward me, then?" I covered my mouth with my hand. "I'm sorry. That wasn't fair."

He shrugged in what I assumed was meant to be a nonchalant way, but it came off stiffly. "It is what it is."

He scratched his eyebrow, a familiar gesture that demonstrated his discomfort. I hid a smile. We once shared such a strong connection that I could almost read his mind, and a part of me was thrilled that I could still read him so well, even after all this time.

We pulled into the shop's parking lot. He backed the truck in front of one of the bays and hopped out. I waited in the cab for him to finish unloading the car, but I jumped when he opened my door.

"There's some stuff you need to sign." Nate nodded to the small office. "Your brother said you were heading to see him. I can take you when you're done."

I grabbed my things and went inside. Not much had changed since Nate had taken over the business. My family had been coming to Sanders's Tire and Auto for as long as I could remember, both out of loyalty and because they were the only mechanic shop in town. As I stepped into the building, I spotted a seating area with some old chairs and an ancient television that was only capable of playing four channels. On the other side of the small room was a desk with a computer, printer, and phone. A man I vaguely recognized was on a call as I approached, and he held up a finger, indicating he would be with me shortly.

While I waited, I replayed the short conversation Nate and I had on the drive over. He and my mother had resolved their differences. I couldn't get over that unexpected revelation. What I wouldn't give to have been a fly on that wall.

"Ma'am?" the man at the counter called out.

I smiled and stepped forward. "My car was just brought in. A blue Ford Focus."

"No problem. Have you been here before?" he asked as he typed into the computer. His graying hair fell onto his forehead, and he shoved it out of his eyes.

"Um, it's been a few years, but I might be in the system. Or it might be under my mother's name. I'm Lanie McAllister."

The man's head shot up, and his green eyes took me in as if seeing me for the first time. I took a wary step back. There were only two reasons why my name would be familiar to this man: either he knew my mom, or he knew my history with Nate. Neither was a welcome possibility.

"Melody's daughter?" he asked.

"That's me," I chirped with feigned enthusiasm.

"I was sorry to hear about her passing. Did you move back to town?"

"Oh no. I'm just here to finalize her estate."

He harrumphed but said nothing else. I bristled. The noise reminded me of my father, whose tick often indicated his disapproval.

Just as I opened my mouth to give him a piece of my mind, the whir of the printer sounded beside him. He marked a couple of places on the paper and slid it over. "If you'll initial here and here and then sign right here, we can get you a new tire."

I scanned the document and filled in the sections he indicated then shoved it back across the counter. The man didn't even blink as he checked to see that I'd filled it out correctly.

Nate walked in through the back door and glanced at the paper. "Thanks for checking her in, Sam." He raised his eyes. "Are you ready to go?"

I nodded, and he opened the door. As I walked toward him, Sam gave a low chuckle, which did nothing to improve my opinion of him. Perhaps he was more familiar with my and Nate's history than he let on.

Nate led the way, but I froze when I saw the car he was headed toward. It was a '69 black Camaro convertible, a car with which I was well acquainted. He opened the passenger door and turned but frowned when he didn't see me directly behind him. My expression must have betrayed my thoughts because he smiled for the first time since he'd picked me up.

"I can't believe you still have this car," I finally said as I strolled over to him.

"She's in mint condition," Nate confirmed, a hint of pride in his voice.

I grinned as I climbed in and set my bags on the floor, feeling like I was stepping back in time. I recalled many evenings with Nate, cruising down back roads and stopping to take in the sunset over the water. It made me wish for a simpler time, before a broken heart and Mom's death completely altered my life.

He slid in, a warm smile pulling on his lips. He had always loved that car, and the change in his mood was palpable. We pulled out onto the road, and I relished the vibration of the rumbling engine as he switched gears. Something about that moment felt more like coming home than anything I'd experienced since my plane landed.

Within a few minutes, we pulled up in front of an unfamiliar building with a sign outside that said McAllister and Associates. What? We'd already arrived? I bit my lip and tried to get control of myself. *Get a grip, Lanie.* The man was giving me a ride, not taking me on a date. I pulled the bag into my lap.

"Well, thanks for the ride." I turned toward Nate with a forced smile. "And the rescue."

"No problem." He nodded toward the bag. "What's all that?"

"My mother's life, essentially." I opened the bag and gestured to one pile. "This is to put her house on the market. The rest is her will and other related documents."

"How long will you be in town?"

"Not long, I hope!" I met his gaze and realized a moment too late I'd suffered from foot-in-mouth syndrome for the second time that morning. The warmth he'd had moments ago disappeared in an instant.

"I hope it all works out for you," he said, his voice hard and cold.

"Nate, I didn't mean—"

"I'll call you when the car is ready." He stared at the road, and I took that as my dismissal.

"Thanks." I snuck one last glance at him, but he refused to look at me. As soon as I climbed out and closed the door, he merged onto the highway, leaving me alone on the sidewalk.

"Welcome home, Lanie," I whispered to myself.

Chapter Two

I WAITED FOR MY brother to finish a phone call. For someone who owned a small-town firm, he had gone to extra lengths to make it feel both professional and comfortable. It wasn't stuffy like some other offices were, and I could tell he had put a lot of thought into choosing the furniture and decor.

From the comfortable reception area with four high-back armchairs to the small oval coffee table covered with various legal magazines, it was clear he'd aimed for a friendly, professional vibe. A window at the front of the room looked out over a recently plowed Main Street. The receptionist's desk sat along the opposite wall, and a petite young woman with dark-brown hair typed rapidly, her brows pulled together in concentration. Though he was just starting out with only his receptionist and a paralegal, he'd left options for expanding, including an empty office for another lawyer—perhaps a partner someday.

Steven's door opened, and he stepped forward, all decked out in a black suit and blue tie. Did he have court later that day, or did he always dress that way? Mom had certainly instilled that we should always dress for work as if we were headed to church in our Sunday best.

"I'm glad to see you made it in one piece," Steven said as he engulfed me in a hug.

"Both the tire and the spare were flat since no one's driven it in six months." I narrowed my eyes as I leaned away from him. "Nate had to tow it to the shop."

"Sorry about that." Steven rubbed his neck. "It never crossed my mind to drive the car."

"I gathered as much," I muttered. Despite my annoyance, I couldn't blame Steven. He wasn't mechanically inclined. Dad had once tried to show him how to change the oil. After Dad completed the demonstration, Steven asked how much it would cost to have someone else do it.

"Nate, huh?" Steven arched an eyebrow. "I didn't expect him to handle it himself." Shoving his hands into his pockets, he rocked back on his heels. "How did, uh, that go?"

I glared at him. My unexpected and uncomfortable reunion, on the other hand, was entirely his fault. "Fine. No thanks for the warning."

"Sorry, sis. I really thought he'd send someone else."

I couldn't stay mad at him, and I didn't want to talk about my ex. "Should we get started?"

To my relief, he took the hint and led the way, indicating a seat for me on the other side of his desk as he sank into his chair. His office was just as nicely decorated as the reception area. Shelves lined the back wall, bowing in the middle from the weight of the law books. Behind his desk, he'd hung his framed degrees.

I struggled sometimes to process just how much Steven had grown up. My memories of the annoying older brother who would pull my pigtails and play silly pranks on me was hard to reconcile with the man sitting before me. He not only owned a successful law practice but was also engaged to marry his college sweetheart, who had all too willingly moved back to Cedar Haven to start her life with him. I smiled at the photo of him and Rose on his desk.

"Did you have a chance to look over the paperwork?" Steven asked.

"Mostly. I finished the real estate documents, but I've barely started the rest." I handed him the completed pile.

After flipping through it to confirm I'd signed on all the requisite pages, he knocked the papers together on the desk and into a neat stack. I removed the will from my bag and held it out to him, but he shook his head.

"I have my own copy here." He tapped a different pile on his desk. "Did you have any questions about the sale of the house?"

I shrugged. "It all seemed pretty straightforward. I appreciate that you were able to do a comparison of recent sales in the area to have a ballpark of the price."

"I didn't do anything. John down at Peak Real Estate handled all of that." He waved his hand dismissively. "He said the market's perfect for selling, and he expects the house will go quick. But before I give him the paperwork, I wanted to talk to you about cleaning out all of Mom's things." He folded his hands on the desk. "Many of the items Mom felt were valuable are covered in the will, but certain personal effects—such as her clothes, pictures, and the like—are to be divided between us. I know you and Mom were the same size, so I have no objection if you want to go through her clothes and take whatever you want. I figure we can donate the rest."

"That sounds fair," I agreed, trying to ignore the lump that formed in my throat.

"There is one thing of value she didn't bequeath that I think we should discuss," Steven continued. "Her car."

"I assumed we would sell that too," I said.

"While you're here, I figured you'd use it to get around. And then you're welcome to keep it if you want, but we would have to go through the process of changing the title to you."

"I don't think I want to drive it all the way out to LA."

His eyebrows drew together, but he didn't address the elephant in the room. "For now, let's just put it on the back burner. We can discuss it when we're closer to finalizing the rest of the estate."

I nodded and swallowed. I appreciated that he didn't pressure me—Dad was doing enough of that for both of them—but I suspected my brother would push the issue sooner or later. I hoped I could delay it as long as possible.

"She bequeathed the furniture in the master bedroom, as well as your old furniture, to you," Steven said, looking over a highlighted copy of our mother's will. "But I know you're not settled yet. I didn't know if you wanted to keep any of it, and I was thinking if you didn't want it, we could hold an estate sale. If you do want it, we could get a storage unit while we wait for the house to sell." He gestured toward the door of his office. "You haven't seen it yet, but the bookshelves from the living room are in my paralegal's office."

My stomach churned, and I took a deep breath. Steven had had a significant amount of time to process everything and had clearly studied the will. While part of me appreciated that he'd already started moving his share of Mom's things, another part resented the time he'd had to do it. His efforts meant we would have less to do to prepare the house for sale. At the same time, I'd worked my butt off to finish school and attempt to piece my life back together, but I'd had to put that on hold to come back and settle Mom's estate. It wasn't fair.

"Lanie?" Steven asked, drawing me back to the present. "Are you still with me?"

"I'm sorry. This is just a lot to take in."

His hazel eyes softened. "I know, and I realize you just got here, but we need to get Mom's house on the market as soon as possible. It's the largest part of her estate, and we can't finalize everything until it's disposed of."

I winced at his wording. It sounded clinical and detached, as if he were discussing a piece of trash and not our childhood home. But I shouldn't judge him. That was just "Steven the Lawyer" talking, and I knew he didn't mean anything by it. He was compartmentalizing everything just like I had at school. Taking a deep breath and letting it out slowly, I picked up my copy of the will and nodded at him to continue. It was going to be a long morning.

⁂

"Well, that was productive," Steven said hours later as he stacked the paperwork neatly on his desk and stretched. "There are still some details I think we need to review, but for now, we're in a good place."

With a weary smile, I rubbed the crick out of the back of my neck. I'd spent most of the morning with my head bent toward the paperwork in my lap. We'd gone through the entire will, making notes of specific bequests Mom had made as well as more general things we would need to divide between the two of us. It hurt my heart to see Mom's entire life reduced to a stack of pages.

Steven checked his watch. "I promised you lunch, and it's about that time. Any preference?"

I shook my head, still too muddled to think coherently. He reached across the desk and held out his hand, which I gratefully accepted.

"The worst is over," he assured me as he gave my hand a squeeze. "Most of this is just a formality. The house should be the last stressful part. Closing out the estate in probate will be easy, since she had such a detailed will drawn up." With that, he stood and shrugged into his black wool coat.

I scrambled into my peacoat and followed him out to the parking lot. We climbed into his car and drove in silence. When we pulled up in front of Bea's Diner, I hid a smile. I'd only come a handful of times since high school, but I wasn't surprised

Steven had chosen it. We used to hang out there all the time, and he had even worked there briefly before heading off to college.

"This good?" Steven put the car in park and switched off the ignition.

"Perfect." We walked into the diner together. Unlike my childhood home, the diner was a place where I welcomed the familiarity. The old jukebox in one corner probably cost more in annual repairs than it was worth, but Bea refused to give it up. I couldn't blame her. It certainly added to the ambiance, and those old songs always comforted me whenever I needed them. After a bad test in high school or, later, when the nurse gave me more bad news about Mom's condition, I went there with a pocket full of quarters and played all my favorites, one after the other. Decorated in a fifties theme, the place had old records hanging on the wall, along with a plastic Elvis swaying his hips in time to the music.

Each booth had its own miniature jukebox so that diners could purchase songs from their seats.

After finding a booth, I began flipping through the songs. I almost always ordered the same thing, so I didn't see the point in perusing the menu.

"Any idea when Mom's car will be ready?" Steven asked as he looked over the options.

With my eyes still on the song selection, I shrugged. "They didn't give me an estimate."

"I can drop you off at the shop after we eat if you want." He smirked at me over his menu. "It might be less awkward than having Nate pick you up."

I glared at him but didn't respond. I hadn't given much thought to how I would retrieve the car, but having Steven drop me off appealed to me more than riding with Nate again. Maybe I would get lucky and pick up the car while he was on his lunch break. Then I could avoid him entirely.

"As I live and breathe," a familiar voice called out. "Lanie McAllister!" Bea rushed over to our table, her gray curls bobbing under her hairnet.

I stood to embrace her.

"Welcome home, girl."

"Thanks, Bea. It's so good to see you."

"You're done with school, ain't ya?"

"I am."

"Oh, I wish your dear mother could have seen it." Bea's blue eyes grew misty. "She was so proud of both you kids."

I swallowed around the lump in my throat and struggled to respond. Steven took one look at me and stood as well.

"What, no hug for me?" he teased, giving me a small smile of understanding as I mouthed my thanks behind Bea's back.

"I see you every day," Bea retorted, waving him away. "Doesn't that fiancée of yours know how to cook?"

"She does, but she's usually exhausted after her shift at the hospital," Steven countered. "You know what it's like being on your feet all day."

Bea pursed her lips and nodded before turning to me. "So, what can I get you? Whatever you want, it's on the house."

"Aw, you don't have to do that," I protested as I sat down. "Steven's buying."

"In that case," Bea said with a twinkle in her eyes. She chuckled and nudged Steven's shoulder. "I'm just messing with you."

We ordered burgers and fries, our usual staple. After Bea left to put in our orders, Steven leaned back and stared at me. I squirmed in my seat. *Here it comes.*

"What?" I asked more defensively than I intended.

"I know you don't want to talk about it, but I wish you would at least consider moving home. Couldn't James find a job out here?"

Like that would ever happen. With a sigh, I turned my attention once more to the songs, avoiding his eyes. "I don't want to argue."

"It doesn't have to be an argument," Steven countered, spreading his hands on the table. "I want to understand your reasoning."

"Why do you care so much?"

"Because you're my sister, and I love you. I missed you while you were away." He ran a hand through his hair. "Besides, Rose and I moved here because we thought it was the best place to start our family. Her parents have returned to South Korea to take care of their parents, and with Mom gone, you and Dad are the only family I have left."

"It's not like you'll never see or hear from me again. We can set up weekly calls and plan visits."

"No offense, Lanie, but if your behavior while you were at school is any indication, I don't trust you'll keep in touch." He raised an eyebrow in challenge.

Ouch. He doesn't trust me? My teeth worried my lower lip. Deep down, I knew he had a point, though he could have approached it with a slight degree of tact. Aside from confirming that I'd received emails or sending back text responses in five words or less, I hadn't maintained regular contact with anyone from home. I already dreaded the dressing-down I expected to receive from my friends when they learned I was back.

Folding his hands on the table, he leaned forward. "Look, I get that you don't want to talk about it, and I'm not here to pressure you. I'd just like to have a better understanding of why you have to move so far away. California is as close to moving out of the country as you could possibly get."

"Hawaii is farther," I joked, trying to lighten the mood. It didn't work. My attention returned to the mini jukebox as I debated my next words. "James isn't a small-town kind of guy, and he's from the West Coast, so he prefers to stay out there. And the job is the perfect start for where I want to go. It'll give me the resources and skills to make a difference for these kids." Neither was a lie, not technically. Maybe it was lying by omission, but did that really count?

"But don't you think you could make more of a difference to children who are struggling in underfunded special education programs here?"

I dropped my gaze and stared at the table. Of course I'd considered that. *Struggled* with it was more like it. The school where I would teach was one of the top special education academies in the country, and as such, it was expensive and difficult to get into. Parents desperate to find the best education for their children waited years to be accepted. That meant some of the children who needed help the most were unable to access it. But even if I wanted to move home, which I definitely did not for a multitude of reasons, I couldn't. Not without breaking the promise I made to Mom. Besides, I'd already run into one of those reasons that morning and hoped to avoid repeat performances of the encounter.

"Does this have anything to do with Nate?" Steven asked as if he could read my mind.

"It has more to do with James," I replied, then I raised my eyes to meet his, trying to gauge if he could see through my half-truths. Seeing Nate that morning had shaken me more than I was willing to admit, even to myself. "But honestly, it's just this town." I waved a hand toward the window. "There are so many memories. I don't think I could bear it." I gave a one-shoulder shrug. "Besides, you know Mom always wanted something more for me. She never wanted me to settle."

I'd never told anyone else about the promise I'd made, not even Steven. When I fell in love with Nate, I'd kept it a secret because I had every intention of breaking the promise. And then after he dumped me, it seemed I would keep it whether I wanted to or not. With Mom gone, it felt even more imperative that I honor my word.

"Are you engaged?"

I blinked at his bluntness but shook my head. "We've talked about marriage, but I think James wanted to wait until everything was settled here. He doesn't want to overwhelm me when I already have enough on my plate. But once things calm down, I expect he'll ask."

"And I assume you'll accept?" Steven cocked his head, studying me.

"Sure," I said, unable to pull any enthusiasm into my voice. I hoped Steven wouldn't notice. "Why wouldn't I? After all, James was there for me when Mom died, and we both know how much she loved him."

"I guess I expected you would be more excited about the prospect of getting engaged." A laugh bubbled out of his throat. "If Rose had had your lackluster attitude about it, I never would have proposed!" His smile faded, and he ran his hand through his hair. "Look, if California is where you want to be, you have my full support. I'll even try to help you convince Dad that it's the best move for you." He rolled his eyes. "Though we both know that's a losing battle. But just... promise me you're not doing this out of some misplaced obligation, to either James or Mom."

Our food arrived, and I silently thanked the server for her impeccable timing. I couldn't look him in the eye and make that vow, not when my last one haunted me like a shadow I couldn't shake. What I'd told Steven was true enough. Mom did love James, not so much for who he was but for what he represented—my ticket out of town to the life she wanted for me. The one I promised her I would live. And after spending so much of my relationship with Nate fighting with Mom, it had been nice to be with someone who earned Mom's approval, regardless of how I felt about it.

James had spent Mom's last weeks with me. He'd stayed for the funeral, then he left and went backpacking in Europe to celebrate finishing his degree. It strained our relationship, and for a while, I considered breaking it off. When he returned to Seattle in the fall, he convinced me to stay with him by helping me study for exams and taking care of necessities like grocery shopping and running errands. His support during my last semester had more than made up for his absence in the months prior, or at least, that was what I told myself.

My phone buzzed. I listened to the voice message, meeting Steven's questioning look across the table. "Just James checking in."

"No word on the car, then?"

"Apparently not," I replied. "But I don't mind going over there and waiting. I can't imagine it will take much longer."

"I'll drop you off when we're done here."

"I'd appreciate that. Is there anything else we need to do today?"

Steven shook his head. "I think at this point, we just need to start preparing the house."

"I can work on Mom's clothes this afternoon, and then maybe this weekend, we can figure out the furniture."

"I'll come by the day after tomorrow," Steven said. "If there are any items neither of us want, we'll need to get them appraised and hold an estate sale. I'd like to do that as soon as possible."

I nodded glumly. Once again, my brother's businesslike approach to Mom's possessions grated on my emotions. I knew he meant well and that his efforts to move things along were just part of the process, but it was difficult for me to follow his lead. Perhaps I was being sentimental, but I thought there should be more reverence for the life our mother had led. An estate sale was just a fancy name for a yard sale, and it lacked dignity.

Bea stopped by our table briefly to say goodbye, then Steven and I bundled up before heading out into the bleak January weather. I prayed I wouldn't run into Nate while I waited at the mechanic's shop. His father had often spent much of his day in the small office above the garage, completing paperwork, and I crossed my fingers and hoped that Nate spent most of his time there as well.

"I'll text you when I'm on my way over," Steven said as he pulled into the parking lot.

"Sounds good. Thanks for lunch and the ride."

"No problem. Good luck with Nate," he replied with a hint of humor in his eyes.

I jumped out of the car and slammed the door. My annoyance at Steven melted when I entered the waiting area and Sam was at the desk. Nate was nowhere to be seen.

"Ms. McAllister," Sam said, picking up a plastic envelope and pointing it in my direction. "I was about to call you. We found some issues with your car, and we're going to need to keep it a few days."

"A few days?" I squeaked. I winced, and my chest tightened. What was I going to do for transportation in the meantime? I cleared my throat. There had to be some mistake. "What else is wrong with it?"

The door opened, and a different man entered from the garage. He had blue eyes and short brown hair and looked like he hadn't shaved in a week. A flush crept up my neck as he gave me an appreciative once-over.

"This is Jeff." Sam gestured to the man. "He can tell you more."

"Why don't you follow me, and I can show you what I've found," Jeff said as he held the door.

"I'm not sure I'll understand what I'm looking at," I mumbled. A quick glance around confirmed Nate was not in the bays either. The tension in my shoulders eased.

"No worries. I'll explain it as I go."

For the next several minutes, Jeff walked me around the car as he described the myriad of problems he'd found. When Jeff finished, my head was swimming.

"How much will this cost?" I asked, my voice unsteady. The estate would reimburse me for the repairs, but I estimated how much money I had in my bank account to cover the cost up front and guessed I might be a few hundred or so short.

"I'm sure I can waive the cost of labor for an old friend," a deep voice said behind me.

I spun around. Nate's dark-brown eyes held a hint of amusement, and my lips quirked up slightly in return. Maybe he was in a better mood.

"I couldn't ask that of you," I protested.

"You didn't ask, and it's not for you," Nate replied. "It's my understanding the estate will pay for any repairs, and I don't think it's necessary to charge labor and a tow for something your mother had no control over."

"Th-Thank you," I stammered as my cheeks burned. Of course, he was doing that in deference to Mom. Nothing more. "I appreciate that."

Nate clapped a hand on Jeff's back. "Jeff has already ordered the parts, and we should have your car ready in a few days."

I nodded then shifted uneasily. Without the car, how was I going to get home? Nate seemed to sense my discomfort.

"Something wrong?" he asked.

"It's just—" I shook my head. It wasn't his problem. I would figure something out. "Never mind. It's nothing."

He rubbed a finger over his eyebrow as if trying to determine whether I was lying. I gave a weak smile I hoped was convincing, and he shrugged.

"We'll call you when it's ready."

I walked through the waiting room and out the door, my mind reeling. *Now what?* I pulled up Uber on my phone, knowing full well I would never get someone out to the tiny town. Sure enough, the app reported no drivers available in my area.

Spectacular. There was yet another reason I didn't want to stay in the tiny nowheresville of Cedar Haven. Who didn't have Uber these days? A longing for Seattle swept over me. I missed the city for so many reasons, but public transit and multiple rideshare apps were among my top five at the moment.

Scrolling through my old contacts, I debated calling my friends, but I dreaded it. I hadn't spoken to any of them in months. When I'd first returned to the West Coast, they checked in on me regularly, but people would leave only so many unanswered voicemails before they gave up.

Cursing my antisocial behavior, I swallowed as I dialed, leaning against the building for support. My first two calls went to voicemail. Kristin Donnovan was an old theatre chum, and Leslie Wilson was a fellow teacher. I left messages for both of them without much hope of a response anytime soon.

My next contact was Mom, and I quickly scrolled away as a ripple of pain spread through my chest. I also skipped Rose, since I knew my future sister-in-law was working.

Next up was Toccara Jenson. We'd been friends since elementary school, and my heart filled with hope. Last I'd heard, Toccara had started her own business, which meant she could choose her hours. Of all my friends, she might be my best shot.

"Lanie?" Toccara answered, and I winced at the incredulous tone.

"Hi, Toccara. How are you?"

A brief silence followed, and I could almost sense the judgment pouring through the phone.

"Um, I'm fine. It's been a while."

"I-I know," I stammered. "I'm sorry about that. Things with school—well, you know how it is."

"Sure," Toccara said, though she didn't sound very convinced. "So, what's up?"

"I wanted to tell you I'm back in town." I paced the sidewalk in front of the mechanic's shop. "I'm home to settle my mom's affairs. And, um..." *There's really no great way to do this.* "Unfortunately, I had a bit of an accident with my mom's car this morning. It's in the shop. I was wondering if you might be able to come pick me up."

Another heavy silence. I crossed my fingers as I waited. I wished I had been more responsive to my friends over the last six months. Then I wouldn't be in such an awkward predicament.

"I'd love to help you out, Lanie, but I'm a bit tied up at the moment."

I rested my back against the wall and slid down. The sidewalk was cold and a little damp. I took a deep breath and forced a cheery tone. "No worries. I understand. Maybe we can catch up while I'm home."

"I'd love that!" Toccara said, and my chest tightened at how sincere she sounded. Maybe she would find a way to forgive me for being a terrible friend.

"Great! Well, check your schedule and let me know when you're free."

"Will do. Welcome home, Lanie."

I ended the call. There was only one person left I felt comfortable calling. I dialed Trudy Jackson, but I didn't hold out much hope. Trudy was the only one of my friends who had taken the plunge and gotten married. I vaguely recalled receiving a birth announcement a few months ago.

"Lanie? Oh my goodness, girl, how are you?"

That was promising. "I'm home."

"You are? For good?"

"Uh, not exactly. I've got to take care of some things, like my mom's house, but probably for at least a couple of months. How are you?"

"I'm doing well. My little Davey is almost six months old now."

"Wow! I can't believe I haven't met him yet."

"You'll just have to come on by," Trudy said.

"About that..." I crossed my fingers again. "My mom's car is in the shop, and I'm kind of stranded. Any chance you might have a moment to come pick me up?"

"Girl, I wish I could, but Davey just went down for his nap, and I've got no one to watch him."

"Right." I closed my eyes as I realized I was stuck there for at least the foreseeable future.

"Wait, are you at Sanders's Auto?"

"Yeah, why?"

Trudy chuckled. "How awkward was that?"

"You have no idea," I murmured.

"I'm surprised Nate couldn't give you a ride home."

"I, uh, didn't ask him."

"Guess I can't blame you there." Trudy laughed. "Well, if you're still there in another hour or so, feel free to call me back. I can come after Davey wakes up."

Dear Lord, I hope I'm not here for that long. "Thanks, Trudy. I'd love to see you while I'm home."

"Definitely! You've gotta fill me in on what's been going on. Call me soon, okay?"

"Will do."

I pushed myself off the sidewalk. It was too cold to stay out there any longer, so I went into the waiting room. I texted Steven as a last-ditch effort, knowing full well he had a lot going on that afternoon. As expected, his response was less than encouraging.

Sam glanced up when I walked in but mercifully said nothing. I plopped into a chair, prepared to wait until Steven got off work or Trudy's son woke from his nap. My one saving grace was that Nate was nowhere in sight, though it would be hard to avoid him if I was stuck there for too long.

Chapter Three

About an hour into viewing a mind-numbing episode of one of those you-are-not-the-father shows, courtesy of the lack of channels on the ancient television in the waiting room, I watched a young woman enter with her son. I glanced up when they first came in but, when I saw it wasn't Steven, turned back to the endless drama on the screen.

Soon after they arrived, the waiting room erupted in chaos. The young mom struggled to respond to Sam's questions and simultaneously tried to console her son, who screeched and ran around the room.

I jumped up from my seat and approached the boy, but he scampered away, shaking his head and yelling incoherently. Without thinking, I kneeled on the floor and removed a toy from my purse. It was a small ball with a smiley face and rubbery hair sticking out of the top. When I worked with kids throughout my master's program, I'd learned to always keep an assortment of sensory toys with me. Meltdowns like that one were pretty common in my line of work.

I tossed the ball from hand to hand. The child continued to run in circles, screeching and pulling at his clothes, but when he got close to me, he turned and watched the ball.

Keeping my eyes on the ground, I rolled the ball to him. He picked it up and tugged at the hair then squeezed it. As he played with the toy, he stopped running around and quieted. He sat on the floor, rocking back and forth.

I softly hummed a simple melody, and the boy mimicked my tune. His mother shot me a grateful smile and finished her business with Sam. As I continued to hum quietly, the boy slowly stopped rocking, though his eyes never strayed from the toy. When his mother was done, she stepped over to us.

"You okay, buddy?"

The boy blinked at her but didn't respond. His mom went to take the toy away.

"He can keep it," I said quickly, keeping my voice low and soothing. "I always keep them on hand for my students."

"You're a teacher?" the woman asked.

"For special education," I said with a smile. "I'm familiar with these sorts of situations."

"Thank you for your help. My husband was supposed to be here by now, but I guess he got held up." A car pulled into a parking spot out front. "Ah, here he is now." She glanced back at Lanie. "Your students are lucky to have you." After she helped her son to stand, they left.

I stared after them, a strange heaviness filling my chest. My last semester hadn't involved any student teaching, and I missed working with my students. In Seattle, I'd found a position in an inner-city school. The children weren't as fortunate as the ones I would teach in LA. Somehow, I didn't think I would have the same opportunities for one-on-one interactions, and the thought caused a pang of regret.

"That was amazing." A familiar voice caused me to jump. I scrambled off the floor, brushing dirt from my pants.

"I-I didn't realize you were watching," I stammered, tucking my hair behind my ears. I supposed I was lucky he hadn't come out to the lobby sooner.

"I didn't want to interrupt." Nate moved closer. "How'd you know to do that?"

"It's what I went to school for." I gave what I hoped was a nonchalant shrug. "Though it's been a while since I worked with a child."

"You haven't lost your touch." His deep-brown eyes searched mine, and I shifted self-consciously. Seeming to realize he was staring, he cleared his throat and gestured to the waiting room. "But what are you still doing here?"

"Oh, um, I don't have a ride." When he didn't respond, I babbled to fill the silence. "I tried to find one, but no one was free."

"Why didn't you say so earlier?"

"I didn't want to bother you." I couldn't quite look him in the eye, fearing if I did, I would blurt out the truth. After putting my foot in my mouth twice that morning, I wasn't aiming for the third time being the charm.

He blew out a breath. "I can take you."

Just what I was trying to avoid. "Are you sure? I don't want to impose."

"It's no imposition. No sense in you sitting around here." He inclined his head to the office. "Let me grab my coat and wallet, and I'll meet you at the car." He left me standing in the lobby, debating whether I should make a quick run for it. Maybe I should take my chances in the bitter cold. Anything had to be better than another round of walking on eggshells with my ex.

But I knew I couldn't leave. Not only would it be rude, but it would also make things worse. I trudged out to the parking lot and leaned against his car to wait.

"It's unlocked," he called as he made his way toward me.

I blinked then rolled my eyes, grumbling under my breath about small-town trust.

Nate snorted. "Guess you forgot what that was like in Seattle."

I climbed into the car and buckled in. An uncomfortable silence settled between us as we left the parking lot. I vowed not to be the one to break it.

"I'm sorry," I blurted out a moment later when it became unbearable. I really needed to work on my resolve. "For being so flippant earlier about being back."

He shrugged. I waited for him to say more, but when he didn't, I glared out the window. *Great. He can't even accept my apology?* If that was what I could expect from him for the rest of the time I was at home, then I needed to make sure to hightail it back to the West Coast as soon as possible.

I stifled a sigh. Things used to be a lot easier. Our conversations once lasted for hours, but suddenly, we couldn't fill a ten-minute drive.

As soon as he'd parked in my driveway, I mumbled a quick thanks and jumped out, not even bothering to look at him. I raced to the door, hoping to put the whole awful experience behind me.

"Wait!" Nate cried out.

I stopped on the porch and spun around, bracing myself for whatever he was going to say.

He ran a hand through his hair. "Is this how it's going to be between us?"

Crossing my arms, I leaned back, assessing him. "I don't know. You tell me."

We stared at each other for a moment, and I resisted the urge to escape into the sanctuary of the house.

He pursed his lips and stepped forward. "I'm sorry about earlier too. I expect it's been overwhelming, coming back here."

"You don't know the half of it," I said, shuffling my feet. I took a deep breath, hoping a bit of honesty might help alleviate some of the iciness between us. "The truth is, I don't know how long I'll be back. We're putting the house on the market, and Steven talked about holding an estate sale." I pushed myself off the side of the house and placed a hand on the porch railing. "But it's not like I have anywhere to be right away. My job doesn't start until May."

His eyes widened. "You already have a job? Where?"

"I've accepted a position at a school in California."

A shadow crossed his face. "I guess you're a West Coast girl now."

"I don't know that I'd go that far." I forced a smile. "But I'm excited about it."

"Well, I hope it works out for you, then." He shoved his hands into his pockets and hunched his shoulders, essentially closing himself off to further conversation.

I took that as my cue. "I should go. I promised Steven I'd go through Mom's clothes today. Thanks for the ride." I started toward the door then turned back. "And for fixing the car."

"My pleasure."

Tears pricked behind my eyes, and I turned away before he could see them. I opened the door and slammed it behind me before collapsing against it.

The universe had a sick and twisted sense of humor. First, my mother chose me to be the executor of her estate, despite the fact that Steven was the oldest and a lawyer. Second, I had to leave the life she'd made me promise to live so I could go home and settle her affairs. Then, upon arriving home, I had not one but two uncomfortable run-ins with my ex-boyfriend, the man I'd thought I would spend the rest of my life with but who, instead, had broken my heart. And for reasons I didn't understand, he not only hated me but apparently could barely stand the sight of me.

I buried my face in my hands as I tried to stop the flow of tears that had started coursing down my cheeks. As if it weren't hard enough to come home. As if I weren't facing the awful task of sorting through my mother's life, in the house that held so many memories. *Nope.* Apparently, the universe needed to throw in constant reminders of the *other* reason I hated the town: Nate Sanders.

The sad thing was, I didn't even hate him. On the contrary, despite how things had ended, I'd tried to be cordial when I came back last spring. The few times I ran into him, he either changed course to avoid me or grunted his way through small talk, disappearing the moment someone else approached. Why he got to play the wounded party when *he* was the one who broke up with *me*, I would never know. But eventually, I gave up and avoided him right back. With my mother's car in his shop, however, that had ceased to be an option. We had to deal with each other, at least until he fixed the car.

Maybe I could avoid him in the meantime. I doubted I would be going anywhere for the next few days since I had so much to do at the house. And whenever the car was ready, I might be able to convince Steven to go get it. Or better still, Nate could just keep it. I could rent a car or beg, borrow, and steal rides. Whatever it took to avoid another awkward encounter.

After grabbing my phone, I scrolled through my contacts and clicked James's name, needing to vent to someone who might understand. But I stopped myself. He was in the middle of his workday and wouldn't appreciate an interruption. The last time I called him while he was working, we had a "discussion" that evening about his policy of not taking personal calls during office hours.

"Only call if it's a real emergency," he had said. "And even then, consider whether I'm the appropriate person to assist."

It sounded so clinical and detached, like he was reading straight from a dry employee manual. Since then, I'd avoided even texting him while he was at the office. I knew his job was important to him, but sometimes, I tired of playing second fiddle.

Pushing thoughts of Nate and James from my mind, I headed upstairs. I'd lost precious time sitting in the mechanic's shop, waiting for a ride. But as I stood in my mother's room, I struggled to decide which area to tackle first. Steven had made it clear we needed to get the house ready to sell as soon as possible. However, he was wedding planning with Rose that evening, which meant I was on my own for the night.

What I hadn't counted on, however, was how overwhelming the task was. It wasn't the amount of clothing I had to go through; it was more the memories each item conjured. A soft gray cardigan hung off the back of the chair in front of Mom's vanity. Toward the end of her life, Mom alternated between hot flashes and freezing, and the cardigan had been the easiest way to regulate her temperature because she could slip it off and on without assistance. My heart squeezed at the memory, and for a moment, I imagined her sitting in front of the mirror on one of her good days, wrapped up in the sweater's warmth as she brushed her thinning blond hair. The skin on her hand was so pale, I could count her veins.

With a sigh, I entered Mom's closet and removed armfuls of clothes before laying them gently on the queen-sized bed. There were warm cashmere sweaters in mostly pink and blue, soft blue jeans, and sparkly sequined dresses in an array of colors. I'd grabbed a few large plastic bags from the kitchen on my way up for the clothes I would donate, but it was agonizing to put any items into them.

I pressed a dark-green sweater to my face and breathed in deep, relishing Mom's faded scent of lavender and peonies. It was one of Mom's favorite pieces because it brought out the green in her hazel eyes. I could almost picture Mom standing in front of her full-length mirror, tugging her sweater into place as she dressed for work, her blond hair in curlers on her head. Steven and I might have inherited Mom's hair color, but our thick locks were a product of our father.

I closed my eyes as a tear slipped down my cheek. Though I knew I would never wear that sweater, I couldn't quite part with it. I set it onto the pile of clothes I would keep.

Next, I picked up a dark-blue button-down dress featuring a heart-shaped lace cutout at the chest. Mom had loved that dress so much, she bought two. The other one was green. I held it up to myself as I stepped to the mirror. I imagined Mom standing behind me, wearing the green one, the fabric hugging her soft curves. I shook my head, and the image dissipated. I decided to keep the green dress and donate the blue one. Each item that went into the bags was placed with a tender reverence.

When all the clothes were sorted, I surveyed my work. Two full bags were tied up and ready to go to the local church. Mom would want it that way. She'd always helped the less fortunate and would be happy to see so many of her treasured possessions going to people in need in the community. While I tried to take comfort in that knowledge, I still had to swallow a lump in my throat.

My stomach growled, and I checked my watch, surprised to find it had taken me about three hours to sort everything. I went to the kitchen and assembled a snack tray of crackers, cheese, and pepperoni with a glass of white wine. Food in hand, I slipped into the living room and sat on the worn red sofa.

As if on cue, the ringtone for James sounded, and I smiled. He must have just gotten off work. "Hey, babe, thanks for calling."

"Of course," James said. "How was your day?"

"Ugh, not great." I proceeded to tell him about my experience with the flat tire, omitting the part about my ex coming to the rescue. I couldn't say why I kept that information to myself. A few hours ago, I would have poured my heart out to my boyfriend, uncomfortable conversations included. Maybe I was too emotionally exhausted to hash all that out again. Or maybe a part of me feared James would be jealous or worried, though he'd never displayed possessive behavior before.

"I'm so sorry. That sounds like quite an ordeal. I can't believe your brother didn't bother with upkeep while you've been away."

"I know, right?" I sipped my wine, feeling vindicated. "But what's done is done. I spent the rest of the afternoon going through my mom's clothes."

"I bet that was hard," he said in a soothing tone.

"It certainly wasn't the most fun thing to do." I tried to sound nonchalant. Clearing my throat, I changed the subject. "How's your new job?"

"It's amazing! I was put on a team working on this huge campaign, and everyone's been very welcoming," James gushed. He told me how awesome the team was and how happy he was at the firm. I tried to ignore the pang in my chest. He sounded so happy and full of life; I couldn't help feeling a little jealous. Why couldn't I be with him, starting our lives together instead of stuck in Cedar Haven, trying and failing to outrun the past that threatened to catch up with me?

My phone beeped, and Steven's name flashed on the screen. A strange but familiar panic set into my bones.

"I'm sorry, James, but Steven's calling. I've gotta go."

"Oh, okay. Well, I hope tomorrow goes better for you. I'll call you soon. Love you."

"Love you too." I clicked over to answer Steven. "What's wrong?"

"Wrong? Nothing's wrong," Steven replied, bewilderment coloring his voice.

I exhaled and covered my face with my hand. Would I ever stop fearing the worst? "Sorry. I've become accustomed to bad news every time the phone rings."

"I get it," Steven said. "But everything's fine. I was calling to see how your day went."

"Pretty well. I managed to sort through all of Mom's clothes."

"That's great," Steven said, but something sounded off in his voice.

"What is it?" I asked.

A deafening silence came from the other end, and my heartbeat quickened. Was my first instinct right?

"Look, I need you to promise you'll hear me out before you get mad, okay?"

I frowned. "Why would I be mad?"

"I asked Nate to help us with the furniture," he exclaimed in a rush.

"What?" My mouth fell open. *What the—* "Why would you do that?"

"There's a lot of furniture to move around," he retorted. "I'd like to break down the beds and move as much downstairs as possible to avoid having people traipsing through the house, messing it up right as it goes on the market. I also thought they could help stage the furniture you and I are keeping for when people come to see the house."

"But wasn't there anyone else you could have asked?" I moaned.

"Nate's guys literally lift heavy things for a living. And they'll do it for a couple of beers and some pizza. It seemed the most obvious choice."

I stared at the ceiling. There was no denying he had a point. It would cost a fortune to hire movers, especially on such short notice. But I didn't want to see Nate again. The car was one thing, and I wasn't above begging Steven to deal with it. But this?

"I can't believe you asked him without clearing it with me first." I tried to sound strong, though my voice trembled.

"Come on. It's just for a few hours."

"No, Steven. Mom made me executor, and I think this task should fall to me." I hated myself for pulling rank, but there was no way I was going to spend another afternoon in uncomfortable silence with Nate Sanders.

"Fine." Steven sounded sullen. "Then what do you suggest?"

I considered my options. "I'll call around tomorrow and price-check movers. And I'll reach out to some of my old friends. Maybe they know someone."

"Well, while you're calling around, you need to find an appraiser as well for anything we want to sell in the estate sale."

"Okay," I said with a resigned sigh. "I can do that too." For what felt like the millionth time, I questioned Mom's decision to make me executor.

"I do have someone in mind, if you're interested. As an attorney, I do work with them often." Steven's tone had moved from sullen to sarcastic.

"Please send me their information," I said, trying to appease him.

He was silent for a moment, and I checked to make sure the line hadn't disconnected.

"I'm sorry I couldn't pick you up earlier. How much was the car?" Steven asked, and my shoulders relaxed at his friendlier tone.

"I don't know yet. They said since it hasn't been driven in months, there are a lot of repairs needed."

"Do you need transportation in the meantime? Rose might be able to drive you around."

"I'm not planning on going anywhere for a while," I said. "But I'll keep her in mind."

We chatted about the day, then Steven had to go. I pulled up an app on my phone and searched for local movers before bookmarking the various sites. I hoped I would be able to find an affordable moving company, but I wasn't above begging friends and neighbors. Anything to avoid spending more time with Nate.

The next day went by without incident. I continued to go through the house room by room. I also took a break to call the movers I'd reviewed the night before and get estimates. Steven's assessment of the expense was accurate, and I feared Nate might be our best shot after all. But I wasn't willing to admit defeat just yet.

I woke up early on Friday, ready to meet Steven to discuss the furniture. As I sat at the table, sipping my coffee, a flash of red caught my eye. A cardinal was perched on the back porch railing, looking in at me. Was it the same one I saw the morning after I'd arrived? I stood and took a few cautious steps toward the window, not wanting to scare it away. The cardinal cocked its head as if it wanted to speak. A smattering of black dots sat near its beak, like freckles, and its wing tips were tinged with black. Something about the bird's presence was soothing, and the tension that I'd carried in my shoulders for the past few months eased. The front door slammed, and I jumped.

"Hallooo?" Steven bellowed.

"In the kitchen!" I called. When I turned back to the window, the cardinal was gone.

"Morning, sis," Steven sang out as he entered the room. He'd already removed his coat and pushed the sleeves of his dark-blue sweater up his arms. "Are you ready for a busy day?"

I smiled and nodded. "Where would you like to start?"

Steven looked around the kitchen. "First, I'd love to have another cup of coffee." He grabbed a mug from the cabinet and made himself a cup before adding cream and sugar. I returned to my seat at the table, and he joined me.

"I've gotten through most of the rooms and have divided up the items but figured you'd want to take a look," I said.

"That sounds like a good place to start. Once we've sorted through the small items, we can clean the furniture and make some decisions."

"I wasn't sure if you and Rose would want any of Mom's dishes or cookware." I gestured to the pots hanging from the ceiling and the pale-white cabinets where the everyday dishes were stored. "She kept the china in the divorce, so there's that too."

Steven squinted through the doorway to the dining room at the cherrywood china cabinet where the light-blue plates were displayed. "We don't have much need for such a fancy set."

"Wedding china certainly seems to be a thing of the past," I agreed. We'd used it only for holidays and special occasions. "You don't think Dad would want it?"

Steven snorted. "What would Dad use it for? He barely even uses real dishes these days, preferring the wonders of paper plates."

I didn't respond. Guilt needled my stomach. I hadn't seen my father since arriving back in town. At least I had the excuse of not having transportation, and truth be told, I'd expected him to come by the house. Steven hadn't mentioned whether Dad would be by that day. My father had been surprisingly helpful for the last few months of Mom's life, and they had parted on good terms. So I thought he would want to pitch in with cleaning up the house. Still, the last awful conversation I had had with him echoed in my mind whenever I thought about seeing him again, and I didn't regret his absence. Seeing him again was bound to be awkward, but I couldn't put it off forever. He was the only parent I had left.

"Maybe you should take it," Steven said, interrupting my thoughts. "California is full of famous people. Who knows? Perhaps one day, you'll have Brad Pitt over for dinner, and you wouldn't want him eating off some run-of-the-mill dish set."

"Hmm, I'm not sure if it's good enough for him," I replied, matching his teasing tone. "What about the pots and pans?"

Steven stood and wandered over to the pans hanging from the ceiling. His eyes narrowed as he scrutinized their quality. I understood why. Mom had loved to cook and continued using the pans well beyond their natural life.

"Honestly, I think these should probably be tossed," Steven finally said after he completed his examination.

I forced myself to nod, though it hurt my heart to do so. While I couldn't hold on to everything of Mom's, somehow, throwing away items she had lovingly touched every day felt wrong. It was as if, little by little, the small remaining pieces of my mother were being chipped away until all that remained were intangible memories.

"We can try to donate them, of course," he hurried on, and I worked to keep my emotions in check.

"It can't hurt to try."

That decided, we finished our coffee and went through each room of the house. There were many things I had set aside for Steven or charity that he seemed to think were too worn. Towels that had begun to sport small holes from overuse, sheets that had faded to pale remembrances of their former brightly colored selves. I couldn't help seeing it all as some twisted, painful metaphor for how my once vibrant and energetic mother had slowly faded away.

The morning passed quickly as we took stock of everything. I had a clipboard to keep track of it all. Once we were finished sorting, we packed up the items bound for donation and loaded them into Steven's pickup. By the time we had dropped everything off at the church, it was lunchtime, and Steven offered to stop by Bea's Diner. I readily agreed. All that work had made me hungry.

We entered the diner, and as I scanned the room for an empty booth, my eyes met Nate's dark-brown ones, and my heart skipped a beat. I glanced away, searching in vain for somewhere else to sit, but the lunch rush was in full swing, and the only available seats were at the breakfast bar. Unfortunately, Steven had seen Nate as well and was already making his way over to his table. I recognized a couple of guys from the shop and noted, without enthusiasm, their table had two empty seats.

"Nate!" Steven called out in greeting. "How's it going?"

"Good. It's going good," Nate replied. He nodded at the vacant chairs. "Would you two like to join us?"

Steven took the seat across from Nate, which left me the seat next to him. I shot a glare at my brother, but it wasn't fair to assume Steven was seating us together on purpose. I knew him well enough to know how oblivious he could be in such situations. As a matter of fact, it had taken him months to notice Rose was interested in him and even longer before he worked up the courage to ask her out.

"How's the house preparation going?" Nate directed his question to Steven.

"Pretty well, actually," Steven replied with a glance at me. "I think we're making good progress." He turned to the other men. "Did you close the shop for lunch?"

"Nah, taking a break," Jeff said. "Nate's buying as a thank-you for agreeing to help with your mom's house."

"Uh, about that." Steven grimaced. "Lanie is looking into movers."

"Why?" Jeff stared at me. "We not good enough for you?"

Warmth crept up my neck. *Gee, thanks for throwing me under the bus, Steven.* "It's not that, but as executor of the estate, I just want to make sure I handle things correctly." I swallowed as I snuck a glance at Nate, wondering if he bought my half-truth. The frown on his face suggested he didn't.

"Why would us helping out not be the correct way to handle things?" Nate asked, a touch of anger in his tone.

I thought fast. Why, indeed? I couldn't very well tell him that he was the main reason behind the change in plans and that avoiding him was my new life goal.

"She's probably afraid old Sam here will drop some precious breakable," Jeff joked, slapping Sam on the back.

"You're the one who has butterfingers," Sam retorted. "Wasn't it you who kept dropping a wrench yesterday?"

I forced myself to laugh along with the rest of the group, relieved the other guys hadn't taken it personally. But Nate's eyes never left my face, and I knew he wasn't buying it.

"Well, if you change your mind, let us know," Nate said.

I shifted in my seat. "Thanks. I appreciate that."

Truthfully, I *did* appreciate their willingness to pitch in. Knowing I wasn't doing everything alone kept me from feeling overwhelmed. But considering how awkward Nate and I were around each other, I didn't want to put us through that again. And I would consider us lucky if we survived lunch without it morphing into an uncomfortable situation.

Fortunately, the conversation turned to other things, and I perused the menu in peace. I was conscious of Nate sneaking glances at me when he thought I wouldn't see, but I tried to ignore him. Even if I wanted to know what those glances might mean, and I definitely did not, I had too much on my plate as it was without overanalyzing them.

"Thinking of trying something different?" Nate asked in a low voice.

I started at the sound then shook my head. "I'd love to say yes, but I think I'm too much of a creature of habit."

"Me too," Nate agreed, sliding his menu to the middle of the table. "Tell me more about your new job. You said you start in May?"

I stared at him, wondering why he was so interested in talking to me all of a sudden. The other day, he could barely even look at me.

"I'm supposed to be there for orientation in May. They have year-round school, and I'll start teaching in June for the summer semester." I side-eyed Steven. He'd said he was on my side, but I still didn't want to rub his nose in the reminder that I was leaving soon.

"Does Steven not know?"

"No, he knows, but he and my father hoped I would reconsider and move home."

"But you don't want to?"

"I have a job lined up," I replied, evading the question. "I'd be unemployed for who knows how long if I stayed here."

Nate stared at his hands for a while, and I hoped that meant he would return to ignoring me. I rummaged in my purse for coins, hoping to steal away to select a new song on the jukebox.

"I understand you have a job waiting for you," he said, drawing me back into conversation. "But I did want to let you know the middle school is hiring a teacher for their special education department. Mrs. Carlisle is planning to retire at the end of this year, and they'd like to bring someone in beforehand to make it a smooth transition for the kids."

I bit my lip. "I appreciate you letting me know."

"But you're not interested?"

I shut my eyes as I debated my next words. How many more times was I going to have this conversation? And why did Nate, of all people, care? Shouldn't he be thrilled at the thought of never seeing me again?

"It's not that. It's just—" I pressed my hands against the table as if bracing myself, though for what, I wasn't sure. "This place doesn't feel like home to me anymore. Not without my mom. There are too many memories."

"They're not all bad memories, right?"

Was he serious? After how he treated me yesterday, I was convinced he didn't have any good memories of me whatsoever. I glanced at him. His question sounded genuine, even if I couldn't understand why.

"No, not all of them." I exhaled sharply. "Being back here, I find it hard sometimes to remember she's gone. At school, it was different. I was so far behind, most of my time was spent catching up. And she only visited the one time, so there wasn't much out there to trigger any memories. But being here, in her house, sometimes I wake up and rush down to the living room to check on her, only to remember she's gone." I bowed my head. "I don't know that I would ever fully let go of that feeling if I stayed."

To my surprise, he reached over and gently took my hand in his. I froze, unable to pull away. The warmth coursing through our hands was all too familiar. Did he feel it too? Before I could say anything, the server arrived to take our order, and I took advantage of the distraction to snatch my hand back.

What was that all about? I breathed in and out, willing my heart rate to slow. He was just trying to comfort me. It didn't mean anything. Besides, it *couldn't* mean anything because I was with James.

But when the server left and Nate raised his eyes to look at me, with that sweet smile that never failed to melt my heart, I started reevaluating everything I thought I knew about Nate Sanders.

Chapter Four

"THANKS FOR LUNCH," SAM said as Steven paid the bill.

"Anytime." Steven turned to me. "Ready to go?"

I nodded and jumped up, desperate to put some distance between Nate and me. I couldn't get over my reaction to him holding my hand. Flushed cheeks and a pounding heart? What was wrong with me?

Deep down, I dreaded the answer, and I shook my head, trying to clear it. Of course, I would always have a soft spot for him. He was my first love, but that was it. I was with James, and we were preparing to start our new lives in California as soon as the estate business was finished. Still, I wondered whether there was something more to the way Nate had looked at me during lunch. Maybe things weren't as settled between us as they should be.

"See you all later." Steven waved to Sam, Jeff, and Nate then gestured for me to lead the way.

My thoughts spun around in my head as I headed to Steven's car. The last thing I needed was to waltz down memory lane. But on the drive home, I couldn't stop thinking about Nate and how everything that had once seemed so right had gone so horribly wrong.

It was funny how I'd gone to school with him for years and saw him every day but never took any notice of him. Then one day, Nate and I were paired to perform a scene from *Romeo and Juliet*. At first, it was awkward. Despite having several classes together, I didn't really know him. We'd been assigned the death scene, though our teacher had shortened it so that we were alone on stage. During rehearsal, we'd practiced both our lines and the actual dying part, but neither of us were comfortable practicing the farewell kisses Romeo and Juliet impart to each other before they die.

When it became clear we were running out of time, I broached the issue with Nate one day during rehearsal. To say he was uncomfortable with the topic was an understatement. I suggested that for Romeo's death, he could just kiss my cheek, and that for Juliet, I could turn from the audience and kiss near his mouth but not on it. Nobody would be able to tell the difference.

It sounded so simple in my head, but I hadn't allowed myself to consider the emotion involved, specifically my emotions. Because during those rehearsals, I'd gotten to know him more than I had during all our intervening years at school. And the more I knew, the more I liked until I was mortified to realize I had a full-fledged crush on my scene partner.

During our final rehearsal, I'd worked up the courage to give him a real kiss. We were alone in the auditorium, and I hesitated a beat after I said my line. His eyes fluttered open as he frowned at me, but he must have seen something in my face because he swallowed. And then... he nodded as if he knew exactly what I'd planned. What I'd intended to be a quick peck on the lips morphed into something much more meaningful as he lifted his hand and slid his fingers into my hair.

Things changed quickly after that. Our rehearsals had caused us both to become interested in acting, so we tried out for the spring play. He got the lead while I won a supporting role. That allowed us to spend most days together after school, and soon, we were inseparable.

Everything wasn't all hearts and flowers, though. Being in high school came with its own sources of drama. Nate had a jealous side, which sometimes clashed with my outgoing personality. But I was committed to Nate. We worked through our differences, convinced we could survive anything.

Even when my mother began to interfere, we held on to that belief. Mom's negative comments started innocently enough. A jibe here about Nate's future prospects, implying Nate couldn't afford to attend college. A snide remark there about being stuck in a small town. Then her comments became more blatant, especially after I made the mistake of telling her I might delay going away to college. I'd been accepted at my dream school in Seattle, but I didn't want to leave Nate. She not only reminded me of the promise I'd made to her, but she also began to criticize my relationship more openly.

Unfortunately, her attempts to break us up backfired. At first, I vacillated between ignoring her comments and defending Nate, but those tactics just led to further arguments. Finally, I got so fed up with her, I moved in with my dad for my last semester of high school, a choice I later regretted.

When I left for college, I thought everything was good between Nate and me. But the calls and texts became more sporadic as the months dragged on. I started suspecting he'd found someone else, and when we broke up over winter break, I demanded he tell me who it was. He swore there was no one else, that we'd just drifted apart. I could never quite bring myself to believe him.

As far as first loves went, I considered myself incredibly lucky, despite the way things ended. Nate had always been a man of few words, but what he did say was thoughtful. Though it took me a long time to break him out of his shell, the end result was worth it for the short time we were together.

"You're awfully quiet," Steven said as he pulled in front of the house.

I blinked as I was jolted back to the present. "Sorry, I was just thinking."

"I'm guessing being back has brought up a lot of old memories for you."

"You could say that again," I murmured as I climbed out of the car then unlocked the front door.

I went up to my room, needing a moment alone with my thoughts. The house was starting to feel emptier, and I didn't want to admit how painful that was. I wasn't sure if I would ever be ready to say goodbye to it, even if I didn't intend to return to Cedar Haven.

A knock sounded at my door, and I called out that it was open. Steven came in and sat down on my bed. He frowned as he looked around the room. It was the one place in the house that hadn't been touched, though I knew I would need to start packing soon.

"Have you scheduled the movers yet?"

I shook my head. "I called a few yesterday, but I was hoping to call a few more next week."

Steven's lips pressed together. "The appraiser I work with is available next week. I'd like to get everything moved once he's evaluated what we plan to sell so we can put the house on the market."

I gave an absent nod. That was good news, even if it didn't feel like it. Each step brought us closer to selling the house and finalizing the estate, which meant I could return to my real life.

"I invited Rose over for dinner tonight," Steven continued when I didn't respond. "I thought you might enjoy the company."

That caught my attention, and I gave him a warm smile. "It's been so long since I've seen her."

"She's missed you," Steven said. "I've got some stuff to take care of, but we'll be back in a little bit. Anything you need while I'm gone?"

I shook my head. Steven gave me a quick hug and left. Moments later, a car door slammed. I breathed a deep sigh of relief at being alone at last.

Climbing off my bed, I decided to wander into Mom's room. I pulled the cardigan off the vanity chair and slid my arms into it, relishing the faded scent of lavender and peonies. After so many busy days, I hadn't managed to get over my jet lag. I lay down on Mom's bed and curled into a ball, promising myself I would close my eyes for only a few minutes.

⁓

The front door crashed open, startling me awake. I stared around the darkened room, disoriented. When did I fall asleep? The faint scent of lavender touched my nose.

"Mom?" I whispered. Of course, there was no response. I rubbed my eyes, wishing I could remember my dream.

"Lanie!" Rose sang out from downstairs. "Where are you?"

"I'll be right down," I croaked, and I cleared my throat, which was thick with sleep. I turned on a light and stared at myself in the mirror, smoothing my dirty-blond hair before I went to greet my brother and future sister-in-law.

"It's been too long," Rose declared as she threw her arms around me.

I bit my lip, guilt sinking in my stomach like a brick. I'd meant to call Rose. But then, I'd meant to call everyone back home. I could blame it on my thesis, but as that wasn't the whole story, I kept silent.

The warm scent of jasmine filled my nostrils as we embraced. Rose had been a godsend during those last few months of caring for Mom. A nurse herself, Rose had managed to coordinate home care to give me periods of respite, and at my request, she translated the medical jargon the oncologist used.

As we stepped back from each other, Rose grasped my hands and gave a sympathetic smile. Her thick black hair fell in sheets on either side of her face, and her dark-brown eyes were hooded with long lashes.

"Rose, it's so good to see you. How have you been?"

"Busy!" Rose shrugged out of her coat before handing it to Steven. "I've been doing a lot of the wedding planning on my own while this one"—she nudged Steven with her elbow—"has been dealing with everything here."

"Well, the house will be on the market soon, and then I'll be all yours," Steven exclaimed, throwing his arm around his fiancée. "Though I thought my only job was to show up and say 'I do.'"

Rose rolled her eyes. "Men."

The doorbell rang, and Steven released Rose and went to answer it. I led the way to the kitchen and began setting the table with plates.

"How's it been, being home?" Rose asked as she got out glasses.

"It's been... difficult." I turned and leaned against the counter. "Did Steven tell you we had lunch with my ex today?"

"He did," Rose replied, her tone hesitant. "But he also said he thought it went well."

Before I could respond, Steven came into the kitchen, carrying multiple boxes. He set them on the table and opened every box. There were two pizzas, breadsticks, and chicken wings.

"Why did you order so much?" I asked. "It's just the three of us."

"There might be one more," Steven said cryptically.

"You didn't!" I cried out. Had he invited Nate for *dinner* too? I didn't think I could handle another awkward meal with him.

The front door opened, followed by heavy footsteps coming down the hall. Something about the sound was familiar, but I couldn't quite place it. I didn't have to wait long, however, before Max McAllister himself entered the room.

My father had always been a forbidding presence, earning the nickname *The Intimidator* from a few of his work buddies who were also avid NASCAR fans. He stood six foot four with broad shoulders and strong arms. Beyond his imposing physique, his bushy black eyebrows seemed to be permanently fixed into a grimace, so even when he smiled, he never quite gave off a happy disposition.

"Hey, Dad." Steven clapped our father on the back. "Glad you could make it."

Dad grunted in response as his brown eyes met mine. His expression darkened, but he allowed Steven to usher him to the table. Neither of us spoke to the other, but the tension between us was palpable.

How long till he brings up California? I snuck another glance at Dad's face. Based on his expression, I would bet about five minutes.

"Lanie, why don't you sit here?" Rose directed me to a seat away from Dad. I shot her a look of gratitude. While there was no avoiding him, I would take all the distance I could get.

Everyone took their seats and filled their plates. The room was silent save the rustling of boxes being moved or a chair scraping against the floor. My heart pounded painfully against my rib cage as the scent of pizza turned my stomach. I couldn't believe Steven had invited Dad to dinner without telling me. As if I hadn't had enough uncomfortable encounters for one day.

"So, what's the plan?" Rose asked.

"I've been calling around to movers, but so far, they're all either too expensive or not available," I began. "But Steven found an appraiser who can be here next week."

"You're going to pay for movers?" Dad frowned. "I'm sure the good people of Cedar Haven would be willing to pitch in."

"I already asked Nate if he and some of his guys could help." Steven shot a pointed look at me. "But *someone* didn't want to go that route."

Rose elbowed Steven, but Dad's frown only deepened, if that was possible. I bit back a sigh as I picked at my food.

"I don't know that Nate would have been my first choice either," Dad said.

My head shot up. As far as I was aware, only Mom had issues with Nate. Dad had never been anything but kind to my ex.

"Regardless of who we use, we need to get someone in soon," Steven said. "If we're going to have an estate sale, we should do that within the next month so we can get the house cleared out and on the market."

"What happens if some of Mom's things don't sell?" I asked.

"Whatever doesn't sell, we can donate," Steven said as he picked up a chicken wing. "We simply need to keep track of everything for closing out the probate case."

"Just let me know when the sale is and what time you want me." Dad lifted another slice of pizza onto his plate.

"You're coming?" Since he hadn't been by once while I'd been home, I figured he hadn't planned on getting involved.

"Steven asked me to help." Dad shrugged.

"We need the manpower," Steven said. "We don't want anyone slipping out without paying for things, and that will give you and me leave to help customers."

Steven and Rose finished their food and began clearing the table while my father and I lingered. For a while, we glowered at each other in silence, neither wanting to be the first to break it and thus admit defeat. Finally, Dad blew out a long breath.

"Why haven't you been by to see me?" His conversational tone had an unmistakable edge to it.

"Well, I don't have a car right now, for one."

"You couldn't find a ride?"

"There's nothing stopping you from coming here." I took a deep breath, willing myself to remain civil to avoid an argument. "But I'm glad you were able to come over tonight."

Dad harrumphed. "Good thing I did. Otherwise, I might not have seen you at all."

"I'm home for at least another month or so, Dad," I chided. "That's more than enough time for several visits." Rose turned from the sink and gave me a thumbs-up. At least my future sister-in-law understood what I was trying to accomplish.

"You could make more of an effort."

I bristled. *Seriously?* "I flew three thousand miles to be here. Is it too much to ask that you close the distance by driving a few?"

"I could," Dad said. "But I wasn't sure what welcome to expect."

"I don't know what to tell you. It didn't seem like you wanted to hear from me after our last call."

Dad shook his head. "You're the one who hung up on me."

With good reason. I glared at him. "Only after you called me a huge disappointment."

"You're twisting my words," Dad retorted, his eyes flashing. "I meant *your decision* was a disappointment."

Unbelievable! "Oh, really? Because that's not what I remember," I shot back, my hands shaking.

Dad sipped his soda. "Perhaps I was too harsh with you, but I think you're making a mistake."

And here we go. To my father's credit, he'd lasted much longer than I'd anticipated. Maybe he was mellowing out in his old age. Unfortunately, it wasn't enough to avoid the argument entirely.

"So you've said, on multiple occasions." I crossed my arms over my chest.

"And if you'd listen to me, maybe I wouldn't feel the need to reiterate my point."

I shoved back from the table. "I don't want to hear it!"

Dad stood and held up his hands, which might be viewed as a sign of surrender, but I knew better. "We need to talk about this."

"There's nothing more to say. You don't want me to move to California, and I don't want to move back here. We're at an impasse!"

"You're running away."

Heat crept up my neck as I worked to keep my temper in check. "I'm not running away from anything. I'm progressing, moving toward something. Why can't you see that?"

"What's in California that's so much better than here? Cedar Haven is full of people who love you and want the best for you." He tapped his hand on the table. "This is your home."

"No, Dad, it *was* my home. Soon, it'll belong to some stranger. We've been over this. My home is on the West Coast, where James and a new job are waiting for me. Why can't you understand that?"

He took a deep breath and shook his head. "What would your mother say?"

"She'd probably cheer me on," I practically shouted, throwing my arms up. "She never wanted me to settle." I opened my mouth to tell him about the promise she'd forced me to make, but then I thought better of it. He would find a way to twist that as well. "And who do you think you are, trying to speak for Mom? You didn't even know her at the end."

Dad recoiled as if I'd slapped him, and I regretted my words. I wasn't being fair, and I knew it, but I'd long tired of having the same stupid argument. While my parents had been divorced for some time when Mom got sick, they had reconciled their friendship before she died. He had helped with transporting her to doctors' appointments and visited her often during her last months.

Steven stepped forward as if to break Dad and me apart, but Rose put her hand on his shoulder. Her eyes met mine with an unspoken warning. Closing my eyes, I counted down from ten. When I was sure I wouldn't lash out again, I looked at my father.

"I'm sorry," I said, my shoulders hunched forward. "I shouldn't have said that. Can we please drop this? I'm building my life in California, with James. Once we've settled Mom's estate, I'm going, and nothing you do or say is going to convince me otherwise."

I stared at him, daring him to keep pushing the issue. He blinked first, and the tightness in my chest eased. I'd won the battle, but the war was far from over.

"At least I know you got one thing from me," Dad said with a wry smile. "My stubbornness."

I laughed, mostly in shock. "Are you sure? Mom could be pretty stubborn too."

"So what you're saying is you got a double dose?" Steven asked with a smirk. He and Rose had come back to the table once the storm had passed.

"All right," Dad conceded. "I'll let it go for tonight, but we're not done having this conversation."

"We never are, Dad," I grumbled as I left the kitchen, seeking the sanctuary of my room. I could hear Dad and Steven hashing out details for the next week, and I needed a moment to decompress.

Sometimes, it bothered me that my dad and I weren't closer, particularly once he was the only parent I had left. But arguments like the one that night reinforced the reason our relationship was strained. He had a very narrow way of viewing the world, and he didn't like for that view to be challenged. By opting to move to the other side of the country, I was directly challenging it. To him, Cedar Haven was the only place worth living in. That wasn't to say he didn't enjoy traveling, but he always said the wonderful thing about traveling was going home at the end. He had expected that once I finished my "travels" at college, I would happily return. My refusal to do so had been a thorn in his side for months, and despite sticking to my guns, I'd yet to make any headway in convincing him to let it go.

Dad left soon after dinner, and I went back downstairs. Rose spent the rest of the evening gushing over her wedding plans and asking for my opinion on everything from the flowers to the food. I welcomed the distraction from all the talk of estate sales and probate court. Before they left, Rose invited me out for drinks the next night, and I readily agreed. Not having a car was starting to get to me.

⁓

The next day passed without incident. I begrudgingly started packing up my room. Or at least, I tried to. In truth, I spent more time flipping through old yearbooks or diaries I unearthed than actually packing, but it was the thought that counted. As evening fell, I prepared for a night out with Rose. I spent more time than I had in a while curling my blond locks and staring at myself in the mirror. Sometimes, I struggled to reconcile the changes I saw from the person I was before Mom got sick with the one currently reflected back to me. I'd never been a high-maintenance person, but I used to put more thought and effort into my appearance. While caring for Mom, I was too tired to bother. I always pulled my hair back into a messy bun to keep it out of my face, and I never bothered with makeup. It was strange, almost luxurious, to be sitting in front of the mirror, pampering myself.

At the same time, my skin prickled like I had something more pressing to do. It was a familiar feeling, one that had never fully gone away even after Mom died. Perhaps it would fade with time. Or perhaps the sense of foreboding, that perpetual waiting for the other shoe to drop, was something that would remain with me for the rest of my life.

As I finished applying lip gloss, the doorbell rang. I slid the makeup back into the drawer of the vanity and went to greet Rose. When I opened the door, I stumbled back at the sight of not only my future sister-in-law but a gaggle of my high school friends as well.

"Surprise!" they all cried out, their arms thrown open and their smiles wide.

"What the—" I gasped. "What are you all doing here?"

"I thought you could use a girls' night!" Rose exclaimed. "Steven helped me reach out to some old pals. They wanted to see you."

I surveyed the group, noting they were all dressed to the nines. My hand nervously smoothed the simple black dress I had picked out. Was I underdressed? But there weren't any upscale restaurants or bars in the tiny town of Cedar Haven. Definitely nothing resembling a night club.

"Well?" Rose pressed, her voice tinged with impatience. "What are you waiting for? Grab your coat and let's go!" That was followed by a chorus of agreement from the rest of the girls. I laughed and did as instructed.

An unfamiliar minivan sat in the driveway, and as I climbed in, I stifled another laugh at the haphazard attempt to clean up crumbs. Trudy was the only one of my friends who was married and had a kid. I recalled Trudy had said her son—Davey, was it?—had just turned six months old.

Leslie Wilson climbed in beside me as Trudy and Rose took over the front seat. Kristin Donnovan and Toccara Jenson were already buckling up in the back row. When I turned to look at them, they gave hesitant smiles.

"It's good to see you," Toccara said, the overhead light from the car highlighting her dark curls. Her deep-crimson coat brought out the reddish undertones in her complexion.

"Seriously, Lanie, it's been ages!" Kristin piped up beside her. Her rich black braids fell forward as she leaned closer. "How long are you home?"

"Not long, I'm afraid," I said. "Just long enough to settle my mom's affairs."

"Where will you go once that's done?" Leslie asked, her blue eyes curious as she turned and joined the conversation.

"I have a job waiting for me in California."

"And a boyfriend as well!" Rose quipped from the front seat. Her sleek black hair was pulled back into a low bun and secured with two sticks.

"Are you still with that guy from school?" Trudy asked as she turned the key in the ignition. Her hooded brown eyes met mine in the rearview.

"Yes, I'm still with James. We're getting a place together in LA," I said, smoothing my hair. In the meantime, James was crashing with some friends. He'd promised to wait until after I returned from Cedar Haven to look for a place.

"He was at your mom's funeral, wasn't he?" Kristin asked.

I nodded, swallowing around the sudden lump in my throat. With a shake of my head, I dispelled the memory. Not tonight. My friends had rallied to take me out and show me a good time, and I refused to let sad thoughts intrude on our fun.

"We'll just have to make the most of the time we have with you." Toccara's wide smile was warm, but it didn't quite touch her eyes. Guilt needled in my belly, knowing how terrible I had been at keeping in touch with my friends. They'd stopped by when I was home caring for Mom, usually with groceries or takeout. I'd lost count of how many casseroles Trudy had made. But I couldn't bring myself to answer their calls while at school. Compartmentalizing was the only way I'd been able to cope.

"I'm sorry I've been MIA this last year," I said. "But I'm sure I'll be back to visit."

"She'll be here for the wedding," Rose insisted, her small dark eyes sparkling as her cheeks brightened.

The car filled with oohs and aahs as we traveled along the dark highway out of town. I squinted out the window, searching for any hint of where we were going. Giving up, I refocused on the conversation occurring around me.

"When's the big day?" Trudy asked.

"September. It's usually a slower time for me at the clinic, and we'll be back from our honeymoon right before flu season." Rose's contagious laugh filled the car, prompting everyone else to join in.

Trudy slowed the car and turned onto a side road, causing me to peer curiously out the window. I still didn't recognize what little I could see of the scenery in the darkness.

"Where are we going?" I finally asked, trying to keep the apprehension from my voice.

The girls all exchanged conspiratorial glances. When no one volunteered any information, I racked my brain, trying to think of long-forgotten places I'd heard of in the surrounding area. Suddenly, the dark road gave way to the brilliant lights of a city, and I recognized where we were.

"We're going to the National Harbor?" I asked. Of all the possibilities, that wasn't one I'd considered. It was like a mini DC but without the long drive and expensive parking.

"They have quite a few nightclubs," Leslie explained with another conspiratorial look around the car. "We thought you should understand what you'll be leaving behind once you move out west."

"They've really built it up since I was last here," I murmured. The city seemed entirely out of place, caught between the river and the quiet suburbs, like the Emerald City at the end of the yellow brick road.

Trudy pulled into a parking garage, and we all filed out of her minivan. Toccara and Leslie linked arms with me, pulling me toward the sidewalk, as the rest of the girls filled in behind us. I was grateful for the pressure on my arms, as it allowed me to take everything in without worrying about tripping on a dip in the sidewalk.

I'd been there once or twice before when it was first built. The Gaylord Hotel had an ice show every year around Christmastime, and my parents had taken Steven and me before they split up. We had also gone ice skating and spent some time shopping around the town.

The group headed in the direction of Bobby McKey's, a dueling-piano bar, and I relaxed for the first time that evening. Seattle had a similar piano bar my friends and I enjoyed visiting. I smiled as the promise of an evening filled with laughter, drinks, and music lifted my spirits.

When we entered the bar, I blinked upon seeing they'd reserved a table. How long had they been planning this evening? I took a seat between Toccara and Rose. Leslie sat across from me at the round table with Kristen and Trudy beside her. I looked around, taking in each of my friends and the changes I had missed. Leslie's mousy-brown hair was shorter than I remembered, cut just past her chin. Kristen appeared to have lost weight, and her arms had more definition, like she had been hitting the gym. Trudy's features had softened from her recent pregnancy; the angles of her face were rounded. An air of wealth surrounded Toccara, from her perfectly manicured nails to her designer handbag. Her new business must be booming.

"Thank you all," I said. "Rose was right. I needed this."

Their faces lit up around the table, filling the void I had struggled with for so long. The moment was interrupted when the waitress came over to get our orders. While the show hadn't started yet, the air filled with anticipation as more people filtered into the club.

"Tell us more about your boyfriend," Trudy said. "I met him briefly at the funeral, but we didn't get a chance to talk."

"James has been amazing this last year," I said. Not wanting to worry anyone, I rushed on, forcing excitement I didn't feel into my voice. "He flew here right after graduation and stayed with me until Mom passed. I don't know what I would have done without him."

"So you guys are moving in together?" Rose asked. "Does that mean he already has a job lined up?"

"He got a position at a marketing firm based in LA right after he graduated and started at the end of last summer," I confirmed. "They have a branch in Seattle, and he worked there while I finished my last semester."

Our drinks arrived, and I took a long sip of the fruity cocktail. If the conversation continued to focus on my relationship, I would need the fortification.

"Will we hear wedding bells in your near future?" Toccara teased, stirring her frozen concoction with a straw.

An image of Nate flashed before my eyes when Toccara said "wedding," but it disappeared the moment I blinked. What was that? Everyone stared at me, and my cheeks flushed scarlet as I tried to articulate a response.

"Oooh, she's blushing!" Kristen exclaimed. "That means yes!"

I shook my head. "No, er, I mean, we've, uh, talked about it." My voice shook as words failed me. My mind had just conjured an image of Nate, and I couldn't imagine what that meant.

"Maybe once you're back out west, he'll propose," Leslie said. "He probably doesn't want to overwhelm you with everything else that's going on."

Though I was grateful for the subject change, her comments put everyone at the table in a somber mood. Their eyes filled with sympathy and concern as they assessed me. I shifted uncomfortably. Maybe I should have played up the potential proposal more, even though it was hard to feign excitement.

"How are you really doing?" Toccara asked, her dark eyes searching my face.

"It's been... difficult," I admitted, sucking in a ragged breath. "Especially being home. Living in her house." I closed my eyes and twirled my hair around my finger. "Sometimes, I wake up and rush downstairs to check on her only to be reminded she's not there." I coughed a bitter laugh. "I even think sometimes I can still hear the beeping of her heart monitor."

A hand closed over mine, and I opened my eyes to see Rose. The other girls reached across the table, and soon my hand was completely covered with the loving touches of my friends.

"I can't imagine what you're going through," Trudy said. The other girls glanced at one another and nodded. I forced a smile. I was the only one of my friends to have lost a parent.

I shook out my curls. "But Steven and I have made a lot of progress, and I think it'll get easier when I'm not living there anymore."

"If you need a break, you're welcome to stay with me," Kristen offered.

"I just might take you up on that." I released their hands and waved, trying to dispel the somber mood. "Ugh, I'm sorry. I don't mean to be such a downer. Tonight's supposed to be fun!"

While my declaration was met with a chorus of cheers and enthusiastic nods, I didn't miss the concerned looks being exchanged by my friends. Luckily for me, the lights dimmed, and the show began.

The rest of the night passed in a blur. Listening to familiar songs played on pianos and hearing the crowd sing along allowed me to let go of all my stress and worry, even if just for one night. My friends and I danced, sang, and took full advantage of the fruity drinks offered at the bar. A bachelorette party was underway, and my heart stuttered at the idea that one day soon, I might celebrate my own pending nuptials. But it wasn't James's face I saw in the vision, and that unsettled me.

Near midnight, we left the bar. Trudy had offered to be the designated driver, and she led the way to the parking garage, where her minivan waited. Though tired, I felt like a weight had been lifted from my shoulders that evening, and I was glad I had gone out. I promised myself to do better at keeping in touch with that wonderful group of friends.

Trudy dropped me off first, and everyone climbed out of the car to give me a hug. Rose's was the tightest and the longest, as if she hoped to imbue me with all of her love and warmth to carry me through the night.

"By the way, the school system is having a fundraiser this week to provide the kids with supplies for second semester," Rose said. "It'd be great if you could come and help out."

"That sounds like a distraction," I teased. "But one I need. Text me the details, and I'll be there."

Rose smiled and nodded then hopped into the vehicle. While I hadn't thought about what it would feel like to go back to the empty house alone, as I waved a last goodbye to the girls, a wave of nausea came over me.

With a heavy sigh, I unlocked the door and flicked on the hallway light. The silence was deafening after the loud music of the bar. I set my purse down on the bench by the door and stepped out of my shoes. Trudging across the floor in my stockinged feet, I headed to the kitchen, flipping lights on my way as if I could block out the melancholy darkness waiting inside me.

I grabbed a bottle of water from the fridge and sank into a chair at the kitchen table. After pulling the cap off, I gulped it down. The last thing I needed tomorrow was a hangover. After I had swallowed half of the bottle, I pulled out my phone. A missed call appeared on the screen. I tapped the voicemail, and James's familiar voice filled the room.

"Hey, babe. It's been a while since I heard from you, so I thought I'd check in. Hope everything is going well. Call me. Love you."

It was too late to call, even with the West Coast being three hours behind. James was an early to bed, early to rise kind of guy, and I knew he would already be asleep. It was just as well. I couldn't shake my discomfort at what had happened when my friends mentioned marriage. While I wasn't ready to marry James, I'd thought that was because I wasn't ready to marry anyone.

But seeing Nate's face unsettled me. Coupled with my reaction to him holding my hand at lunch the other day, I clearly had some things to sort out before I spoke with James again. More importantly, I hoped to resolve my feelings by the time I next saw Nate, which, if I had my way, wouldn't be anytime soon.

Chapter Five

Sunday morning dawned much too early after the late night before. My phone chimed, waking me. With a groan, I rolled over and tapped to open a group text from Trudy, which gave details about the fundraiser Rose had mentioned. A semiannual event for the local schools, it included an auction, and they were seeking donations.

I rubbed my eyes then reread her message. Mom had a few items I thought might work. And Steven would be thrilled to get rid of some things, especially if they went to a good cause.

Hey, Trudy, I can donate some odds and ends of my mom's. Where should I meet you?

After climbing out of bed with my phone, I padded down to the kitchen in search of coffee. My water chugging had staved off a hangover, but I was still bleary-eyed and exhausted from being out so late. As the coffee brewed, my phone pinged again.

Awesome, Lanie! Can you stop by the high school this afternoon?

In one text, she'd reminded me of my lack of transportation. A glance outside confirmed the weather wasn't conducive to walking, and even if it had been, it would be quite a walk, as the school wasn't nearby. Besides, I would need help carrying everything.

Ping. I glanced down, and my stomach dropped.

Hey, Nate here. I need to drop off my contribution as well. Happy to pick you up on the way, Lanie.

I set my phone down and grabbed the mug, gulping down the scalding liquid and instantly regretting it. My throat burned, and for a moment, I thought I might be sick. But I yanked a chair out and slid into it, laying my head on my hands. The nausea passed, and I took another tentative sip of coffee. Still too hot, but the warmth and caffeine helped to wake up my brain.

What should I do? On the one hand, I needed a ride, and Nate's offer was more than gracious, though I suspected he felt obligated since my car was still in his shop.

On the other hand, my attempts to avoid Nate had so far been unsuccessful, and agreeing to a ride would be the equivalent of admitting defeat. How many more awkward conversations could one person be expected to survive?

I weighed my options. Rose and Steven were both off that day. However, they were planning to visit a caterer for a tasting. While they could likely drop me off on their way, I would be stuck at the school until they were finished, giving the universe ample opportunity to throw Nate in my face again. Perhaps it would be better to accept my fate and meet him willingly. Then I would avoid any surprises like the other day at lunch.

Torn over what to do, I picked up my coffee and stepped to the window. My eyes swept over the backyard, taking in the shortening shadows as the sun rose in the sky. A familiar flash of red caught my attention, and I leaned toward the glass. The little cardinal was back, perched on the railing and staring right at me.

"Am I crazy to see him again?" I asked. The bird flitted closer and settled on a branch right outside the window. I'd never seen a cardinal so close before. The distinctive black dots resembling freckles were clear near its beak, confirming it was the same cardinal I'd seen before.

"It feels like a bad idea," I continued as the little bird flitted closer to the window.

"Maybe I should say no and take my chances with Steven and Rose." The bird cocked its head and chirped. Was it my imagination, or was there a hint of disapproval in the bird's song? Shaking my head, I tried to snap out of it, but something about the tilt of the bird's head and the way it fluffed its wings was eerily reminiscent of a look Mom used to give me.

Before I could process the resemblance, the bird flew away, and I was left disquieted. I ran a hand over my face. Great, I was talking to birds. Was I going crazy? I returned to the table and drained the last of my coffee. The weird resemblance between the cardinal and Mom meant nothing. My confusion over Nate was causing me to wish my mom was there. That was all. With that justification, I rinsed out the mug in the sink.

As I picked up my phone, Nate's message stared at me, waiting, mocking. With a sigh, I typed a message back, hoping I wouldn't live to regret it. *Sounds good. Thanks, Nate.*

After confirming what time he would pick me up, I headed upstairs to get ready. About an hour later, I was sitting in the living room, awaiting his arrival and trying to ignore my pounding heart. How ridiculous. It'd been six years since we'd broken up. Shouldn't I have been over it by then? I'd thought I was, but the memory of the spark I felt when we'd touched haunted me. What was wrong with me?

The doorbell rang, pulling me from my thoughts. I pasted on a smile and opened the door, but one look at him caused the breath to catch in my throat. He wore a black leather jacket and jeans, his dark hair combed neatly back, still damp from a shower. His clothing accentuated his muscles much more than the bulky winter coat he had on the other day, confirming my earlier assessment he had filled out significantly since high school.

"Morning," he said with a shy smile. His eyes swept quickly over me, and I hated how pleased I was when he raised an appreciative eyebrow.

Nate offered his arm. "Ready?"

As I'll ever be. I grabbed my bag of donations and accepted his arm, carefully stepping out over the frozen ground.

"Thanks for giving me a ride," I said as I slid into his car.

"Figured it was the least I could do, since it's my fault you're stranded," he replied with an impish grin.

See? Obligation. Nothing more. Some of the tension in my shoulders eased, but I still had an awkward ride ahead. I glanced at him out of the corner of my eye. He seemed in a much better mood. Maybe it wouldn't be so bad after all.

"More like Steven's," I said with a shrug. "If he or my dad had bothered to drive the car once in a while, it wouldn't have so many issues."

"Can't argue with you there." Nate put the car into gear and backed down the driveway. As we pulled onto the street, my neighbor, Cassandra, went out to pick up her newspaper. I waved and blinked when Cassandra's wrinkly face broke into a smile as she waved back.

"Steven and I were convinced she was a witch when we were kids," I said.

"She's certainly a character," Nate agreed. "Whenever she comes to the shop, she brings a homemade gift. Sometimes, it's cookies, but then others, it's some sort of satchel filled with herbs to ward off evil spirits, bring good luck, or help find love." His cheeks flushed at his last comment. "Not sure any of it has worked for me."

"What? No hot dates?" I teased as Nate's blush deepened. "I find that hard to believe."

He glanced at me before turning his attention back to the road. "Believe what you want." His voice had an edge to it. Maybe I had gone too far. Just what I needed, to make things more uncomfortable.

"I'm sorry. I didn't mean anything," I murmured.

"Sorry. I know you didn't." Nate sighed. "Sore subject."

I stared at my hands, unsure of what to say. Part of me wanted to ask why he'd called it a sore subject. After all, he broke up with me, not the other way around. While he'd sworn that there was no one else, I'd often wondered if he'd lied to spare my feelings. Though I knew I shouldn't care, I itched to know if he was involved with anyone. But a huge elephant sat in the car between us, and neither of us wanted to be first to address it. The longer the silence dragged on, the more desperate I became to fill it.

"What made you decide to work at the shop?" I finally asked, praying I'd chosen a safe subject. "You always talked about being a vet."

"Well"—Nate's shoulders visibly relaxed—"I enjoy working on cars. And you know my dad wanted me to take over. When I finished my associate degree at the community college, I switched to a trade school to study automotive technology." He shot me a look. "Besides, I didn't have a lot of money, and not going to a West Coast school saved me a bundle on student loans."

Heat crept up the back of my neck. We were treading dangerously close to that elephant again. I thought fast, hoping to steer the conversation back to safe subjects.

"I'm sure your dad was happy to keep the business in the family."

"Of course he was." Nate rolled his eyes. "He wasn't planning on retiring immediately. I was going to transition into the role over time. But then he had his heart attack." He shook his head. "Following old dreams didn't seem as important anymore."

I turned toward the window and choked on a sudden onset of tears. I understood what he meant. Sometimes, the line between my dreams and what Mom wanted for me blurred. Guilt stirred inside my chest, and I snuck a quick glance at him. I wondered what Mom would say about my spending time with him. I didn't really need to ask because Mom had made her feelings about Nate clear. Her words echoed in my head. *Promise me you won't settle here. Promise me you'll build your life as far away from this town as you can. Don't make my mistakes, Lanie.*

"You said you made your peace with my mom," I blurted out suddenly, forgetting my plan to stick to safe subjects. "What did you mean by that?"

"Nothing," he responded a little too quickly. He meticulously pulled into the parking lot of the school and avoided my gaze. "It's not important."

Before I could press the issue, he climbed out of the car and moved around it to open my door. His chivalry distracted me. When I stepped onto the pavement, he offered his arm again, and I took it gratefully, sliding the bag of donations onto my shoulder. The parking lot was plowed and salted, but the temperature had dropped below freezing the night before. I suspected black ice blended in with the pavement, and the last thing I needed was to slip and fall.

"What are you donating?" I inclined my head toward the folder in his hands.

"Coupons," he said with a wry grin. "Free oil changes, tire rotations, stuff like that." He nodded at my bag. "What about you?"

"Some old knickknacks of my mom's that Steven and I don't want and that don't have much value anyway."

When we reached the entrance, Nate held the door open, and we walked to the auditorium. The buzz of activity grew louder as we drew near, and a wave of nostalgia came over me. Nate and I had spent most of our relationship there. Over in the back corner, Nate had asked me to be his girlfriend. And the stage was where we'd shared our first kiss. I tried not to focus on those memories, but as I looked around the room, they were impossible to ignore. Nate tensed beside me. Was he remembering our time together as well? I shook my head and forced myself to focus. Trudy had taken over the stage and was directing people left and right to set up. School was closed for the Martin Luther King holiday the next day, which made that the perfect time to host the fundraiser, right before the new semester started.

"Lanie! Nate! Thank you so much for coming," Trudy exclaimed when she saw us. She rushed over and gave us each a brief hug. "What'd you bring me?"

Nate handed her his folder. "Coupons, as requested."

Trudy flipped through it quickly and beamed. "Thanks, doll." She turned to me.

"I've got some old figurines of my mom's and a few other trinkets that may spark some interest."

I pulled out a few statuettes. "Unfortunately, I couldn't bring much because we have to wait for the appraiser, but I thought this would help."

"It's perfect," Trudy assured me. "I'll set these up over here. Feel free to have a look around."

"Do you mind?" I asked Nate. When he gave me a questioning gaze, I hurried on. "We don't have to stay if you have somewhere to be." I didn't want him to get the wrong idea.

"I'm free as a bird." Nate gave me a slow smile that made my traitorous heart skip a beat. "We can stay as long as you like."

I wandered around the different tables, noting Trudy had been busy that morning, setting up the area for bids. Homemade crafts were on one table, jewelry on another, and various other businesses had donated coupons like Nate did. Bea's Diner had donated a free dinner date, complete with a three-course meal, prime seating, and bottomless sodas. A laugh bubbled out of my throat before I could stop it. Nate had won a similar date for us during our senior year. We'd gone together on Valentine's Day, and it had been a fun evening, despite the cheesiness of the location.

"Something funny?" Nate asked.

"Just remembering a simpler time." I pointed at the coupon.

"Right. That was a fun night. They tried to make the diner seem like fine dining, but they didn't quite pull it off."

I looked up at him and saw the same wistfulness that filled my chest. My breath caught in my throat, and I spun away. The elephant had returned.

"Nate, it's nice to see you," a voice said behind us. We turned to find a petite older woman with a plump face and salt-and-pepper hair.

"Mrs. Carlisle, what a pleasant surprise. What brings you to school on a Sunday?" Nate asked.

"Thought I'd help with the fundraiser one last time before I retire," she said. "Ah, Lanie, how are you, dear?"

"I'm well, Mrs. Carlisle." *Oh no.*

"I'm glad I ran into you," Mrs. Carlisle continued. "I understand you've finished your degree in special education."

I gave a wary nod. I knew where the conversation was going, and my stomach churned with dread. A quick glance at Nate's clenched jaw confirmed he was following it to its natural conclusion as well.

"The school would like to hire my replacement before I leave." Mrs. Carlisle's kind smile only increased the nausea building within me. "I'm not sure if you've heard, but I'm retiring at the end of the year. Are you staying in Cedar Haven? If so, you should think about applying. I think you'd be a perfect fit."

I gulped, trying to suppress the panic rising in my chest. Nate refused to meet my gaze. *Awesome.* Yet another sore subject between us, though I couldn't understand why he cared whether I stayed. I thought he'd accepted my reasoning at lunch the other day. Apparently not.

"I'm actually not staying," I squeaked. *Ugh. Get a grip.* I cleared my throat. "I have a job waiting for me in California."

"Ah," Mrs. Carlisle said, her face falling "Congratulations on the position. We'll be sad to see you go, but I understand." She forced a smile. "It was lovely to see you both." After giving my shoulder a brief pat, she turned and walked away.

"I know you have a job waiting," Nate said, his tone clipped. "But an interview wouldn't kill you."

"What's the point when I've already accepted another position?" I demanded with my hands on my hips. But my heart flip-flopped in my chest. I didn't want to have that conversation, well... ever, but especially not there, not in *that* room.

Nate finally looked at me, and his warring emotions were clear on his face. He took a deep breath and closed his eyes. When he opened them, they were calmer, though something still raged behind them.

"It's none of my business, of course," he began. "I just think you could do so much more here for kids who don't have the same opportunities as the ones at the school in LA."

I turned away and resisted the urge to rub my temples. He sounded like Dad, and it took a great deal of effort not to rail at him as I had my father the other night. Besides, as tired as I was of the argument, it wouldn't be fair to take my aggravation out on Nate. He wasn't aware of the unfair pressure my father was putting on me.

"I'm sorry," Nate said when I didn't respond. "It's not my place."

"It's okay." I sighed. "You're not the first person to make this argument. You probably won't be the last." I gave him a weak smile. "Are you ready to go?"

A shadow passed over Nate's face, but it was gone as quickly as it had come. Without a word, he nodded and offered his arm again, and we walked out of the school together. I reflected on the last time we'd left the school arm in arm like that. It was just after graduation, and I thought the world lay at our feet. I'd been so naïve. And though it had been years since our breakup, I couldn't ignore the overwhelming sense of loss that came over me as we crossed the parking lot.

"Are you okay?" he asked when we reached his car. The concern in his eyes caught me off guard. Again, I wondered why he cared.

"Just... thinking."

"It's weird, being back here." Nate stared behind us at the school.

"That's one way of putting it," I murmured. My heart ached, and all I wanted to do was return home and lick the wounds that had reopened after spending time with Nate. He might have said the words, but I knew that my decision to leave him for college had been the catalyst for our breakup. I was a fool to think we would make it.

My mother was right. A sharp pain, like a knife, twisted in my gut.

He looked at me sharply. My face must have betrayed my thoughts because he rounded the car and tentatively wrapped his arms around me. The movement felt wrong and right all at the same time. Without thinking, I slid my arms around his waist, and he tightened his hold. He smelled the same, a mixture of Old Spice and Ivory soap.

"I'm sorry, Nate," I choked out, unsure whether he would understand my apology or where my memories had ended up.

"It's not your fault," he assured me, his hand stroking my hair.

I pulled back to see his face. "How can you say that? I'm the one who broke us."

As Nate shook his head, his eyes betrayed an emotion I couldn't place. I frowned and leaned closer. When he dropped his gaze, it hit me. He was hiding something.

"What is it?"

"Nothing."

I reached up and held his face in my hands, forcing him to look at me. "Tell me."

"It's nothing. Just forget it."

"Does this have to do with my mother?"

"Lanie." He said my name like a caress, his voice pleading. "Please, just let it go."

I held his face for a moment longer, ignoring the warmth coursing through my hands. When I released him, he sighed, whether in relief that I'd dropped it or because he felt that same warmth, I didn't know. I was also afraid to find out.

"Fine, I'll drop it… for now," I said, glaring up at him. And I meant it. Sooner or later, I would make him tell me whatever he was hiding, especially if it had to do with my mom.

He stepped back from me and opened the door. With one last glare in his direction, I climbed into the passenger seat, and he drove me home.

The next day, I lucked out in not needing to rely on Nate for a ride. Trudy herself picked me up for the fundraiser, and I vacillated between enjoying myself and wanting to hide. Between the condolences for my loss and the questions about my plans, I longed for the obscurity I'd had in Seattle, where I could walk through a crowd and disappear.

Of course, the one person I wished to talk to most avoided me for the entire event. Nate attended the fundraiser as well, but he was always one step ahead of me. Whenever I started to approach him, he would find an excuse to be somewhere else. Was he afraid I would start asking more questions about whatever he was hiding? Or was it as painful and awkward for him to be around me as it was for me to be around him? On the one hand, I appreciated that he gave me space, but on the other, his avoidance hurt more than I wanted to admit.

When I woke the day after the fundraiser, I had another visit from the cardinal. I'd thought by that point, with the lack of food in the yard, it would have moved on. But there it was, as bright and curious as ever, perched on the back railing, gazing in at me. It stayed longer that time, watching me go through my morning routine, but we were both startled when my phone rang.

I recognized the number from the shop. "Hello?"

"Hey, Lanie, it's Nate. Your mom's car is ready."

"Okay, great," I said with enthusiasm. I would no longer have to rely on the kindness of others to get around. But then reality hit, and I chewed on my bottom lip. How was I going to pick up the car?

"I can come pick you up if you'd like," Nate said as if reading my mind.

Ugh, another awkward ride with Nate. Just what I didn't need. Then again, maybe that was a good thing. He couldn't avoid me in the car.

And I was tired of dancing around the elephant between us. I was stuck there for as long as it took to sell the house and settle the estate. I really didn't want to walk on eggshells every time I ran into him, which, in our tiny town, was sure to be often.

"You sure? I don't want to interrupt your workday."

"It's no problem. Is now a good time?"

"Yeah, that's fine. Thanks, Nate."

"Be there soon."

I got ready to go, vowing that I wouldn't let him weasel his way out of a difficult conversation again. We were both adults. There was no reason we couldn't at least tolerate each other.

When he arrived, I was waiting on the front porch. He jumped out of his car and opened the door, but I was already there. I didn't want to be distracted by his chivalry. With a curt nod, I slid into the car. He hesitated outside before climbing into the driver's seat.

"Thanks for the ride," I said.

"No problem. I'm sorry the repairs took so long."

I shrugged. "It's fine. Having no transportation gave me time to sort through my mom's things, and I've made a lot of progress."

"That's good to hear."

"I saw you at the fundraiser," I blurted, my voice accusatory.

He shot me a wary look. "I saw you too."

"Why didn't you say hello?"

Nate blew out a breath and ran a hand through his hair. "I wasn't sure if you wanted me to."

"Just because you're keeping something from me doesn't mean we can't be friends," I shot back.

He winced, and my resolve faltered. What right did I have to demand he tell me his secrets? Was my rabid curiosity really enough for me to justify treating him this way? What if whatever happened was something deeply personal? I wasn't being fair.

"I'm sorry," he replied before I could retract my words. "I shouldn't have avoided you." He braked at the stoplight and turned and looked at me. "I wasn't sure where we'd left things, and I didn't want to upset you."

"You could have just asked." I raised an eyebrow.

The light turned green, and he returned his attention to the road. "Next time, I will. I promise."

"I'm sorry too."

His eyebrows shot up. "What do you have to be sorry for?"

"Your relationship with my mother is none of my business," I said, though it pained me to do so. If Mom had wanted me to know whatever transpired between them, she would have told me. "I shouldn't have pressured you."

His throat moved as he swallowed, and his hands tightened on the steering wheel. Curiosity raged within me, but I pressed my lips together, mentally repeating the mantra that it wasn't my business.

"What will you do with your newfound freedom?" he asked in a clear attempt at a subject change.

I decided the gracious thing would be to follow his lead. "Not much. The appraiser is coming tomorrow to look over everything. Steven expects that will take most of the day." I glanced out the windshield. "And then I still need to find movers."

"No luck with your search?"

I shook my head. "Everywhere is so expensive. I didn't think it would be this difficult."

"The offer still stands for the guys and me to come by and help."

"I appreciate that," I said. And I did, but if we could barely get through a short errand without arguing, I didn't hold out much hope of doing so for an entire day. "But I'm sure I'll figure something out."

"All right," he said slowly. "But it might alleviate some of your stress to have that out of the way."

I hated that he was right. The house couldn't sell until we moved the furniture we were keeping and staged the rest. If I had any hope of getting back to the West Coast in the near future, I needed to get that over with and soon.

"You have a point."

"But?"

He always could see right through me.

I blew out a breath. "Won't it be awkward?"

He barked out a laugh that warmed my chest. "More awkward than it's been so far?"

With a grin, I nodded. "Fine. You win. If you guys are free, we're planning the move for Monday."

He pulled into the parking lot of the shop and slid the car into a free space. "I'll check with the guys and let you know, but I don't think it'll be a problem." He walked me to the building and held the door. "Sam will take care of you. I'll be in my office." Then he scurried away without another word.

I stared after him. While we still hadn't addressed the elephant, I considered the conversation a success. At least some if not all of the air had been cleared, and as I approached Sam, my steps were lighter.

Chapter Six

THE NEXT FEW DAYS flew by. After the appraiser spent the better part of Wednesday at the house, Steven and I prepped as much as we could for the estate sale. He stopped by most nights to go through the rest of Mom's belongings. My brother treated the process much more clinically than I did, and sometimes, I wondered if he even noticed I was in the room.

Sunday night, Steven came over to remove his share of the smaller items. We sat in the living room, packing up boxes of old books, photo albums, and a few trinkets.

"Do you remember our last trip to Disney before Mom and Dad split up?" Steven asked as he flipped through old photos.

"When we all spent a day or so in the hotel, suffering from heat exhaustion?" I shook my head. "Who could forget?"

"I know it wasn't the best experience," Steven said, his voice low. "But it's one of my favorite memories."

I stared at him as if he'd grown two heads. "Seriously? Why?"

He shrugged as he flipped another page. "Hindsight, I suppose."

"Hindsight?"

When he looked at me, his hazel eyes were filled with sadness. "We didn't know then it would be our last family vacation." He looked at the album. "On the one hand, I wish it had turned out differently so we would have a better memory to share. But on the other, I think the fact it was so awful made it more meaningful, in a way. Instead of spending day after day trudging through the parks and standing in endless lines, we were forced to rest and spend time together with little to distract us."

I moved over to the couch and settled in beside him. Tucking my knees under me, I glanced at the photos. There was one of the four of us, standing in front of Cinderella's Castle. My parents had Mickey ears, Steven had bought a ridiculous Goofy hat, and I wore a tiara. The happy smiles hid the darkness beneath the surface. My parents' marriage had been on the brink of divorce for years. In some ways, that vacation was their last-ditch effort to stay together. In others, it seemed a fitting farewell.

"We did play a lot of board games," I said.

"And I've hated Monopoly ever since," Steven grumbled.

I giggled. "That's just because Dad is ruthless." Leaning back against the couch, I stared at the ceiling. "But no worse than Mom at Uno."

"Ugh! I forgot about that." Steven smacked his forehead and groaned. "I swear she hoarded those draw-four cards. And she always threw them down—"

"Right when one of us would yell 'Uno,'" Steven and I said simultaneously then laughed.

As he resumed packing the photo albums for Rose to look through for a wedding collage, I continued to mentally reminisce about that last vacation. Steven was right. Despite how awful it had been to get sick at Walt Disney World, that vacation had briefly made me believe everything would be okay. My parents had continued to try for another year before they finally separated.

"You know how you said you didn't know why Mom chose you as the executor when you first got back?" Steven's voice broke into my thoughts.

"Yeah?"

He leaned back against the arm of the couch and looked at me. "I think she knew you needed to be here."

I raised an eyebrow. "For what?"

"Closure."

"What do you mean?"

With a deep breath, he continued, "Even though you were here for Mom when she was sick, I think the two of you tiptoed around a lot of issues. You two used to fight all the time. You even moved out and lived with Dad for your last semester of high school." He glanced at his hands. "But when she got sick, that stopped. Things changed. You dropped everything to come help her."

"She needed me," I protested.

Steven held up a hand. "I'm not finished."

I crossed my arms with a frown, unsure where the conversation was going.

"You were right to come home. She did need you, and I'm sorry I wasn't more helpful back then. It was difficult to visit while I clerked in Baltimore, but I wish I had done more." He fixed me with a probing look. "But come on, Lanie.

Can you honestly tell me you and Mom hashed everything out before she died? When you first came home, I could see you were holding back, biting your tongue in favor of keeping the peace. Like if you bottled up all your anger at some of her comments, it would prevent her from getting worse."

Worrying my lip, I considered his words. I thought I'd hidden my emotions better than that but perhaps not. If my brother had seen through me so easily, did that mean Mom had as well?

"I just... I thought we'd have more time," I whispered. "I thought, once she got better, we'd—" A single tear slid down my cheek. "But she—she never—"

Steven pulled me into his arms as I struggled not to lose it. "Shhh, it's okay, Lanie. I know." He rubbed my back as his voice cracked. "We all thought we'd have more time with her."

It was the first time since the funeral that I had seen my brother grieve. My arms tightened around him, and I hoped he felt as comforted by my embrace as I was by his. He was, after all, the only other person in the world who could truly understand what I was going through because of the loss we shared.

When we finally broke apart, red-eyed and sniffling, Steven gave me a watery grin. "This is why I wish you would stay in Cedar Haven. I can't bear to lose you too."

"I'm moving to California, not dying," I tried to joke, but my voice caught in my throat. I'd been so busy thinking of how hard it was for me to be home, but I hadn't stopped to think about what my brother was going through. While he had seemed to be doing well, maybe it was just a façade he put on to get through the day.

He snorted. "You know what I mean. It hasn't been the same while you've been gone these last six months. I missed you."

I nodded, not trusting myself to speak. I'd missed him too. The distance I gained when I returned to school helped push my grief to the back of my mind, but it'd been hard to be away from my family.

"You can always come visit me in LA," I said. "We could try out Disneyland, see how it compares."

"It won't. It's too small," Steven teased. "But I'm sure Rose and I will make it out there after the wedding craziness is over." He stretched and stood. "Speaking of, I should probably get on my way. She's been chomping at the bit to get these albums."

There was an unopened box on the floor by the couch. "What's in that one?"

Steven shrugged. "It looks like an old file box. Probably has old bills and whatnot. You can put it in a closet for now, and we'll take a look at it later."

As I helped Steven carry the boxes to his car, I couldn't stop thinking about what he'd said. Had Mom made me executor to force me back here to deal with everything we'd left unsaid? Was I being selfish by wanting to put this small town in the rearview? But Mom made me promise to leave, to never settle here. If she changed her mind, wouldn't she have told me?

⸎

I woke up the next morning with my heart in my throat. I went downstairs and grabbed a mug from the cabinet. The little sleep I'd had was filled with confusing dreams about Nate. With the mug in hand, I stepped over to the back window. My cardinal friend was flitting along the railing.

"Hello there." I waved. The cardinal cocked its head at me, displaying those familiar black dots near its beak. "Today is a big day. We're getting the house ready to sell."

The cardinal chirped and fluffed its wings as if it approved. Maybe it was hopeful the new owners would be better about filling the bird feeders. After he flew away, I finished my coffee then headed upstairs to get dressed.

When I returned, Steven was already at the kitchen table, waiting.

"Ready for this?" Steven asked with a grin.

"Ready as I'll ever be," I muttered. "What time will they be here?"

Steven checked his watch. "Any minute now."

I nodded absently as I went into the dining room and grabbed some newspaper. There were a few things I still needed to box up that I planned to keep. After grabbing a few of the moving boxes Steven had brought from his office, I slipped into Mom's room, wrapped some of Mom's treasured knickknacks, and placed them carefully into the box. The doorbell rang, and Steven's voice drifted up the stairs as he greeted the men. Packing up these items was the perfect excuse to be upstairs when they arrived. I needed a moment to compose myself before I saw Nate.

It bothered me more than it should have that he was hiding something. Of course, he was under no obligation to tell me anything. I kept telling myself it wasn't my business, but when he'd mentioned making peace with Mom, he'd said it so matter-of-factly I couldn't help being curious. I wondered what had been said between them and when. Was it before Mom got sick?

As I lifted a small carousel horse replica, I sensed a presence behind me. I spun around and found Nate standing in the doorway, watching me with a peculiar expression on his face. When our eyes met, he straightened and ran a hand through his hair.

"Sorry, I didn't mean to startle you," he said. "Steven sent me up here to break down your mother's bed." He nodded to the stripped queen bed against the back wall.

"I can move this stuff out of here so I won't be in your way." I hastily stacked the remaining items into my arms to move to another room.

He touched my shoulder gently, and the wave of unexpected heat tingling down my arm almost caused me to drop everything. I glanced at him, and his face softened with the sweet smile that used to take my breath away.

"You're fine, Lanie. You're not in my way."

As I slowly faced him, the air separating us crackled with electricity. Gazing at him, I watched as the warmth in his eyes gave way to a fierce heat. My heartbeat quickened, and suddenly, I felt like I was sixteen again: a mix of nervousness, elation, and desire making me tongue-tied. Drawing a ragged breath, I realized I'd stopped breathing.

Nate blinked, and when his eyes refocused, the fire in them was gone. He reached out with a half smile and took a couple of items from my arms before setting them on top of the dresser.

"Do you need help with these?" he asked absently as he lifted a figurine.

I stared at the familiar item, a single dolphin jumping a wave. It was the last Christmas present

Nate had given me before we broke up. I hadn't seen it in years. What was it doing here, among my mother's things?

I took it from him without thinking. "Where did you find this?"

"With the rest of the stuff you were wrapping," he replied, raising an eyebrow as he waved his hand over the assortment of knickknacks.

"I thought I lost it," I murmured as I turned the dolphin over in my hands. Such little dust had accumulated on it, almost as if it had been lovingly cared for in my absence. I wondered how it had gotten there and why I hadn't noticed it while sorting through everything before.

Nate was still staring at me, frowning, though whether from confusion or because he recognized the figurine as well, I didn't know.

"Do you remember this?" I asked.

"Remember it?" Nate scoffed. "Do you know how long I agonized over what to get you?" He shook his head with a rueful smile. "I went to so many stores. I looked at jewelry, electronics, clothing, just trying to find the perfect present. But when I walked into that Hallmark store and saw this, I knew I'd never find anything better."

"It really was perfect," I agreed, turning it over again. "I've always loved dolphins."

That Christmas, I gave him a football jersey of his favorite team. We hadn't been able to spend the day together due to plans with our respective families, but he had texted me a photo of his family in front of the tree, and he wore that jersey. My heart ached for that simpler time.

A throat cleared behind Nate, and both our heads shot up to find Steven standing in the doorway. I set the dolphin down and took a step back.

"I thought you came up here to break down the bed," Steven said, struggling to keep an amused grin from his face.

Nate nodded. "I was helping Lanie wrap up these breakable items. I didn't want to risk knocking anything over."

Steven quirked an eyebrow. "Mm-hmm, well, we need you downstairs when you're done." His assessing gaze made my cheeks burn before he turned and left us alone again.

"I really should move this stuff to another room," I hedged as I gathered the figurines once more. "It sounds like they need you downstairs."

Nate stopped my hand with his, and that familiar spark hit me all over again. "They can wait, Lanie. I'm happy to help." He picked up a figure of a little girl in a green dress and laid it in some newspaper then carefully wrapped it before placing it in the box.

Torn between wanting some distance and not wanting to offend him, I suppressed a sigh as I grabbed a sheet of newspaper and wrapped another item. I couldn't deny the packing was more efficient with two pairs of hands, and before

I knew it, we were finished. Without speaking, we moved over to the bed, lifted the mattress, rested it against the wall, and followed up with the box spring. Then I watched as Nate knelt at the frame and unscrewed the bars.

His hands moved deftly as he worked, reminding me of how they felt on my shoulder. The spark that ripped through my body confused and thrilled me. But I didn't understand why I was having all those feelings whenever he was around. I've heard that old saying that people never forgot their first love, but it felt like more than just never forgetting him. The connection went much deeper, almost as if old feelings I had buried deep within for years were reawakening.

"Penny for your thoughts?" Nate's voice broke through my reverie, and I jumped. Not trusting myself to speak, I forced a smile and shook my head, hoping to hide the guilt churning in my stomach.

"I saw Mrs. Carlisle again," Nate said, his eyes flicking to mine briefly. "They're having a hard time finding a teacher to replace her."

"I'm sorry to hear that," I said flatly. All the warmth from a moment ago evaporated. I stood and walked over to the mattress before picking up one end. "We should get this downstairs."

A shadow passed briefly over Nate's face, but he nodded and went to the other side.

"After you," he said brusquely, causing my heart to sink a little. I didn't mean to blow him off, but I really wasn't in the mood for another conversation about staying there.

We carried the mattress, box spring, and bed frame downstairs to the space Steven had left for it. Then I ran upstairs to pack more items and get away from Nate. Whatever old feelings I was having weren't enough to keep me there, so there was no point in even entertaining them.

Hours later, I finally finished packing the last of my mother's knickknacks and headed downstairs to check on their progress. The couch was the only furniture remaining, as we had plans to donate it, but everything else was gone. They'd set up Mom's bed on the opposite side of the living room from the couch, right under the spot where the TV used to be. Steven and Nate must have removed it from the wall while I was upstairs.

I moved into the kitchen, looking for the guys and Steven. Voices floated into the room, and I stepped to the kitchen window. Nate and Steven were talking out on the back porch, and a slight feeling of déjà vu came over me as they stood by the railing where the cardinal had visited earlier that morning. While I couldn't make out what they were saying, I had a distinct feeling it had to do with me. Especially when Nate lowered his head, his expression pained.

Doesn't he see how hurt Nate is? My heart ached for him. Maybe I should have just eaten the costs of movers and not put Nate and myself through it all. Spending time together was bound to stir up the past, which wasn't healthy. We needed to move forward.

Before anyone caught me staring, I headed upstairs to make sure we hadn't missed anything. Seeing the house so bare caused a pang in my chest. That was my childhood home; I'd grown up within those walls. I walked to my room. How many times had I taken solace in that sanctuary? How many tears had I poured into those pillows? How many laughs had echoed across the ceiling? A choked sob escaped my lips as tears sprang to my eyes.

"Lanie?" A voice came from behind me in the darkened hall. I quickly wiped away my tears and turned.

"Lanie, the guys are—" Steven stopped short. "Hey, are you okay?"

"I'm fine," I replied quickly. "The guys are what?"

"Heading out," Steven said, his eyes searching my face. "I can tell them goodbye for you."

"No, I'll be right down." I ducked into the bathroom, leaving Steven staring after me. With the door closed, I leaned heavily against it, taking deep breaths. I went to the sink and splashed cold water on my face, patting my eyes to help clear the red splotches. When I had hidden all traces of my grief, I sucked in one more deep breath and descended the stairs.

The guys were all suited up to head out into the cold winter air. I pasted a warm smile on my face as I looked them over. When my eyes met Nate's, he frowned, and my smile faltered. He always could read my emotions like the back of his hand.

"Thank you all so much for helping us get the house ready," I said, relieved that my voice sounded steady. Steven came over and threw his arm around me. "We appreciate everything you did today."

"It was nice to get out of the shop!" Jeff declared.

"Certainly smelled better," Sam joked.

"Well, maybe if you bathed more often, that wouldn't be a problem." Rob playfully smacked Sam on the back.

Not to be outdone, Sam turned and pulled Rob into a headlock while rubbing his fist on Rob's head. Rob hollered and struggled to pull away, and when Sam released him, he staggered back a few steps as he tried to smooth his hair. The rest of the guys laughed at the roughhousing, except for Nate. His eyes never left my face.

My phone rang, catching everyone's attention. I looked at it then up at Steven. "It's James. I'm sorry. I need to take this."

"Come on, Nate." Jeff put a hand on his shoulder. "Let's go grab a drink at The Point."

Nate started to protest, but something in Jeff's demeanor made him stop. His eyes met mine, and a dark cloud passed over his face before he followed the guys out the door.

I turned away and answered the phone.

"Lanie!" James's voice rang out. "I'm so glad I caught you. I feel like we've been playing phone tag for days. How are you?"

"I'm okay. The time zones are throwing me for a loop," I said. It was partially true, and James's preference for going to bed early certainly didn't help things.

"I get that," he said, his voice filled with sympathy. "Listen, I know you've got a lot going on, but I wanted to tell you I found the perfect apartment."

"You already found a place?" My stomach dropped, and I struggled to keep my voice even.

"Yeah. Look, I know we talked about me crashing with friends until you return and then we'd find a place together, but I think you're going to love what I found. It's a great complex with a gym and a pool, and the apartment has all the latest amenities. It's three bedrooms, which I know seems like a lot, but we could each have our own office."

I sank to the floor and covered my mouth with my hand, fighting a wave of nausea as James continued his ecstatic exclamations about the apartment. It was beginning to feel like my real life was moving on while I remained in some sort of limbo, tying up loose ends. I could see the logic in him apartment hunting without me, but the news still hit me like a ton of bricks. Especially since James wasn't known for being prudent when it came to financial decisions.

"Honey? Are you still there?"

"I'm here," I said, shaking my head as I tried to clear it. "That all sounds great, but are you sure we can afford it?"

James scoffed. "We'll figure it out."

That wasn't very comforting. I gnawed on the inside of my cheek as I debated my next words. "Do they at least have a website I could look at?"

"Of course they do. I'll email it to you, and we can talk more later after you have a chance to review everything. Sound good?"

It didn't seem like I had much of a choice. I closed my eyes and took a deep breath. "Thanks, James."

"No worries. I got you."

You've got me, but how about a budget? Perhaps I wasn't being fair, but James had a habit of jumping into things with both feet without fully thinking them through. I had asked him to wait for me to look for places to avoid that exact situation. From all the amenities he'd listed, I was pretty sure we were going to be in over our heads.

"How are things going?" James asked when I didn't respond.

I stood and stepped over to the front window. All the cars were gone save Mom's and Steven's. "It's been stressful."

"Any idea how much longer you'll have to be out there?"

"Actually, things are moving a lot quicker than I anticipated," I said. "Steven and I have divided up the furniture and other things. And today we had some help getting ready for the estate sale this weekend."

"Wow, that is fast. And good news. I miss you."

"I miss you too." I meant it, mostly. I missed having him to lean on, the way he distracted me from my pain just when I needed it most.

"Have you seen your dad yet?"

"I had dinner with him the other night."

"I'm glad to hear that. I know things have been rough between you two recently," James said with enthusiasm. "So, who helped you move the furniture?"

"Um, Steven asked a few guys he knows," I responded meekly. I didn't want to get into who the guys were right then. While I'd told James about Nate, I wasn't sure whether he would put two and two together. Something told me to keep that information to myself, at least for the moment.

"Well, that's nice. Hey, I'm sorry, hon, but I've gotta go. I'll send over the apartment complex's website. Give me a call after you take a look, okay?"

"I will. I love you."

"Love you, too, babe." My phone beeped three times, and I suddenly felt every mile of the distance between us.

"'A few guys I know,' huh?" Steven asked as he stepped back into the hallway. "That's not quite how I would describe them."

I leaned against the wall with one arm and pressed my forehead against it. "It just didn't feel like the right time to tell him."

"Is he aware your first love still lives here?"

"We've had the whole 'exes' conversation, but I'm not sure if he'd remember who Nate was." I pushed off the wall and walked by him into the kitchen. "It's been a long day."

"A long but productive day," Steven countered, following me. "I was thinking of ordering a pizza for dinner and inviting Rose to join us." He gave me a critical once-over. "Unless you're tired of people."

"That sounds nice, and I'd love to see Rose!"

"All right, I'll give her a call and put in the order. Pepperoni and pineapple?"

I nodded as I got a glass of water. Steven was right—it had been a productive day, and I was amazed at how fast we were accomplishing everything. If we were able to sell the house as quickly as we had readied it for sale, I would be back on the West Coast in no time. That knowledge should have made me happy, but for some reason, it didn't. To be fair, I had expected to be there a while, which was why I had told the principal of my new school I couldn't start until the summer. It would be nice to have some time off to relax and enjoy some downtime.

Between caring for Mom, finishing school, finding a job, and then dealing with Mom's estate, I hadn't had much time to just be. Then again, whenever I did have a moment to myself, it was harder to keep the crushing weight of grief at bay. I preferred to stay as busy as possible.

At least I would be with James, and maybe having some distance from Cedar Haven would help me to move on. Besides, I reasoned, I'd be busy enough setting up our new home and establishing myself in California. That last thought brought me up short. It shouldn't bother me so much that James was looking for a place without me, but it did. I wanted to be part of the process, especially to ensure he didn't get something out of our price range. Lately, my life felt out of control, like I was just going through the motions. Choosing where I would live gave me a sense of purpose and a tether to the future I wanted to create.

I stared out the kitchen window and watched as the shadows lengthened with the setting winter sun.

Chapter Seven

MY TREPIDATION ABOUT THE apartment continued into the next morning. I was still stewing over it when the doorbell rang. Who on earth would be stopping by so early? With a sigh, I shoved away from the table and went to greet my visitor. My eyes widened when I opened the door and found my neighbor, Cassandra Winters, standing on the front porch, dressed in all black, her gray hair cascading down her shoulders. She held a picnic basket, and the tantalizing scent of baked goodies wafted through the air.

"Mrs. Winters," I said. "What a pleasant surprise."

"Good morning, Lanie." She held out the picnic basket. "I thought you might want something other than toaster pastries for a change."

I blinked. "How did you—?" But before I could continue, a cardinal landed on the porch railing.

"Well, hello there, little fella," Mrs. Winters cooed, holding out her finger to the bird. I half expected the cardinal to hop onto it. Maybe I'd been wrong all those years about my strange neighbor. Maybe she was really a Disney princess in disguise. The bird cocked its head and chirped. I recognized the black spots near its beak.

"That little bird has visited me almost daily since I've been home," I said, shivering as the frigid air cut right through my thin shirt. "Ah, where are my manners? Would you like to come in?"

Mrs. Winters glanced up, startled, as if she had forgotten I was there. "Actually, I think you need to come with me."

"What do you mean?" I tilted my head, frowning at the change in her tone.

"There's something I want to show you," she said. "Would you join me for a cup of tea?"

"That would be lovely, Mrs. Winters, but I—"

"Oh, my dear, I think you're old enough to call me Cassandra now." She gave a wink before spinning on her heel, startling the cardinal in the process. It flew overhead as she walked down the driveway. I debated whether to follow her, my blood chilling in my veins and not from the winter air. But curiosity got the better of me, so I quickly grabbed a coat and shoved my feet into my shoes before I hurried after my eccentric neighbor.

I hesitated on the porch, my muscles tense, but I took a deep breath and forced myself to step into the notorious home of the neighborhood witch. Even as an adult, I found that Cassandra's decor made me uneasy. Herbs hung from the ceiling, and the house still smelled like sage. The walls were painted in the rich colors of nature, a dark earthy brown in the hall giving way to a vibrant green in the kitchen. It felt like stepping into some enchanted forest instead of a house.

Cassandra indicated a seat. Sinking into it, I let my eyes dart around the room as I looked for evidence that would confirm my childish suspicions. While I didn't see a cauldron on the stove, I wouldn't have been surprised to find a broom perched in the corner, ready to take flight.

"I'm not going to turn you into a newt," she said with a chuckle.

I jumped at the sound of her voice then bowed my head sheepishly. "I'm sorry."

"Oh, it's all right. I can understand why you children were afraid of me all those years ago. I've been called worse than a witch," she replied with a mischievous gleam in her blue eyes. After filling the kettle, she set it on the stove to boil then reached into her oven and pulled out a tray of scones.

"Were you expecting company?" I asked.

"You never know." She set out two small plates then took the seat across from me. "I understand you're selling your mother's house."

"We have an estate sale this weekend, and then it will go on the market." At first, I nibbled at the scone, but the sweet, flaky pastry was too delicious, and before I knew it, I had gobbled up two.

The kettle whistled, and Cassandra stood and poured the water into two cups. She placed a bag of peppermint tea into one and handed it to me. After grabbing a sugar bowl, some honey, and spoons, she sat down again.

"I was so sorry I couldn't visit more often with Melody before she passed." Cassandra's eyes were moist with unshed tears. "She was kind to me. The baked goods she sent over with you kids were always a welcome treat."

"It's hard," I said, swallowing around the lump that formed in my throat. "Living there without her."

Cassandra slid her hand across the table, and I clasped it.

"Your mother will never truly leave you. She'll always be in your heart."

I forced a smile and cleared my throat. "You said you wanted to show me something?"

"Oh yes, it was about that little cardinal on your porch." She stood and stepped over to her small kitchen window, where a shelf was filled with books. "Ah, here it is." After setting it on the table, she flipped through to a faded black-and-white photo of a bird. "Cardinals are said to be visitors from heaven."

I leaned forward, staring at the page she pointed at. The cardinal in the photo looked exactly like my bird, though without its telltale red. Beneath the photo were stories, the stuff of old folklore and legends.

"As I said, your mother will never leave you." Cassandra pointed at another line on the page. "'Cardinals represent light during the darkest of nights, provide hope to the sorrowful, and are a source of warmth in winter's cold embrace.' Here, it says, 'Red cardinals are a sign that a departed loved one is attempting to connect.'" She sat down in her chair, letting her words sink in.

I shook my head, not for one minute believing any of it. Cardinals were just birds, and their presence was noticeable only because they were a vibrant red.

"It's just a coincidence," I insisted, even while a small kernel of hope grew in my heart. "The only thing that bird wants to communicate is it's past time to refill Mom's old feeders."

"If it were about food, the cardinal would have moved on long ago." Cassandra sipped her tea, regarding me over the lip of the cup. "You said you've seen it regularly since you've been home."

"Maybe it has a nest in our yard and doesn't want to travel in the cold," I argued. I wasn't a religious person, and that just sounded like one of those things people told one another as a source of comfort, a way to ease the pain of losing someone they loved.

"You can choose not to believe." She shrugged. "But I suspect that little bird has a purpose."

Lifting the cup to my lips, I barely tasted the tea. My mind was running through logical arguments against what she was saying. No way would I believe Mom was trying to communicate with me from beyond the grave. And even if she was, the only message I was getting from the visits revolved around Nate, since they always seemed to occur right before I saw him.

"But she hated Nate!" I blurted out, then I covered my mouth with my hand.

Cassandra cocked an eyebrow as she wrapped her hands around her cup. "Perhaps she has a message for you about this Nate." She pushed the plate of scones toward me. "Eat. You look pale."

I automatically reached for another scone and took a bite, not fully registering what I was doing. I didn't linger long in Cassandra's house, my unease increasing the more time I spent there. While my imagination was more grounded as an adult, her otherworldly demeanor still unsettled me. After thanking her for the scones and tea, I went to my house to prepare for the day. All the while, I tried to push Cassandra's crazy cardinal theory out of my mind.

It didn't work. I thought back over the times I'd seen the cardinal. The first was when the car got a flat tire and Nate came to rescue me. Then it appeared again before that awkward lunch at Bea's Diner when Nate told me about that job. It showed up a third time when he took me to drop off items for the fundraiser, and another visit happened right before he arrived to help with the move. And then I'd seen it that morning, so did that mean…?

I shook my head. I was being ridiculous. It was just a bird, not some messenger from the great beyond.

But then I thought back to what Steven had said the other night. He asked if Mom and I had really settled everything between us before she passed. I believed we had, at least as much as anyone could hope to. There would always be things I wished I'd said or done differently, but when she died, I felt we were on solid ground. Our relationship was never perfect, but I didn't have any regrets.

As I pretended to pack up my room, I glimpsed a photo stuck in the mirror frame that I'd never had the heart to take down. Nate and I were in formal attire. It was just before prom. We looked like we'd been caught kissing, but really, my friends had staged it in a way to get a better view of the back of my dress and hair.

Pulling it off the mirror frame, I studied it. Nate's eyes were looking at the camera, but mine were on him. His arms were wrapped tightly around me, and his smile was bright, but it didn't quite reach his eyes. I recalled my mother had stood nearby when this photo was taken. Even then, he stared at my mom with a wariness that broke my heart. But he'd told me they had made their peace. What did that mean? What did peace look like for Mom and Nate? And did it have something to do with why the cardinal visited me?

I put the picture back and pulled out my computer. James had sent the apartment information, and I decided it was as good a time as any to see what he'd found. When I clicked on the website, my stomach dropped. Just as I'd suspected, the cheapest apartment they offered was way more than I had planned to pay monthly. If I hadn't already done my own research, I might have accepted that it was just the price of housing in LA. But I knew better. While the apartments I had bookmarked to check out when I got back to the West Coast had fewer amenities, they were affordable.

With a sigh, I closed my eyes and rubbed my temples. Based on the number of exclamation points in James's email, he was excited about the complex, but the math just didn't add up. We could either rent that apartment or we could eat, but we couldn't do both. I supposed I could get a part-time job, but that seemed unnecessary when I had already found several apartment options that would work instead, even if they didn't have all the bells and whistles James raved about.

Maybe I should consider finding my own place. James and I had been together for years, and it made sense for us to take that next step and move in together. As I'd told Steven, he would likely propose once Mom's estate was no longer hanging over my head. It might not even make sense for us to get separate apartments, knowing we would be moving in together once we were married.

I cringed at the thought. Marriage. We'd discussed it at length, of course, but it had always seemed like some abstract thing we would get to eventually. But with grad school behind us, James had brought it up more frequently than before I went home. Part of me wasn't even sure I ever wanted to get married. It wasn't like I'd had the greatest example. My parents' divorce had been awful, but I reminded myself they were friends in the end.

But was it really marriage I was struggling with or a life with James? Did I even *want* to move to California? Sometimes, I wasn't sure. Because of my promise to Mom, my plan had always been to live somewhere other than Cedar Haven, and when the school in California offered me a position, it made the most sense.

I could stay in Cedar Haven, though I winced at the thought. The idea of breaking the promise to my mother hurt my very soul. And yet, there was a job there, still doing what I loved. Okay, sure, it would be significantly less money than I would make in California, but I could bunk with my dad for a while until I got settled.

Could I live in Cedar Haven with all the painful memories? Nate's question echoed in my head. *They're not all bad memories, right?* And he was correct. Over the past few days, I'd been reminded of happier times by going out with Rose and my friends then hanging out with Steven and reminiscing about our childhood. Even driving with Nate was a sweet echo of a time I wouldn't want to forget.

After navigating to the local middle school's web page, I found the job posting for Mrs. Carlisle's position. When I finished reading it over, I knew I was a perfect fit. My stomach knotted as I filled out the application, convinced my mother's ghost was about to pop out from some dark corner of the room to scold me for breaking my promise. But I reasoned that Mom also had always encouraged me to keep my options open. What better way to do that than to apply for the position? It couldn't hurt, and we miss one hundred percent of the chances we don't take, right?

Hours later, I drove to the school with a folder containing my résumé, transcripts, and letters of recommendation. Soon after I submitted the application, someone from the school called and asked me to interview. Well, I'd already gotten my feet wet, and my life didn't feel like mine anymore. Between James's decision to find us a home without my input, being stalked by a bird, and my confusion over Nate, I needed to take control of something in my life. Applying for the job was my way of doing just that. Besides, an interview didn't mean I would accept. It wouldn't stop me from going to California as planned. But it might provide an alternative to the life I thought I wanted.

What I didn't know was what my choice would mean for James and me. I loved him, or at least, I thought I did, but the apartment episode had made me realize that I hadn't been happy with him for a while. And his latest decision could have a huge impact on my life, at least financially. I promised myself I would talk to him about the situation before I made any rash decisions. One interview wasn't enough for me to upend all my plans, and besides, there was always a chance they would turn me down.

As I pulled into the parking lot of the school, I breathed easier at the sight of clear, dry pavement. The last thing I needed was to slide on black ice, face-first into a snowbank, when I wanted to make a good impression. Squaring my shoulders, I marched to the front of the building and rang the bell, ready for whatever future the decision might bring.

After the interview, I stopped by the grocery store to find something for dinner. It'd been ages since I last cooked. I gathered some basic ingredients while I decided what I wanted to make. When I rounded the corner after grabbing a pint of ice cream, I had to swerve to avoid a person striding toward me. A flash of dark hair caught my eye, and I turned. Nate's eyes widened as they met mine.

"I'm sorry. I didn't see you there," he said.

"It's my fault I was tearing down the aisle like the Indy 500," I quipped, glancing into his cart. "Frozen dinners?"

"What's wrong with that?" he demanded.

"It just screams 'bachelor,'" I replied with a wry smile.

"Well..." He waved his bare left hand. He peeked into my basket. "What are you getting?"

"Odds and ends, though I feel like cooking something tonight. Haven't decided what yet."

"Need suggestions?" he asked.

I raised an eyebrow. "Are you trying to procure an invite?"

"Maybe." That slow, heart-melting smile stole over his face. "If you're offering."

That was... unexpected. But I wasn't about to waste his good mood. "Hmm, I could be persuaded."

"How about we make a trade? You cook, and I'll buy your groceries?"

I wasn't one to turn down a free meal, even if I was technically paying for it with my labor. "It's a deal." I dumped my things into his cart and slid an arm through his elbow.

"When did you learn to cook?"

I bit my lip and stared at the ground. "My mom taught me some things growing up, but I guess I learned most of it through trial by fire when she was sick."

He patted my hand but didn't respond. Perhaps he didn't know what to say. As the awkward silence between us lengthened, I searched for a safe subject.

"I was thinking I'd make shepherd's pie."

"Sounds like the perfect meal for a cold winter's day," he agreed.

I blew out a breath, and we wandered through the rest of the store as I added to our supplies. To my surprise, the conversation flowed easily while we shopped. Nate paid, and I blinked at the cost, but when I opened my mouth to protest, he waved me off. Business must be good, though I supposed with it being winter, I likely wasn't the only person who had fought a pothole and lost.

We headed to my house, with Nate following in his car, and he helped carry the groceries inside. I poured two glasses of wine then turned on some music while I began preparing the meal. Singing along to the tune, I caught Nate staring at me and flushed at the intensity of his gaze. I suspected what he was thinking as the memory flashed through my mind as well—late nights on the phone when I'd serenaded him before he slipped off to sleep.

While I worked, I debated whether to tell him about the interview. On the one hand, he'd told me about the job in the first place, so it wouldn't be weird for me to share my news. On the other hand, I hadn't told anyone else, and somehow, I worried that telling Nate might imply I planned to stay. I wasn't sure why I thought he would care beyond my filling a potential void in the town's education system.

Once I slid the shepherd's pie into the oven, I lowered the volume of the music and took a sip of my wine, steeling myself. My heart thumped in my chest, but whether from excitement or nerves, I didn't know.

"I have something to tell you," I whispered conspiratorially, leaning toward him.

"What's that?" he whispered back, his eyes twinkling as he played along.

"I had an interview today," I said.

He blinked and raised an eyebrow. "An interview? For what?"

"Mrs. Carlisle's position," I replied with a wink before lifting my glass and gulping down more wine. Why had I just winked at him? What was I thinking? I supposed that was the problem—I wasn't thinking. The alcohol went straight to my head, which did little to help the situation.

"What?" Nate asked, his eyes wide. "You applied? When?"

"This morning." I smiled, though I wasn't sure what to make of his reaction. Shock etched across his face, but was it good or bad? And for that matter, why did I care?

Nate leaned back in his seat and stared at me in silence. I gave him a moment to process my news, but as the silence stretched on, everything started to itch, and I couldn't stop myself from fidgeting. Why wasn't he saying anything? Did I make a mistake in telling him? But he'd told me about the job, so shouldn't that be a good thing? Unless he didn't trust that I would follow through. My head was swimming, and I struggled to remember the last time I'd eaten. Was it the scones? I should have paced myself with the wine.

"What changed your mind?"

His words brought me back to the present, and I worked to keep my face neutral while my shoulders sagged in relief. Curiosity danced in his eyes, along with another emotion I couldn't place, but at least he didn't seem angry or upset.

"You wouldn't believe me if I told you." I laughed, shaking my head. "Let's just say a little bird told me I should."

He rubbed his chin, and a slow smile broke over his face, stealing my breath. But he still hadn't said what he thought, and that worried me.

I frowned. "Aren't you going to say anything?"

"I'm a little speechless," Nate admitted. He slid his hand across the table, and I tentatively placed mine in it. "And I'm not sure what's... safe to say."

I cocked my head. "Safe? What do you mean?"

"Just that, well, the other day, you wouldn't even consider applying, and now, you've applied and interviewed." He pulled away and ran his hand through his hair. "I guess I'm trying to understand what changed."

The oven timer beeped, and I jumped up to toss the rolls in the oven, grateful for the interruption. I wasn't sure how I should answer him. To blame it on James and the apartment felt childish and reckless. Besides, I wasn't even sure if Nate knew about James. We'd never talked about him.

And I couldn't very well tell him that my neighbor thought my mother's spirit was trying to communicate with me through a bird. My joke about it earlier had been more for my benefit than his.

When I returned to him, he stared at me with that same intensity again, and it was all I could do not to fidget. I decided that a half-truth was better than nothing.

"My dad is dead set on me staying in Cedar Haven," I said, forcing a smile. "And I feel like I owe it to him, as the only parent I have left, to at least see how that would work. I'm not making any promises, but it might get him off my back for a while."

"Did they say when they would make their decision?" Nate asked, and I breathed a little easier.

"As soon as possible." I shrugged. "But you know the government. I'm sure there are levels of approval they'd need to go through. It went well, though."

"I'm glad to hear it," Nate said. "If you stay, do you think you'll still sell the house?"

"Probably. I can't afford to buy Steven out of his share of the estate, and I don't know that I'll ever feel comfortable here without her." I took another sip of wine. "I haven't really thought about that. It was an impulse decision, and I hadn't expected to be interviewed so soon."

"I don't think they've had a lot of applicants," Nate said. "Not many people looking for small-town life these days. I'm glad you applied. It's good to have options."

I spun around at his words, and he gave me a wary look. Swallowing, I cleared my throat. "I'm sorry, it's... I... I, er, that's something my mom would say."

Nate sat perfectly still, and I had the distinct impression that he was choosing his next words carefully. All the air seemed to leave the room as I waited, wondering if he was about to reveal whatever secret he'd been keeping from me.

"Perhaps I heard her say it once or twice," Nate finally replied, his voice strained. "But it's a common saying."

I nodded, choosing not to force the issue. The oven timer went off behind me, and I bent to check dinner.

Nate stood and got plates and silverware while I set out the shepherd's pie and rolls on the table.

I refilled our wineglasses, though the last thing I needed right then was more alcohol, and took a seat, gesturing for him to serve himself. After spooning out a healthy portion, he passed the spoon, grazing my fingers. His eyes met mine briefly before looking away.

"This is delicious." He scooped up a mouthful of mashed potatoes.

"Better than a TV dinner?" I teased.

"Not even in the same neighborhood."

"You never learned to cook?"

He shook his head. "I'm afraid the most I do is grill."

A laugh bubbled up in my throat. "Cooking is just grilling indoors."

"I disagree," he said as he reached for his wine. "There's something about burning something over an open flame that brings out the caveman in all of us."

I snorted. "'Burning something'? So what you're saying is, you're not good at grilling either?"

"Hey now, I said I grill. I never said how the food turned out!"

"Did you learn your skills from Max McAllister? He never met a hamburger he couldn't turn into a hockey puck."

"I don't believe I ever had the pleasure of your dad's, er, culinary experiments." His mouth twisted as he stumbled over the words, and I laughed again.

"Hmm, that's right." I pointed my fork at him. "You only enjoyed my mom's taco nights."

"When she set me up to see how many I would eat?" Nate glared at me. "Yeah, I haven't forgotten that."

I covered my mouth to hide my giggling, but his answering grin assured me he wasn't offended. That was what I missed the most since we'd broken up. The joking around, harmless teasing, and playful banter. Nate had always been closed off from the world, aside from a few close friends. But I had discovered a different side of him when we were together. His sense of humor and boisterous laughter warmed my insides.

He scraped his plate, clearly enjoying every last bite, and I hid a smile as warmth blossomed in my chest. I missed cooking. When I was back in Seattle, I'd never found the time to cook for James and me. We usually ordered takeout, as he had never learned to cook for himself.

"Well, since you made this amazing meal, it's only fair I do the dishes," he announced as he took his plate and mine to the sink.

"You don't have to do that." I stood to stop him.

"Nonsense. I was raised to do my part." He placed a hand on my shoulder and gently nudged me back into my seat. "Besides, I'm hoping I'll earn another invite in the future."

"You can count on it." My lips curled into a soft smile as I watched him fill the sink and begin washing the dishes. *I could get used to this.* I blinked at the thought, hoping to dispel it, but instead, a whole different future filled my mind. I pictured coming home to him after a long day at school, him washing the grease and grime off his hands before joining me in the kitchen while I made his favorite meal.

I shook my head, and the image vanished. What was wrong with me? Why had I allowed myself to entertain such a vision of my future? And more importantly, why was Nate in the starring role instead of James? What did that say about me?

"I need some fresh air." I rushed out of the kitchen, leaving Nate calling after me.

I stepped out onto the front porch, crossing my arms over my chest as the first bite of winter's chill cut through my thin shirt. Breathing in the crisp air, I closed my eyes. Perhaps it was only natural, being there without my mother to guide me, that I would fall into old habits. Maybe I was making too much out of nothing. So what if I still had feelings for Nate? It wasn't like I would act on them, especially since I had no evidence he felt the same way about me.

A moment later, the front door opened, and Nate slid in beside me. I could feel his eyes searching my face, and I worked to keep my expression neutral. He slipped his hands into the pockets of his pants and hunched his shoulders.

"It's freezing out here."

I nodded, not quite trusting myself to speak. My skin felt tight, my muscles tense at his closeness. It was one thing to admit that I still felt something for him, but it was quite another to have those feelings welling up in my chest while he stood next to me. I shoved them down and turned to him.

"Thanks for cleaning up," I said, forcing a smile.

"Thanks for dinner." His brows pulled together. "Are you... okay?"

"Of course. Why wouldn't I be?"

"You ran out of the kitchen and have been standing out here in the cold."

"The house was warm after the oven was on," I lied. "I needed to cool off a bit."

"Oh." His frown deepened as if he could see right through me. "Well, I guess I should go."

"Wait," I said, internally cringing. I should let him go. Spending time with him wasn't helping anything, but I didn't want to be alone. "Why don't you stay a minute and have another drink with me?"

He gave me a dubious look but nodded, and a small part of me filled with hope. I squashed that part. We were friends. At least, I hoped we were moving in that direction. And frankly, I needed all the friends I could get.

We went inside and sat on the couch, where we faced each other. A charity was coming to pick up the couch at the end of the week, and I savored the little time I had left with it. It was funny, the things we got attached to when someone we loved passed on. Some tangible items had no real monetary value but possessed such priceless sentiment.

He glanced at me with a teasing grin. "It's nice to sit here with you without the threat of yellow police tape."

I threw back my head and laughed so hard I almost spilled my wine. He caught my hand to steady the glass, and my eyes flew open as I met his gaze. The air seemed to surge with an electric intensity. But it didn't last as my cheeks flushed, and I pulled away.

"I forgot about that," I murmured. "Mom and her threats." I gave a weak smile. "You were always a good sport about her antics. The tacos, the police tape."

Nate shrugged, and I could feel his discomfort growing. I supposed we were approaching one of the many elephants in the room. I stifled a sigh that quickly morphed into a yawn.

"I'm so sorry." I covered my mouth with my hand.

"It's fine. I know it's getting late." He stared at the floor, his lips pressed into a thin line. "I should be heading home. I've gotta open the shop early tomorrow."

We stood, and he set his glass in the kitchen before making his way to the front door. After shrugging into his coat, he surprised me when he grasped my hand and gently pulled me to him, wrapping his arms around me. My heart thudded as I rested my head against his broad chest.

Too soon, he pulled away enough to look at me, and a desire to press my lips to his took over me. But I knew better. I stepped away and opened the door. When I glanced back, he had a bemused look on his face as if he was overcome by the same pull.

He blinked and recovered. "Bye, Lanie. I'll see you later."

Instead of responding, I waved and closed the door behind him before leaning against it. I listened as his car door slammed and the engine sparked to life. A moment later, the wheels crunched on the snow-covered driveway. Then silence.

I couldn't put it into words, but somehow, I knew that things between us had changed that night. Whether that was a good thing or not, I suspected I would find out soon enough.

Chapter Eight

ON THE DAY OF the estate sale, I woke up groggy and disoriented. I'd dreamed of my old apartment in Seattle, and I didn't recognize my childhood bedroom at first. As I sat up, everything rushed back to me, and I groaned when I remembered what day it was. I wasn't looking forward to the throngs who would be traipsing through my childhood home in a few hours.

Before my mom died, I considered myself an outgoing person, but in the last six months, I'd become more withdrawn and introverted. When I returned to school, I avoided social engagements, though I had the excuse of catching up on all the schoolwork I'd missed. Since I'd been home, preparing the house had kept me busy, but it was harder to escape socializing in such a small town.

Memories from the night before drifted through my mind. I'd enjoyed spending time with Nate, reminiscing about the past. I believed we were well on our way to being friends again. I hadn't realized just how comfortable I was with him until that hug at the end of the night. It felt like old times. Maybe too much like old times. At one point, I thought he might kiss me, and it scared me that part of me wanted him to.

I winced, silently rebuking myself. What about James? We were planning to move in together, for goodness' sake. What was I thinking? The truth was, I hadn't thought about James much at all yesterday. After my residual anger regarding the apartment had driven me to apply for a job I shouldn't want and didn't need, I hadn't given him a moment's consideration. That had to be a bad sign. Shouldn't I have at least told him about the job interview?

I pushed the thought from my mind and tried to focus on the day ahead. James and I would have plenty of time to talk later. Climbing out of bed with a heavy sigh, I straightened the covers then set out my outfit for the day. I chose a navy-blue pantsuit in hopes of appearing like a capable salesperson. More like a suit of armor against what was going to be an emotional day. While I'd made my peace with the things we weren't keeping, it wasn't going to be easy to watch them go to strangers. On the flip side, I expected the town to come out in full support. Perhaps seeing some familiar faces would lessen the blow.

When I stepped out of the shower a little while later, voices drifted up from the floor below. A quick peek out the window confirmed Steven had arrived. I quickly dressed, ran a brush through my hair, and pulled the damp strands into a ponytail.

"Well, good morning, sleepyhead," Steven called as I descended the stairs. "I tried calling you last night, but you didn't pick up."

"She was probably exhausted, poor thing." Rose's voice carried from the living room. "She hasn't had a chance to catch her breath since she arrived."

As I entered the living room, I caught Steven's eye, and he shrugged. "It had to be done, and since she's in such a hurry to get back to her West Coast lifestyle, it's good we're moving quickly."

Some might have taken offense at that last comment, but I knew my brother. He'd accepted my decision to move to California, but that didn't mean he wouldn't get a few digs in before I left.

"Could you stop talking about me like I'm not here?" I demanded, hands on my hips in mock anger.

"Somebody woke up on the wrong side of the bed," Steven teased.

I shot him a glare before I turned to see what they'd done with the downstairs. Steven and Rose had set up the room in a way that directed the flow of traffic. All of the items had price tags according to the appraisal they had received. My heart fractured as memories of each piece flooded my mind.

"Dad will be here soon," Steven continued, writing on his clipboard. "You can help Rose set up things in the kitchen."

I nodded absently, following Rose as instructed. The plan was to put Mom's china on full display. Some of the pots and pans had been deemed acceptable for sale, but we'd tossed most of them.

"Why don't you grab a cup of coffee and some food before we get started?" Rose indicated the box of doughnuts on the counter. I gave her a grateful smile and helped myself, standing over the sink to avoid getting crumbs everywhere.

"How are you feeling about today?"

I gave a noncommittal shrug. "I'm trying to stay indifferent, but it's difficult."

"I understand," Rose murmured softly. "After everything you've been through this last year, it's got to be hard to say goodbye."

"I think it's more I feel like I'm losing another part of my mom." I sipped my coffee as I surveyed the kitchen, committing every little detail to memory. "It'll be hard to leave all this behind."

"You're definitely set on moving, then?"

I gave her a wary look. "Why? Has someone told you differently?"

Rose's responding laugh was infectious. "Clearly, you know your family well."

"Steven says he's accepted my decision, but my dad..." I shook my head. "Part of me wonders if I'm making a mistake, but I feel like I have to at least try, you know?" I didn't mention the application and interview for the local teaching position. No reason to get anyone's hopes up. "I appreciate their concern, but I think it's for the best."

"And not even a certain someone will change your mind?" Rose asked innocently, but I saw right through her.

"Did Steven put you up to this?" I retorted with a glare.

"No. Like you said, he's accepted your decision." She grinned. "But I'm not blind. I've seen the way Nate looks at you."

"I don't know what you mean," I said, turning away from her. Lucky for me, Steven and my father entered at that moment. I wasn't ready to address my conflicting feelings toward Nate.

My dad gave me a nod before he walked over to the table and surveyed the china. He picked up various pieces and turned them in his hands, his eyes far away. I wondered if he was remembering happier times with Mom.

After cleaning the crumbs from my fingers, I moved next to Dad at the table. He had lifted a gravy boat and was fiddling with a small crack at its base. I touched his arm gently, and he turned to me with a sad smile.

"Your mother cracked this when she slammed it down on the table one Thanksgiving," he said, his eyes wistful. "I don't remember exactly what I did, but I do recall she was hopping mad with me."

When I rested my head on his shoulder, he set the dish down and wrapped his arms around me. We stood there together, lost in our memories, our ongoing argument about my plan to leave momentarily forgotten. It touched me to know that despite everything that had happened, my parents had never stopped loving each other. What their marriage had taught me, above all else, was that love wasn't enough. Good relationships required work, communication, and a hefty dose of humility.

I stifled a sigh as realization swept in. James and I needed to talk, and the sooner the better. If I planned to have a future with him, I needed to hear him out on the new apartment and discuss my concerns like a rational adult. Not jump feetfirst into a job opportunity just to prove I could. And who knew? Maybe talking to him would help me sort out whatever was going on between Nate and me, assuming there was anything going on. It could be all in my head.

"You'd better get started on pricing everything," my father whispered, pulling me back to the present as he extracted himself from our embrace. "You know how your brother is."

I nodded and turned to Rose. The men left the kitchen to continue preparing the rest of the house. Working with my future sister-in-law was exactly what I needed for the day. We shared a comfortable silence, only sporadically broken by a comment on an item here or a shared memory there. It was peaceful, and I appreciated the lack of unnecessary chatter.

Soon the sale began, and Steven opened the front door to welcome the customers. I blinked when I saw the line already waiting outside, but I recognized many of them. Dad stationed himself by the back door, managing the cash box and tablet with a card reader attached. Rose and Steven worked the floor, helping customers. They both had previous sales experience, and they were naturals.

I opted to stay in the kitchen, helping customers who wandered in but wanting to maintain a low profile. Some people sought me out to express their condolences, but most seemed to understand my need for solitude. I hoped the day would pass quickly and successfully.

⁓ ℓℓ ⁓

"Thanks for staying, Rose," I said as we finished cleaning up from the sale. What few items remained were destined to be donated.

"No problem," Rose replied as she set a Sold sign on the kitchen table. "Got any plans tonight?"

"A night in my jammies with a glass of wine sounds like heaven."

"You two should go out," Steven said as he came into the room and surveyed our progress. "You've earned it."

"Don't you have plans?" I tried to disguise the desperation in my voice. I could use a quiet night at home after the exhausting day I'd just had.

"Nope, she's all yours," Steven said as he slipped an arm around Rose and gave her a quick squeeze. "Tonight, Dad and I are helping load some of the furniture that sold." He gave me an appraising look. "Unless you want to help us, I suggest you two go have some fun."

"What do ya say, Lanie? I hear Seabreeze has karaoke," Rose suggested.

The last thing I wanted to do was spend a night listening to awful singing, but Rose looked so hopeful, I couldn't bring myself to turn her down. And karaoke night was one of the most popular events at the bar. I would be able to disappear into the crowd.

"Sure, sounds great," I said, forcing myself to sound enthusiastic.

"Perfect!" Rose exclaimed. "Let me just run home to change. Pick you up in an hour?" Rose embraced me without waiting for a reply and rushed out the door. With a resigned sigh, I trudged up the stairs to get ready.

I chose an off-the-shoulder pink dress that hugged me in all the right places. It wasn't exactly the best option for blending in, but after being so underdressed for Bobby McKey's the other night, I didn't want to risk it again. No chance of that in this dress. I curled my hair and applied a little makeup. Before I knew it, the front door opened, and Rose's voice drifted up the stairs.

I slid my feet into a pair of matching heels and met Rose in the hall. One look at Rose's outfit made me second-guess my choice. Had I overdone it? I pursed my lips. Did I care? The dress could be my armor, and something told me that tonight, I would need it.

Steven dropped us off at Seabreeze, which was already packed. Seeing all those people caused conflicting emotions to bubble up inside me. As we walked toward the bar, Rose linked our arms, and I was grateful for the support. The distinct sound of steel drums poured out from within, and I resisted the urge to roll my eyes. A Caribbean paradise, right in the middle of quiet Cedar Haven. Sometimes, the town tried way too hard to be something it wasn't.

Once inside, we searched the crowded place for empty seats, and my traitorous heart skipped a beat when I saw Nate. He sat at a table with a couple of the guys from the shop and a few women I didn't recognize. A burning sensation spread through my chest, and I froze. What was wrong with me? I had James, so I had no right to be jealous.

Before I could assess the feeling further, Nate's eyes met mine, and the slow smile that came over his face took my breath away. He had rolled up the sleeves of his shirt, and his well-defined arm was draped over the back of his chair. I gave him a shy smile in return then scurried after Rose to a booth along the wall of the bar.

"Thanks for coming out with me tonight," Rose said as we sat down. "I've been hoping to get a chance to talk to you alone."

"What's up?" I asked as I shrugged out of my coat and set it on the bench beside me.

"I know Steven has asked you to read a poem at our wedding, and initially, we weren't planning on having a bridal party, but I was wondering..." Rose's voice faltered.

I searched her face, frowning at her nervousness. "Yes?" I prompted, my curiosity getting the better of me.

"Would you be my maid of honor?"

"Oh my gosh, Rose! Of course, I would love to," I gushed. Rose's shoulders visibly relaxed as I grabbed her hand. "I'm even more excited for your wedding now!" I cocked my head. "But why were you so afraid to ask me?"

Rose blew out a breath. "It's just... with everything you have going on, I didn't want to add to your plate."

"But this is a fun thing, and I could use more of those."

The server came, and we ordered our drinks: a cosmopolitan for Rose and a Long Island iced tea for me. I needed something strong, especially if Rose had any plans to participate in karaoke.

While we waited for our drinks, we chatted about Rose's job and what I had missed while I was in Seattle. Through it all, I shamelessly snuck glances at Nate when Rose wasn't looking and was rewarded many times with another heart-stopping smile. The women at the table with him kept trying to engage him in conversation, but from what I could tell, he didn't pay them any attention. I hated how much that pleased me.

"That boy has got it bad," Rose said, catching me off guard.

"What? Who?"

"Don't look now, but Nate Sanders hasn't taken his eyes off you since we walked in."

Blood rushed to my cheeks as I dropped my gaze to the table. I was saved from a response when the server appeared with our drinks. I gulped down mine, hoping Rose would drop that line of conversation. Nobody knew about the dinner Nate and I had shared, but I knew that in such a small town, nothing stayed secret for long.

"Is something going on between you?" Rose pressed.

Oh boy. There's not enough alcohol in the world for this conversation. "N-No. Why would you think that?"

"Because you turned about five shades of red when I told you he was staring at you," Rose replied with an arched brow.

I sighed. If we kept making eyes at each other across the bar like that, it wouldn't be long before the whole town shared Rose's suspicions. The best thing to do would be to come clean and avoid any nefarious rumors.

"He, uh, I mean, we had dinner together the other night."

"Um, okay, and why am I just now hearing about this?" Rose demanded as she leaned forward, her sleek black hair curtaining her face.

"I haven't told anyone," I protested. "It was an impromptu thing. We ran into each other at the store, and I invited him over." Lifting my shoulders in what I hoped was a nonchalant shrug, I forced a smile. "No big deal."

"The way his eyes are burning holes into that dress of yours suggests otherwise."

That was no exaggeration because I could feel the heat of Nate's gaze from across the room. It took all my willpower not to sneak another glance in his direction. With a deep breath, I focused on Rose.

"If I tell you something, do you promise not to tell anyone? Not even Steven?" I pleaded.

Rose nodded, her brown eyes wide. How do I approach this? Was this even the right thing to do? Probably not, but I needed an outlet, a sounding board. Keeping my feelings bottled up wasn't helping anything. I racked my brain on how to broach the subject. Perhaps I should start where all the trouble began, with that darn bird.

"Do you believe in legends?" I blurted out.

Rose's brows knitted together, and I imagined that was the last thing my future sister-in-law had expected me to say.

"Legends? What do you mean? And what does this have to do with your ex?"

"Just"—I held up a hand—"answer the question. Do you think there's any truth to myths or legends? Folklore?"

Rose rested her pointed chin on her hand as she appeared to seriously contemplate my question. "I guess there's some truth to every legend, isn't there? It had to have started somewhere, right? So it's likely it began with a real story that took on mythical proportions over time." She fixed me in her steely gaze. "Please explain what the heck this has to do with Nate."

"I know this is going to sound crazy." I hesitated. "But I've been seeing this bird, a cardinal, often over the past several weeks. I went to see Mrs. Winters. You know, my mom's neighbor?"

"Oh my! Steven told me about her." She lowered her voice. "Isn't she a witch?"

"She's not, well—" Cassandra had never confirmed or denied her witchy reputation. Not that it really mattered. I waved my hand. "Anyway, she told me legend says cardinals are visitors from heaven."

"Visitors from... Wait, do you think your mom was reincarnated as a bird?" Rose asked incredulously as she signaled to the server to bring another round.

"Not exactly," I hedged. I wasn't explaining things very well. "Cassandra says they represent a deceased loved one who's trying to make contact."

"All right. Let's say I buy this. What does your mom want to contact you about?" Rose asked. "This isn't Casper. She doesn't have any unfinished business that I'm aware of."

I threw back my head and laughed. "Wow, what a reference."

"I was a Devon Sawa fan back in the day," Rose said with a wink. "What do you think your mom wants, though?"

"The thing is," I continued, stirring what was left of my drink and struggling to find the right words. "The cardinal tends to show up right before I run into Nate."

"Oh? Did you see it today?"

"I think I saw it briefly this morning, but things were hectic, and I wasn't really paying attention."

Rose swallowed the last of her drink in silence as she digested everything I'd said. I silently pleaded with her to understand and not dismiss me as crazy. It mattered in that moment that someone believed me. I needed someone else to understand what I was going through.

"But... didn't your mom hate Nate?" Rose finally asked after the server had set down our drinks and removed the empty glasses.

"She did," I replied, and I couldn't hide the pain in my voice. "I never fully understood why other than that she and my dad were also high school sweethearts and she seemed to see my dad in him, but that's the part that doesn't make sense."

"Maybe she's warning you away from him?"

"It doesn't feel that way," I admitted. "And Cassandra suggested my mom might have had regrets."

"Ah, so she does have unfinished business, just like Casper," Rose quipped with a grin.

I snorted. "I suppose that's one way of looking at it."

"And how do you feel about Nate?"

I squirmed under Rose's scrutiny. "I, well—" But I was cut off by the sudden appearance of the man in question.

"Hello, Lanie." His voice, low and deep, sent my heart careening into overdrive.

"Fancy meeting you here," I replied, pulling my lips into an easy smile, which faltered when I met his gaze. His eyes were filled with that same fire from the other night.

"Would you like to join us?" Rose asked innocently as I shot her a death glare.

Nate didn't move, his eyes locked on me. Unsure what else to do, I scooted over on the booth's bench and patted the spot beside me. His slow smile caused another wave of heat to sweep over my face.

"Are you planning to do karaoke?" Rose directed her question at Nate while I resisted the urge to kick her under the table.

"I'm not much of a singer," Nate said with a chuckle. He turned his dark-brown eyes back to me. "But I wouldn't object to hearing you sing."

"Oh, I don't think so." I shook my head vehemently. "I don't sing in front of strangers." *Or exes.*

"You sang at your mother's funeral," Rose pointed out.

"That was different," I murmured, breathing deeply through the sudden pang of sadness at the memory. Nate gently laid a hand on mine, a move that didn't go unnoticed by Rose.

"It was a beautiful song," Nate told her, his voice sincere.

"I think you should sing, Lanie," Rose insisted.

"I'm going to need a few more of these if I'm going up there," I quipped, shaking my glass.

With a wicked grin, Rose waved our server over.

The laid-back atmosphere of the bar gave way to excitement as the stage was set up for karaoke. Cedar Haven didn't have much to offer, but karaoke night was a town favorite. I downed my drink quickly, hoping to imbue some liquid courage before I dared to climb up on stage in front of the town.

"All right, how's everyone doing tonight?" the DJ called out over the microphone. A chorus of cheers erupted in response.

"The sign-up sheet for karaoke is open now. Come on down and show us how much talent Cedar Haven has!"

Multiple people stood up and rushed to the front, but I made no move to join them.

"Come on, Lanie. Whatcha gonna sing for us?" Rose asked.

"I was thinking something fun, maybe '22' by Taylor Swift."

"Ooh, that sounds perfect!" Rose agreed and motioned for Nate to move. He slid out to let me pass. His encouraging smile did nothing to settle my nerves. Swallowing my fears and my pride, I teetered down to the stage, very aware of just how much alcohol was currently making its way through my system. After a cursory glance at the list, I signed my name along with my song choice. The DJ had Taylor Swift's newer albums as well. Maybe it was the alcohol, or maybe it was Nate's influence, but for whatever reason, I found myself signing up for a second song.

Most of the singers that night weren't half-bad, though I probably wouldn't have noticed, as I was too focused on my own performance. The closer it got to being my turn, the more my hands shook. At one point, Nate laid his hand over mine and gave a gentle squeeze, which did nothing to calm me down. If that kept up, I would pass out before I ever made it on stage.

"All right, all right, all right," the announcer said. "Next up, we have Cedar Haven's own Lanie McAllister performing Taylor Swift's '22.' Give it up for Lanie!"

More cheers came, the loudest ones from Rose and Nate, as I walked up to the stage. I concentrated on the screen, ignoring the crowd as I waited for the first notes to play. My first few lines were a little stiff, and I swayed to the music to try to loosen up. By the time I hit the chorus, I was in my element, flashing two fingers and dancing across the stage.

When it was over, my face flushed from both exertion and excitement. I took a quick bow and returned to my table. Nate and Rose greeted me with huge smiles.

"That was amazing!" Rose grabbed my hand. "Please tell me you'll do an encore."

"Well," I replied hesitantly. "There was one other song I signed up for."

"Which is?" Rose demanded.

"It's a surprise," I said with a sideways glance at Nate.

He raised an eyebrow but didn't comment.

We sat and enjoyed another round while others performed, then it was my turn again. Still riding the high from my earlier success, I felt less nervous about the performance. But I was apprehensive about the song I had chosen. For one thing, I didn't know it nearly as well as the last one, and for another, when I'd first heard it, it reminded me of Nate. To sing it with him sitting just a few feet from me would be a whole new experience.

Would he read anything into it? More importantly, did I want him to? Last night had felt like old times in so many ways, and I wasn't sure how to process those feelings I was having toward him. If he did read something into it, would he tell me? Was I about to ruin the tentative friendship we'd formed?

As the first notes of "The 1" began to play, I cleared my throat and swayed to the beat. I searched the crowd until I found him. He smiled encouragingly at me as I sang through the first verse, but when I arrived at the refrain, his brows pulled together briefly before his whole countenance softened. The song was about a past love, and the narrator talked about how she wished the relationship had lasted. How sad she was that things had ended between them and how nice it would have been if it had turned out differently.

I sang the last two lines with my whole heart. Cheers erupted from the other patrons, but I only had eyes for Nate.

When I returned to our table, Rose was ready to go. She had texted Steven to come pick us up. My stomach clenched in disappointment. I'd hoped to have a moment alone with Nate, but as

I followed Rose to the door, he discreetly grabbed my hand and gave it a squeeze. A promise. Of what, I wasn't sure, but I hoped to find out more soon.

"What was that?" Rose demanded once we were outside and alone.

"What was what?"

"You know what." She crossed her arms. "That song. The way you looked at Nate. Lanie, what's going on? I know I've teased you about Nate, but I'd meant it as a joke. Now, I'm wondering if I was a lot closer to the mark." Shaking her head, she stared at me. "I thought you were with James?"

Her words were like a bucket of ice-cold water over the warmth of my high. She was right. *What am I doing?* Guilt settled in the pit of my stomach. I hadn't been thinking about James at all.

"I-I don't know," I moaned, covering my face with my hands. "I'm so confused."

Her face softened, and she put a hand on my shoulder. "I can't empathize, as I've never had any doubts about your brother, but I can sympathize. Do you still have feelings for Nate, or is this stemming from the cardinal?"

I stood there, unsure how to respond. Did I still love Nate? Perhaps the better question was, had I ever *stopped* loving Nate? Deep down, I knew I hadn't, but it wasn't the same as being in love with him. He was my first love, and as the saying went, "You never forget your first love." Was that all that it was? Was I pining for what might have been? What never could be?

"Both, maybe?" I finally said with a sigh. "Please don't tell Steven. I'm afraid he'd let it slip to Dad, and then I'd never hear the end of it. He has more than enough fodder for his campaign to convince me to stay. This would just add fuel to the flames."

"I've told your father he needs to let that go." Rose rolled her eyes. "But I promise I won't say a word to either of them."

Her eyes were so filled with pity, I couldn't bear to meet them.

"You need to figure this out and soon. Before someone gets hurt."

I nodded and dropped the subject as Steven's car pulled up. Rose slid into the passenger seat while I claimed the back seat. I looked forward to having some time alone with my thoughts. Rose was right. I was playing with fire, and someone, probably me, was going to get burned.

When I arrived home, I saw I had missed a call. Nausea swept through me when I saw it was James and not Nate. But maybe it was for the best. We needed to talk, and while it was too late to call him back, I did it anyway. I couldn't keep avoiding him.

"Lanie?" His voice was groggy, confirming I had woken him up. "It's late. Is everything okay?"

"I'm not sure," I mumbled.

"What's wrong?" he asked, and my heart broke a little at the sincere concern in his voice.

"I need to tell you something," I said, debating exactly what I wanted to say and how I wanted to say it.

"I'm listening."

"I—" An internal battle raged within me until I finally made a choice. "I applied for a job in Cedar Haven."

Coward. But I couldn't bring myself to tell him about Nate over the phone. We'd been together for all of our adult lives. He deserved better. We both did.

The silence on the other end did nothing to assuage my guilt. *What is he thinking?* The springs on his bed squeaked, and I could almost see him sitting up, rubbing his eyes, and trying to make sense of what I'd said.

"Why would you do that? You have a job here."

"I know." I covered my eyes with my hand. "It's just, the other day, when you told me you'd found us an apartment, I felt like my life was moving on without me. I needed to feel like I was in control of something. I'd heard about this job from some of my fr-friends." I winced as I stumbled over that word. "I thought I would keep my options open."

James exhaled slowly. I'd never hated myself more. First, I woke him up, then I couldn't even fess up to the real truth, the one that mattered. But I supposed that was fitting, since I wasn't even ready to admit that truth to myself.

"I thought you said you didn't want to move back there because it's too painful. I... I thought I was doing you a favor by finding us a place."

"I know, babe, and I appreciate it, but the place you found... It's too expensive." I blew out a breath. "I want to be part of the process."

"All right, well, we can wait until you're here, then. I just don't understand why you applied for a position there. You do still want to move in together, right?"

I closed my eyes, wishing I could give him a better answer. I wasn't sure about anything at that moment. Despite the issues we'd had recently,

James had been a good boyfriend. We had a lot in common. But there had always been something missing, and that night, sitting beside Nate with my heart jackhammering in my chest, I realized the thing that was missing was passion. I didn't feel passionate about James. Sure, I cared about him, but how I felt didn't hold a candle to my feelings for Nate.

"I do," I assured him, and at that moment, I meant it. What I wasn't clear on was whether that would change. "I just—look, there's something I need to…"

"Hey, listen, you don't have to explain anything to me," James cut in. "I know you're having a rough time, what with your mom's estate and selling the house. If waiting to find a place until you're here will alleviate some of your burden, I totally get it."

"Thank you for understanding," I replied, sagging against the wall. The war going on inside me was wearing me down. "I'm sorry for waking you."

"Hey, I'm here for you. Whatever you need."

My eyes welled with tears, and I forced them back, desperately trying to keep my voice even. "Go back to sleep. I'll talk to you later."

"Good night, my love."

I winced as I ended the call. The truth had been right there on the tip of my tongue. Why hadn't I told him about Nate? I was all mixed up inside. My head fell back as I stared at the ceiling. What was I going to do now?

Chapter Nine

"YOU'RE COMING TO THE Valentine's Day dance this weekend, aren't you, Lanie?" Rose asked as we sat together on my bed, pretending to pack. It was a convenient excuse for hiding from Steven and Dad as they continued preparing the house for sale. The real estate agent planned to list it the next morning, and I struggled to come to terms with the idea that someday soon, my childhood home would be in the hands of strangers.

"I'm not really a Valentine's Day person." I flipped through an old magazine I'd found when going through my desk drawers. "Besides, isn't it for couples and singles? My plus-one is on the other side of the country.”

“It's for anyone who wants to attend,” Rose replied with exasperation. “Come on. You have to go. You know it raises money for the fire department. Who cares what your relationship status is?”

“Ugh, this town has too many events!” I cried as I shut my eyes and mimed banging the back of my head against the wall.

“I heard Nate is going,” Rose said a little too innocently as she flipped a page in her magazine. Her eyes flicked briefly to mine.

I kept my face blank, picking up the magazine again and feigning interest in an article. “I'm trying to keep my distance.”

“Is that what you're doing?”

Glowering at Rose, I climbed off my bed and tossed the magazine into the trash. At the rate we were going, I would still be packing when the new owners moved in. How had I accumulated so much stuff in my short lifetime?

"Have you talked to him since karaoke?"

"No, as that would defeat the entire purpose of keeping my distance." I opened a drawer and pulled out a pile of papers, mostly old notebooks from my emo poetry phase. After shooting a quick glance over my shoulder, I paged through them, cringing at my angsty rhymes.

"Well, you shouldn't let it fester. Half the town saw the sparks flying between you two, and I imagine they'll be keeping a close watch on any interaction you may have at the dance."

"Which is why I have no intention of going," I retorted, debating what to do with the notebooks. Tear them up and save face, or save them for a laugh when I was back on the West Coast?

"Lanie," Rose said, her tone gentle.

With a sigh, I turned and looked at her.

"You need to talk to him. Things are clearly not as over between you two as I thought."

"As long as I'm with James, there can be nothing between Nate and me," I insisted. At least, that was what I kept telling myself.

I ripped out the most cringeworthy poems and shredded them before tossing the rest of the notebooks into a box. Upon opening the next drawer, I found a heavy book.

"Ooh!" Rose squealed. "I love old yearbooks." She waved her hands, gesturing for me to hand it to her. After I did, she flipped through the pages and skimmed the signatures, reading a few of particular interest aloud. "Oh my gosh! There's one from Nate in here."

I spun around. "Don't read that!"

"'Dear Lanie,'" Rose read, oblivious to my growing distress. "'I can't believe we're graduating soon. It's going to be hard when you go off to college in a few months, but I know we are meant to be together. We're strong, and we can survive the distance.' Wow. It's like a weird version of foreshadowing."

"Please stop," I whispered as I sank to the floor.

Rose closed the book and stood. "Hey, are you okay?"

I shook my head, willing myself not to cry. I knew that message by heart. While I was home caring for Mom, I'd found the yearbook and read the message over and over, desperately clinging to a happier time in my life. Even after our relationship's disastrous ending, I had never loved anyone as much as I'd loved Nate.

And even back then, I'd probably known that what I'd felt for Nate had never gone away. There were times when I was home last spring when I would go into town to buy groceries or pick up a prescription, and out of the corner of my eye, I would catch a glimpse of dark hair. Each time, I turned, my heart fluttering in my chest. It was almost never him, and the few times we had met, our conversations were brief and brutal. All that time, I thought what I felt was dread. But what if it was hope?

"I'm afraid I'm still in love with him," I murmured, not realizing I had spoken aloud.

"Oh, honey." Rose knelt on the floor, wrapping her arms around me and pulling me close.

I raised my eyes to meet Rose's. "I don't know what to do."

"What do you want to do?" Rose asked.

Leaning back against the bed, I sighed. "Part of me worries that I'm just setting us both up for heartbreak again." I rolled my head to look at her. "Even if I break things off with James, I still have that job in California waiting for me."

"I'm sure we could find you a job here. There's bound to be a teaching position at one of the schools."

I kept the news about my interview to myself, mostly so I didn't jinx it. But even if they offered me the position, it wasn't so simple. I still had my promise to my mother hanging over my head. The idea of ending things with James and choosing to stay in Cedar Haven made my skin tight and itchy.

Would she ever forgive me if I broke my word? Or would she find a new way to haunt me, one that was less peaceful than a small red bird?

"You're thinking about your mom, aren't you?"

When I glanced at Rose, she was staring at me with a gentle smile. "Am I that transparent?"

"Yes," she said with a laugh, then her face sobered. "And no. I don't pretend to know every complicated detail about your relationship with your mom, but I've learned enough to understand the pressure she put on you." She laid a hand on my shoulder. "She also talked about it once or twice."

I raised my eyebrows. "She did? When? What did she say?"

"Oh, I don't remember the specifics. She wasn't very lucid at the time, but it was more her tone." Rose's eyes softened. "I think she regretted pushing you. She wanted you to be happy. By the end, she seemed to understand that what she thought would make you happy and what actually does are two very different things."

"I'm just so worried that I'll disappoint her." I covered my face in my hands. If seeing me stuck in a loveless marriage was her worst fear, then mine was breaking my promise and smashing her dreams for me.

"As long as you follow your heart, Lanie, I doubt you could ever do that."

I stared up at her, wishing I could believe that, but the truth was, I knew my mother better than that. Maybe she regretted some things when death came knocking, but I couldn't imagine she would ever release me from the promise I'd made.

Rose stood and moved toward my shelves with a box. I wanted to protest that I would take care of the books, but I stopped myself. If we didn't pack something, I might have to pay rent to the new owners.

She paused as a card fluttered out of one of the books. Her forehead creased as she stared at it.

"What's that?" I asked, going to my dresser and pulling out an armful of clothes.

"A business card." She turned to me, one hand on her hip. "For the therapist I recommended."

"Oh, yeah, um, about that," I said, avoiding her gaze.

"Did you even try to go?"

"Yes." I dropped the clothes onto the bed and crossed my arms. "I didn't like her."

"How many appointments did you have?"

"Just the one." At her expression, I rushed on. "But it was enough. Trust me." Turning back to the clothes on the bed, I continued, "Besides, I don't need therapy. I'm fine."

"Sure you are," Rose retorted sarcastically.

I ignored her, folding the clothes and packing them into a rubber bin I'd found in the attic. But I couldn't stop the memory of that awful appointment. Or the image of Dr. Grace Kelvin, with her spectacles halfway down her nose and her eyebrows raised in the most judgmental expression.

"What did she say that was so awful?" Rose asked, her tone gentler than before.

My fist clenched around the hem of a sweater, and I took several deep breaths before responding. "She thought I should confront Mom about all the things she did wrong before it was too late. Dr. Kelvin said that I was shoving my feelings deep down inside and not dealing with them in order to keep the peace."

Rose laid a hand on my shoulder. "And what about that was wrong?"

I whirled around, my mouth dropping open in shock. "How can you say that? I had mere months to spend with my mother, and you think I should have spent them in a constant battle?"

"No." She took the shirt from my hand and placed it in the box. "But I do think you're pushing your feelings away, even now that she's gone. You won't say an ill word about her, despite the fact that even I know there were unresolved issues between you."

My anger deflated, and I sank down onto the bed. "I'm not sure what good it would have done."

"Perhaps not, and maybe Dr. Kelvin was wrong to insist you confront your mom." She sat beside me. "But don't you think you owe it to yourself to work through those issues in a safe and professional environment? Dr. Kelvin can be harsh, but I do believe she saw what we all do, what simmers within you beneath the surface."

"I won't go back, not to her, anyway," I said. "If you have other recommendations, I'll consider them but not her."

"I understand." Rose patted my hand. "It may even be better if you go to someone outside of the community, who doesn't know you at all."

"And what am I supposed to talk about?" My tone was haughty, but I suspected even Rose could see that it was to mask my fear. What would I learn in therapy about my mother, about myself? What did I stand to lose with that knowledge?

"If you're not comfortable talking about your mom, you could talk about Nate, James, whether you should make California or Maryland your home." She shrugged. "It's your hour, but I do think you should try again."

"Fine." I finished packing up the pile of clothes on the bed before I removed another armful from the dresser. Talking about Nate almost sounded worse than discussing my complicated relationship with my mother. Almost.

"This may all be for nothing," I said, trying to lighten the mood. "Who says Nate still feels anything for me? It could all be in my head."

She gave me a dubious look. "Anyone who saw the two of you at karaoke wouldn't believe that for a second."

"But—"

"Well, you can always ask him," Rose cut me off. Her face brightened. "At the Valentine's Day dance!"

"You're relentless," I growled, but deep down, I knew she was right. Nate and I had been dancing around the elephant between us for long enough. Even if it turned out he felt nothing for me, it was better to know, wasn't it? And if that was the case, it would be good for me to have a shoulder to cry on, even if I was paying for that shoulder.

⁓∼ℓℓ∼⁓

After the house went on the market, the real estate agent suggested we hold an open house. I thought the idea came rather last-minute, but Steven agreed. So I spent the week vacuuming the downstairs and clearing away the dust that had gathered. I also forced myself to finish packing my room. I couldn't put it off any longer.

Saturday morning, I woke early and checked to ensure the pamphlets the real estate agent had dropped off the day before were set out on the table in the hall. Steven was bringing muffins, scones, and coffee to be served to potential buyers, and I threw a tray of cookies into the oven for good measure. No one could resist the smell of freshly baked goods, and it might entice someone to make an offer on the spot. At any rate, it couldn't hurt.

My cardinal friend appeared, and I hoped that meant Nate would be at the dance that evening. After the conversation with Rose, I thought it was the best venue to have the talk we needed, though a part of me hoped he would show up at the open house. Either way, I felt that seeing the cardinal was a good omen. Maybe that night, I would finally make some sense of all the conflicting feelings I'd been having lately.

Steven arrived promptly at eight, his arms filled with bags of goodies and a box of freshly brewed coffee. I opened the door for him, and he sniffed the air appreciatively.

"Are you baking in here?" He moved toward the kitchen.

I followed close behind. "I thought it might help add to the appeal."

He smiled and grabbed some paper plates from the cabinet before setting out the various muffins on the counter. Should we have kept the kitchen table until after the house sold? I hadn't minded eating while standing up or carrying food to my room, but perhaps the table would have helped for staging purposes. I shook my head. It was too late.

"You don't have to stay, you know." Steven took one of the muffins and peeled back the paper. "People are just going to be wandering through the rooms and talking to their own agents, if they have one."

"I don't really have anywhere else to be."

He raised an eyebrow. "Aren't you going to the dance tonight? Don't you need to get your hair or nails done or something?"

I laughed. "I'm not going to the prom, Steven. It's just a dance."

He shrugged. "Well, Rose will be here later, and I figured the three of us could go together if you wanted."

"That works for me."

The open house was set to begin at nine, and I made sure I finished getting ready before people started arriving. Steven had brought folding chairs to make up for our lack of furniture.

A few minutes before nine, John, our real estate agent, arrived. I had met him briefly at the estate sale, but Steven had handled most of the real estate stuff. John stood in the living room, scrutinizing every detail with a furrowed brow. His dark hair was cut short, and his small eyes seemed to narrow each time they moved to another corner of the room. I hoped my cleaning hadn't been in vain, though if it didn't live up to his standards, I couldn't imagine what he'd thought of it before.

"When people arrive, try not to bombard them with information. Be available for any questions they might have, but otherwise, let them wander the house at their leisure." John turned to Steven. "I imagine we'll get an offer within a week or so."

"Good," Steven replied. "The sooner we can sell the house, the better."

A sharp pain twinged in my chest, but I forced a smile when John's dark gaze fell on me. No sense in him knowing how much it hurt me to see my childhood home sold. Besides, what else did I expect us to do with it? I was leaving, and Steven had already bought a place for him and Rose to live after they married.

People began drifting in about half past nine, and I kept the smile pasted on my face. I didn't recognize any of the potential buyers, which only served to increase my anxiety. But it made sense that someone outside of town would be interested. Everyone who already lived in Cedar

Haven had a home, and I hadn't heard anyone say they were looking to buy.

Steven and John fielded most of the questions, which left me with a lot of time on my hands and not much to distract me. Maybe I should have found something else to do that day, but as the executor, I felt an obligation to be there.

Around noon, Nate entered the house with a frown as he scanned the room. When his eyes met mine, they lit up, and he crossed over to me.

"Good crowd," he said. "Any offers yet?"

I shook my head. "John thinks we'll get one within a week or two."

He glanced at me. "How do you feel about that?"

"I don't know." Were it anyone else, I might have lied. But Nate knew how hard being there was for me. I slipped my hand in his and gave him a squeeze. "Thanks for coming."

"Anything for you."

My heart skipped a beat, and I turned away. I still hadn't talked to either him or James, and I hated myself for it. Well, I'd planned to talk to Nate that night at the dance, but maybe right then was my chance. I opened my mouth to tell him everything when Steven joined us.

"Hey, Nate, thanks for stopping by. You wouldn't happen to be in the market for a new home, would you?"

Nate laughed and shook his head. "Even if I was, I couldn't afford this."

"Well, don't let Lanie here keep you hiding in a corner. We've got a great spread of baked goods in the kitchen." He put a hand on Nate's shoulder and led him away. Nate glanced at me, worry in his eyes, but he didn't resist Steven.

Part of me was glad for the moment to collect my thoughts, which made me a bigger coward. Why couldn't I just tell him? Even if he didn't feel the same, it was better to know that now before I blew up my whole life, wasn't it?

I mustered up my courage and headed to the kitchen, hoping to steal Nate away for a moment alone. But when I arrived, he was gone.

⁓ℓℓ⁓

That evening, I picked out a simple red dress. I curled my hair and pulled half of it into a silver butterfly barrette. I was still puzzled about Nate's sudden departure earlier in the day, but I assumed he'd needed to return to the shop. Still, it was odd that he hadn't at least said goodbye.

As I reached into my jewelry drawer for a pair of earrings, my hand hovered over a small box. With hesitant fingers, I pulled it out and flipped it open, knowing full well what was inside: a silver locket with the initials NL engraved on its face. Nate had given it to me on the anniversary of our first date.

Let's not be too obvious. I placed the box back into the drawer. I grabbed a pair of earrings and started to close the drawer, but something told me to wear the locket. Shaking my head, I picked the box up and slipped the chain around my neck before I could change my mind. It did go well with the dress, and maybe it would give me the courage to tell Nate how I felt.

The front door opened, and Steven called for me. While I was happy to ride over with him and Rose, I hoped Nate would give me a lift home and I could broach the conversation then. After grabbing my purse and sliding my feet into a pair of red heels, I went downstairs.

"Well, well, well. Don't you look nice this evening." Steven smiled warmly. "Trying to impress someone?"

I rolled my eyes and slipped into my coat, gesturing for him to lead the way. After he flipped the porch light on, we headed to Steven's car. Rose sat in the passenger seat and gave me two thumbs up. I forced a smile as I climbed into the back seat.

"You look amazing!" Rose gushed.

"Thanks. So do you," I replied, reaching forward and giving Rose's arm a squeeze.

"And of course, I look awesome," Steven teased as he settled into his seat and backed the car down the driveway.

"As always, darling," Rose said sweetly, and I pretended to gag.

The drive to the fire station's hall was short, and I struggled to calm my pounding heart as we pulled into the parking lot. I didn't immediately see Nate's car, but since the whole town was there, that wasn't a surprise. Steven helped me out of his car, and I followed him and Rose into the hall.

Cedar Haven liked to go all out for their events, and the Valentine's Day dance was no exception. The hall was decorated with red and pink balloons. Rich ruby tablecloths were dotted with sequined hearts, and the lights were even shaded to give the room a warmer hue. I smiled wistfully. Despite my earlier grumbling, I had missed those events since going away to college. Even when I was home and caring for Mom, I hadn't had time to attend any town affairs. Growing up, I had a love-hate relationship with Cedar Haven's desire to celebrate every little thing. While holidays like Christmas and Halloween were normal, the town also put on a Presidents' Day play, a May Day celebration, and even a Flag Day parade. Sometimes, it felt a little too much, but I suddenly had a new appreciation for the town's eccentricities.

Trudy and her husband, Russell, sat at a table together, watching the crowds. I left Rose and Steven to go say hello. They greeted me with warm smiles as I took a seat next to Trudy.

"We thought we'd grab a table now, before the crowds take over," Trudy said. She gave me a brief once-over and a raised eyebrow. "You look spectacular."

"Thanks," I replied, a warm flush stealing over my cheeks. I tried to keep my excitement in check. So far, it seemed like the town's rumor mill hadn't caught on to Nate and me, and I hoped to keep it that way.

"Where's the baby tonight?" I asked Trudy, trying to distract myself, though my eyes kept sliding to the door.

"With my mom," Trudy replied with a smile. "She's been chomping at the bit to have an overnight with him, so I thought tonight would be perfect."

"And let me tell you, it's awesome to be off duty," Russell said, clinking his glass with Trudy's. "Parenthood is no joke." He drained his glass. "I'm going to get another one. You want one, babe?"

Trudy shook her head, having barely touched the drink in front of her. I saw that as an opportunity to scout the hall for Nate, and I jumped up to join Russell.

I ordered a glass of wine and tried to discreetly search the room. Rose and Steven were chatting with Bea. I had heard that Bea was cutting back on her hours at the diner and might be looking to sell it soon. Without any close family nearby, she didn't have anyone to take over. I hoped when the time came, someone in town would step up and keep the place the same.

Wine in hand, I started to make my way back to Trudy when I saw him. He stood near the entrance to the hall, talking to some of the guys from the shop. My heart in my throat, I placed the glass on an empty table then rushed over to him.

"Nate, I'm so glad you're here. I'd hoped to catch up with you at the open house, but you left without saying goodbye."

"Lanie," Nate replied, giving a brief nod.

I frowned. "Are you okay?"

"Fine. Excuse me. I forgot something in my car." He turned and stalked away.

For a moment, I stared at his retreating back, shocked at his cold and distant demeanor, then I raced after him.

"Wait!" He didn't turn, and I scrambled to catch up. When I finally did, I grabbed his arm. "Hey, what's going on?"

"Nothing. I told you, I forgot something." But he refused to meet my eyes.

"It looks like you're leaving."

He shrugged. "Maybe I am. There's no point in my being here."

"Why not? The whole town is here, and you're part of the town," I teased, but my joke fell flat. "Please tell me what's going on." I tried to sound firm, but my voice cracked, and I shivered—whether from the winter air or his frigid reception, I couldn't say.

His face softened. "Go back inside before you freeze."

"Come with me. I'd love to dance with you, like old times."

That struck a chord. His eyes darkened, and he pulled his arm free. "Maybe you should dance with your boyfriend."

I staggered back as the air left my lungs, like someone had punched me. "You know about James?"

"Your brother told me." His lips set in a grim line. "*You* should have told me."

He was right. Of course I should have told him. I knew why I hadn't, but I was too much of a coward to admit that to him, even then.

"It just never came up," I said with a shrug. What a terrible excuse.

He shook his head. "This whole time, I thought it was the job taking you to California, but it's not, is it? It's him."

"That's not true! I do have a job lined up." At his raised eyebrow, I blew out a breath. "But yes, James is part of it. He and I have plans to move in together."

Nate inhaled sharply, and I hurried on.

"But things have changed," I said. "These last few weeks, spending time with you, I realized—"

"I don't want to hear it, Lanie," he retorted, backing away from me.

"Nate, please!" I cried, grasping for something to make him understand. Lifting the locket, I held it out, and it glinted in the streetlights. "I wore this tonight for the same reason I sang you that song at karaoke."

His eyes widened when he recognized the locket. "B-But what about your boyfriend?" His tone was rough, and I could see the anger in his eyes dissipating as he stared at the necklace.

"I..." What *about* James? That was the question of the moment. I wasn't being fair to either man. There I was, trying to assure myself of Nate's feelings when I had someone waiting for me in California. How selfish could I possibly be?

Before I could formulate a response, a throat cleared behind me. As I whirled around, my hand flew to my mouth, and I gaped as a familiar figure stepped from the shadows.

"Hello, Lanie."

"James?" It came out more like a whisper. The shock of seeing him stole my breath.

He chuckled as he moved closer to us. His thick dark hair was parted to the side, though I struggled to make out his expression as the light played across his full beard. Pushing his glasses up his nose, he stuck out his hand to Nate.

"I don't believe we've met," James said, his tone cool.

Nate stared at his hand for a moment before he accepted it. I monitored their every moment, both men grim-faced as they shook hands. When they stepped back from each other, they both turned to me. I tried to arrange my features into a blank expression, but I wasn't sure I achieved it. Blood pounded in my ears as I processed the situation.

I swallowed the lump forming in my throat. "What are you doing here?"

James raised an eyebrow. "I came to surprise you."

Well, he'd certainly done that. I glanced at Nate, but his eyes were alighting with the anger that had just disappeared a moment ago. My only hope was to prove how surprised I was by James's sudden appearance, though the fact that I hadn't been up front about James's existence wasn't going to help things. But I would deal with that later.

"It's good to see you," I said, keeping my voice light but detached. "But I wish you had told me you were coming so I could've prepared."

James smirked. "That wouldn't have been much of a surprise, now would it?" He glanced from me to Nate. "After our last phone call, I was worried. Applying to a job here when you have the perfect position waiting for you in California?" He shook his head. "It just wasn't like you. I had a meeting with our DC office anyway and thought it might be nice to conduct it in person. So I booked a flight and figured I'd swing by to visit with you for the weekend."

The tightness in my shoulders eased ever so slightly. While he was in town, at least he wasn't staying long. After he met with the DC office on Monday, he would be back on a plane to California either Monday night or Tuesday morning.

As I processed all that, Nate shifted uncomfortably beside me. I opened my mouth to ask James to give us a minute, hoping I could salvage the conversation we were about to have. But before I could do so, Nate straightened his spine and turned to me.

"It sounds like you two have a lot to talk about," he said, his tone clipped. "I was just leaving anyway." He was stiff and formal as he inclined his head to James. "It was nice to meet you."

"You as well," James said as he came to my side and threw an arm over my shoulders. "Have a pleasant evening."

Nate looked at me then, and I silently pleaded with him to give me a chance to explain. But either he didn't understand the message I was trying to convey, or he didn't care because he spun on his heel and stalked away. A lump lodged in my throat. *Can this night get any worse?*

"Well, this wasn't quite the welcome I'd hoped for," James said, turning me away from Nate and heading toward his rental car. "Here I thought I'd arrive at the dance and you'd come running into my arms. Instead, I interrupt what sounded like a passionate lovers' quarrel."

Heat flooded my cheeks, and I pushed away from him. "You should have told me you were coming."

His expression darkened. "Why? Because I ruined your moment with him?"

When I didn't respond, he continued.

"That's your ex, isn't it? I thought the name sounded familiar. Is that why you applied for that position here?"

I stared at the ground, refusing to respond and confirm everything he'd said. Though I knew I had no right to be angry with him, a flush spread across my body, and my skin tingled. Maybe I wasn't angry. Maybe I was ashamed. No, that wasn't true either. I was angry, but the only person I was angry with was myself.

James ran a hand through his hair and sighed. "Look, we clearly need to talk, and I'd rather not do it in a parking lot while we both freeze. Can we go back to your house?"

With a nod, I opened the passenger door and climbed in. He went to the driver's side and joined me. We drove in silence, the darkness seeming to close in around us. I dreaded the conversation we were about to have.

I sent a text to my brother and Rose, letting them know I had gone home, but I neglected to mention James's arrival. It would only cause more questions I didn't want to answer. I was already facing two difficult conversations. No reason to add another one until it was absolutely necessary.

When we arrived at the house, I got out of the car and marched to the front door, not even bothering to help with James's luggage. Part of me hoped that he would leave it and drive back to DC, but I doubted he'd bothered to get a hotel. My family lived within commuting distance of the city, and I assumed James had planned to stay in Cedar Haven. Whether that would change remained to be seen.

Sure enough, he came in a moment later with his carry-on and a garment bag. He left both by the door and stared at the now-empty house. All that was left were the few things I would take with me. A recliner from my mother's bedroom sat in one corner. The worn-out red couch was gone.

I gestured to the chair, and I sank down onto the stairs. "You can sit there if you like."

He looked from the chair to me before he came over and sat beside me. There wasn't a lot of space on the steps. For a moment, neither of us said anything. I had no idea how to have that conversation or what I wanted to say. As if I wasn't confused enough, my mother's voice echoed in my head. *James is going places. He can take you with him and give you a life you've never dreamed of. Don't let him go. Whatever you do, hold on to that one.*

But was it fair to James, to me, to hold on to him? And did I need him to help me leave? I had gotten the California job on my own merit. I could easily find my own place in LA and still live those old dreams my mother and I had discussed, even without being in a relationship. Besides, what did it say about me if I stayed in a relationship just so I had a guaranteed ticket out of town?

"Do you still love him?" James asked, breaking the silence.

The question caught me off guard, though I couldn't imagine why. One thing I'd always appreciated about James was his directness. I never had to wonder what he thought or where we stood. He was honest and forthcoming, sometimes to a fault.

"I..." Answering that question was harder than I expected. Admitting my feelings to Rose was one thing, but to say them to my boyfriend, the man I was on the precipice of moving in with, was quite another. I swallowed. "I do."

The sentence held a certain irony that I hadn't intended. We weren't engaged, though up until recently, I'd expected we were heading that way. It was what my mom had hoped for, and I thought she was a little put out that James hadn't proposed before she died. But James knew I wasn't ready for marriage back then.

His face contorted as he processed my words. The dark anger in his eyes gave way to pain and sadness, and the hard line of his mouth morphed into a pout. Maybe I should have softened the blow—hemmed and hawed a bit or told him I wasn't sure—but with James, I tried to meet his directness with my own. While I didn't always succeed, I knew he wouldn't want me to spare his feelings. He wouldn't appreciate being placated.

"I see," he said, his voice hoarse. "And I assume that he's the reason you decided to apply for a position here?"

"He's part of it." Also true, though not the whole story. "But it's... complicated."

He waved his hand. "I've got all night."

We stared at each other as I struggled to formulate the words. Figuring that I didn't have much else to lose, I took a deep breath.

"As I told you on the phone, I applied to the position after you told me you found an apartment."

He shook his head. "I just don't understand why it was such a big deal for you."

"We were supposed to go apartment hunting together," I said. "You promised me you would wait until I got back."

"Are you serious?" He gaped at me. "I know what we said, but you had so much on your plate.

The least I could do was to have a place for you to land, all ready when you returned."

For some women, his care and attention would seem like a blessing, but for me, it was just another example of an area of my life in which I had no control. I didn't know how to express that without sounding like I'd lost my mind, so I decided to just go with it.

"I appreciate what you were trying to do," I began. "But your actions chipped away at the one area in my life that was still mine." When he frowned at me, I sighed. "I didn't want to come back here." I threw my arm out on that last word. "I had no desire to be my mom's executor, to go through her things like this, to settle her life like it was some legal transaction. Steven was the obvious choice for executor, but for reasons I may never understand, she picked me. And so, I had no other option but to come back here and face all the memories I've been trying to avoid."

A knot settled in my stomach, but I ignored it. "I held onto the knowledge that when I returned to the West Coast, I would finally be able to make the life I wanted for myself. We talked about getting an apartment together, and I was so looking forward to doing that *with* you, but then you told me you found one." I shut my eyes, taking deep breaths to control my temper. "And of course, it wasn't just any apartment. It had to have all these amenities that we'll probably never use. You chose something so far out of our price range, I expect we'd be living on ramen noodles for the next decade."

It dawned on me at that moment that the problem in my relationship with James was not me or James or even Nate. Our problem was compatibility. James and I had never fully been in sync. After Mom died, when he left me to backpack across Europe, I bottled up my feelings because I didn't want him to miss the trip of a lifetime. But someone who knew me, who understood me, would have recognized how much I needed a shoulder to lean on, a hand to hold.

"We'll manage," he said with a careless shrug.

Ugh. Definitely not *compatible.* I shot him a withering look. "I don't want to just 'manage.' With all the options for housing, why can't we start somewhere smaller? Less expensive?"

"Fine!" he retorted. "Then we'll keep looking, but that doesn't explain why you took such a drastic action. Why can't you just admit it's because you want Nate?"

"Because it has nothing to do with Nate!"

He raised an eyebrow. "How can you say that when you just admitted you have feelings for him?"

I buried my head in my hands. "You didn't let me finish."

For a moment, I thought he was going to argue that point as well, but he leaned against the wall and gestured for me to continue.

"I agree with you that I should have spoken about my reservations. There's no excuse for why I didn't. All I can say in my defense is that I've been under a lot of pressure since I arrived to get things squared away with the house."

He didn't respond, and I was grateful to have a moment to organize my thoughts before I went on. "Nate told me about the position, and then I ran into the teacher who's retiring. The town is really struggling to find a teacher to replace her. When you told me about the apartment, something inside of me just snapped." I left out the part about Cassandra and the cardinal. My reasons were already questionable at best. James would have me committed if he thought I was looking for signs in nature. "So, I applied for the position, and they wanted to interview me the same day, but I haven't accepted anything. I haven't even been offered the job."

"But you will be," he muttered. "And it sounds like you've already made your choice."

In that moment, I realized I *had* made a choice, but it wasn't about my professional life. Regardless of whether I stayed in Cedar Haven or moved to LA, regardless of whether Nate and I found our way back to each other, one thing was certain: I needed to let James go.

"I haven't made a choice about the job," I hedged.

He saw right through my half-truth. "So, that's it, then?" His brown eyes were sad as he looked at me. "You're getting back together with him?"

"I don't know what will happen with Nate," I said, and that was true. After the way he'd left that night, I didn't even know if Nate would speak to me again. "But I'm not being fair to either of you."

It was James's turn to put his head in his hands. His fingers riffled through his hair. "This is not at all how I expected this night to go."

"I'm sorry," I said, knowing all too well how inadequate my apology was.

He leaned back on the stairs and slid a hand into his pocket before pulling out a small black box. "I know it's cliché to propose on Valentine's Day, but you sounded so down on the phone, I thought it'd be a nice surprise to lift your spirits." He gave me a rueful smile that didn't reach his eyes. "Guess I misread that situation entirely, huh?"

My heart was heavy as I met his gaze, tears brimming behind my eyes. "I really am sorry, James. I never meant to hurt you." I took his hand. "I was going to tell you everything the next time we spoke."

"Well, I suppose this was better than a Dear John letter or a text."

I bumped his shoulder with mine. "I wouldn't break up with you over text."

"Appreciate that." He sniffled, and I could tell he was barely holding it together.

"Look, why don't you crash here?" I pointed up the stairs. "You can have my bed, and I'll sleep in the recliner. It's too late to drive back into the city."

With a sad smile, he stood. "I need some time alone."

The knot in my stomach grew, but I nodded. I understood why he wouldn't want to be around me right then, but I hoped that I would see him again. I prayed that one day, he would forgive me. He had been there for me through some of my darkest moments, and I didn't want him to disappear from my life completely.

We walked to the door, and he put his hand on the knob, hesitating. When he turned back to me, the tears he had been fighting were streaming down his cheeks.

"I hope you figure it out, Lanie, and that you live the life you want, not one someone else dreamed for you."

I was taken aback by his words, but before I could formulate a response, he stepped into the cold winter's night and shut the door behind him.

I didn't know how long I stood there in the empty hallway, staring at that door, but eventually, my back began to ache from lack of movement, and I moved to the kitchen.

Checking my phone, I felt my chest tighten when I saw I had no messages. I debated texting Nate but decided against it. My emotions were chaotic enough after the conversation I'd just had with James. No need to put my heart through the wringer a second time that evening.

I could text Rose, and I knew she would rush right over, hold my hand, and see me through my grief. But the one I wanted to talk to most of all was the person I could never talk to again. My chest ached, and I placed my hand on the wall to hold myself up.

"Oh, Mom," I whispered to the empty house. "What have I done?"

Chapter Ten

SLEEP ELUDED ME WELL into the night. I tossed and turned for hours until I finally gave up and just lay on my bed, staring at the ceiling. What was I going to tell Nate about James? More importantly, *how* was I going to tell Nate? Would he even agree to see me? Would he even care? Last night, he was so cold and distant, even before James arrived. Sure, I should have told him about James sooner, but it wasn't like he'd been clear about how he felt about me either. One minute, he acted aloof and detached, and the next, he gave me one of those sexy smiles that melted my heart.

And he still hadn't told me whatever secret he was keeping about my mom. I'd pushed it out of my mind, choosing to focus on our time together, but it ate away at me. Lately, it felt like my mother was a puzzle I couldn't solve, as if I struggled to piece together the woman I knew and the one I'd discovered only after her death. The puzzle remained unfinished without the information Nate had withheld, a mystery that wouldn't be resolved until that last piece revealed itself.

The pitch-black of my room lightened to a dull gray as if even the sun refused to shine on me that day. I supposed I deserved that. My eyes burned from lack of sleep, and I dragged myself from bed in hopes a cup of coffee or five might help me make it through the day.

When I entered the kitchen, my gaze immediately strayed to the window, searching in vain for my cardinal. The one time I could really use a message from the beyond, and it was nowhere in sight. *Figures.* Maybe the cardinal's absence conveyed a message in and of itself.

After I poured my coffee, a flash of red caught my eye. I hurried over to the window. My little friend perched on the sill, staring in at me with its small black eyes. It chirped, and I could swear I heard a hint of annoyance in the song.

"What do I do now?" I asked.

The bird chirped again then flitted along the windowsill, its feet clinging to the edge. When it reached the end, it fluttered down to the back porch, and I moved to the sliding glass door in the dining room. It hopped closer to the door and cocked its head at me.

"Did I make the right decision, breaking up with James?"

Another chirp came, that time a short syllable. I shook my head. Why did I expect some poor bird to understand the complexities of my life when I could barely make sense of them myself?

My phone pinged, and my heart jumped into my throat. But it was a text from Rose.

Come dress shopping with me.

I laughed, though it sounded hollow. *Don't you already have a wedding dress?*

Not for me. For you. We need to get you an MOH dress.

When I glanced at the window, the cardinal was gone. A shopping trip was exactly what I needed to avoid wallowing all day. And who knew? The cardinal had shown up before I saw Nate countless other times, so maybe I would run into him again that day. I confirmed I'd meet her at the mall that afternoon and rushed to get ready.

After I'd showered and dressed, I checked my phone. But I still didn't have any messages from Nate. With a sigh, I dialed his number, crossing my fingers. It went straight to voicemail. Sinking onto my bed, I debated what I wanted to say.

"Hey, Nate, it's Lanie." I paused. "We need to talk." That was the understatement of the year, but I didn't want to pour my heart out in a voicemail. "Give me a call when you get the chance."

Did my tone convey everything I wasn't saying? Probably not, but at least it was a start. I'd taken the first step. The ball was in his court, which did little to comfort me. I could only hope he would give me another chance, though I had no reason to expect him to. I'd likely exhausted my quota of second chances.

Rose was already browsing dresses when I arrived. The warmth of her embrace chased away the dark thoughts from the morning, and I knew I had made the right decision in escaping the house.

"What are your wedding colors?" I joined her in flipping through the options on the rack in front of us.

"Lavender and blue with pink and yellow accents." Rose's brown eyes brightened whenever she talked about the wedding. "I want it to look like a late-summer sunset."

"Okay." At least I had several options to work with. "What color were you thinking for my dress?"

"Not yellow," Rose said, wrinkling her nose. "I've never been a fan of yellow dresses, and with your skin tone, it would probably wash you out."

A shocked laugh bubbled up in my throat, but I knew she didn't mean anything by the comment. My gaze strayed to a sleeveless dark-blue dress, and I pulled it out and held it up for her to see.

"I was hoping for purple or pink, but I'm not opposed to blue." Rose fingered the material. "But maybe something paler?"

With a nod, I returned the dress and continued flipping through the options. "Is Steven having a best man now that you've chosen me for maid of honor?"

"To be honest, I'm not sure. He has several options, but I think he was leaning toward asking your father."

"Oh, he'd be honored." I smiled. "Well, he may not show it, but I know he would be, deep down."

Rose chuckled. "Your father definitely fits the bill for the strong, silent type." She held up a pink number with ruffles down the front. "Too frilly." As she slipped it back on the rack, she turned. "Do you think he'll ever remarry?"

The question caught me off guard. I chose my words carefully. "Doubtful. It's been so long since the divorce. If he was going to remarry, I expect he would have done it by now."

"Maybe he held out hope your mom would find her way back to him," Rose said. "And now that she's really gone, he'll finally move on."

I shrugged, not entirely comfortable with the direction the conversation was taking. "He's never said anything to me about it, and as far as I know, he doesn't date."

"Speaking of dating." Rose pounced on the opening. "How's James?"

"He, uh, he was here." I walked over to a different rack and hoped my words would be too mumbled for her to make out.

"Wait, James came to visit you? When? Where?" She rushed after me, grabbing my arm and spinning me around. "Why didn't you tell me?"

"He showed up at the Valentine's dance." I shifted away from her, focusing all my attention on the various materials in front of me. The taffeta, silk, and cotton flowing through my fingers kept me grounded.

"Well?" Rose tapped her foot. "What happened?"

I sighed. Since no one else had seen James, I'd hoped to keep his appearance between him, Nate, and me, but I couldn't see a way out of the conversation.

I grabbed Rose's hand and led her away from the sales floor. While the store was technically just outside of Cedar Haven, it was the only bridal store nearby. I didn't want any prying eyes or listening ears to spread gossip about me back in town.

Once we were safely ensconced in a corner, I relayed the whole sordid tale, making sure to include the awkward moment James appeared and Nate's cold shoulder afterward. With every word I said, Rose's eyes seemed to grow wider.

"You broke up?" She yanked me to her and wrapped me in a tight embrace. "Oh, you poor thing. Why didn't you tell me?"

"You have enough on your plate with the wedding." Well, that, and somehow, saying it out loud made the whole situation that much more real.

"Have you told Steven?"

I shook my head. "You're the first person I've told. I want to tell Nate, but he's not speaking to me at the moment."

"Are you hoping to get back together with Nate?"

I pressed my lips into a thin line. "Right now, I'd just like to *talk* to him. Explain what happened with James and apologize for not mentioning him sooner." I glanced behind me, but we were still blissfully alone. "But you can't tell anyone about James. The last thing I need is to add fuel to the fire of my father's campaign to convince me to stay here."

"But will you?" Rose's forehead creased. "I mean, if you and James aren't together, what reason do you have to return to California?"

"I still have my job opportunity." I crossed my arms. "And I did promise my mother I wouldn't settle down here."

She rolled her eyes. "I don't think she can very well hold you to that now."

"I promised her, Rose, and that means something to me." As she opened her mouth to protest, I held up a finger. "I'm not saying I won't stay, but I have some soul-searching to do before I make up my mind." I blew out a breath. "Besides,

I can't very well ask her to release me from my promise now."

"Well." Rose smirked. "You could ask the cardinal."

Nate still hadn't responded to my voicemail by the time the sun rose Monday morning. He also hadn't responded to my five text messages, two emails, or my failed attempts at telepathy. Could I blame him? Of course not, but I still hoped he would let me explain.

It would have been nice to get that chance before my therapy appointment, but it didn't look likely. With a groan, I dragged myself out of bed and into a hot shower. I was running too late to have my usual leisurely coffee in the kitchen. As I ran out the door with my hair still damp, a spot of red caught my eye. The cardinal was perched on my mother's car, staring at me.

"Here to wish me luck before I face my doom?" I asked it as I opened the driver's-side door and tossed my purse in.

It chirped at me before flying away. Much as I wanted to take the cardinal's appearance as a good omen, Nate's refusal to respond to any of my attempts at communication made me second-guess the purpose of the cardinal's visits. Maybe Cassandra was wrong. Maybe it was just a bird looking for its next meal.

As I drove to the therapist's office, I questioned my decision to forego breakfast. On the one hand, my anxiety had convinced me I wouldn't be able to keep down any food. But on the other hand, the burning in my stomach would only increase the longer I went without.

I almost chickened out. After parking my car, I breathed deeply, trying to settle the panic clawing up my chest. It was just one appointment. If I hated it, I never had to go back. But I didn't want to face my grief. Not yet. Let me get through the sale of the house and probate court. Then, I promised myself, I would take the time to grieve.

Gritting my teeth, I forced myself out of the car and marched with stiff legs into the office. The receptionist gave me a kind smile as I approached the desk.

"How can I help you?"

"I'm here for my appointment," I said. "Lanie McAllister."

She nodded and pushed a clipboard on the counter toward me. "If you'll just fill this out, I'll let Dr. Brooks know you're here."

I took the clipboard and found a seat, grateful that the waiting room was empty. The first few questions on the form were easy, asking about family history and insurance. More difficult to answer were the sections on symptoms. I did my best, unsure whether I was answering things in the right way or if I'd put myself at risk of being committed. When I finished, I stumbled to the reception desk and shoved the clipboard back, wanting to get it as far away from me as possible.

"Thank you," the receptionist said. "Dr. Brooks will see you now." She motioned for me to go through the door behind her.

Every inch of me wanted to run, but it was too late. Dr. Brooks herself opened the door. She was a petite redhead with her hair clipped in a twist behind her head. Her peasant dress flowed loosely down her body, giving her a Bohemian air. I contrasted her appearance with my memories of Dr. Kelvin. Maybe the stark differences were a good sign the visit wouldn't be a repeat of my last attempt at getting help.

"Welcome, Lanie. Come in and make yourself comfortable."

Her office had several different chairs and a couch set up, allowing patients to choose to sit where they were most comfortable. What did a choice say about me? If I sat on the couch, would she expect me to lie down? Or if I chose a chair with a straight back, would she think I was rigid and incapable of change?

I opted for the chair that looked the most comfortable, with green cushions and wooden legs. It sat directly across from the office chair I assumed was hers.

As she settled into her chair, I hid a smile. What did the office chair say about her? Was it simply easy to maneuver back and forth between her desk and the area where her patients sat? Or did it give her a sense of authority?

I shook my head. Maybe I *was* going crazy, thinking so much about nonexistent messages from a stupid chair.

She smiled at me. "Why don't you tell me what brings you in today?"

"Well, my mother passed away this summer—"

"Oh, I'm so sorry," she said. "That must have been difficult." Her face softened, and her tone was kind and genuine.

"Yes, it was. I mean, well, we knew it was coming. She had cancer, and I'd come home to take care of her." I cleared my throat to stop the babble train coming out of my mouth. "Anyway, I'm back now because she appointed me executor of her estate, and I guess I'm struggling?"

Why did I end that speech with a question? "At least, my sister-in-law, who is a nurse, suggested I should go to therapy."

"Have you tried therapy before?"

"Once, while caring for my mom." I hung my head, though I couldn't say why I felt ashamed. Did it count as failing at therapy if I went to only one session? Was it *possible* to fail therapy?

"Why did you stop going?"

I shifted in my seat. "I felt like the therapist was judging me."

She nodded and made a note in her clipboard. *Oh great, now she probably thinks I'm paranoid.*

"I mean, I'm sure she wasn't," I hurried on. "But I was in a vulnerable place, and I didn't take some of her suggestions very well."

Her head tilted. "What did she suggest, if you don't mind my asking?"

"My mom and I didn't always get along." I stared at my hands. "And since she died so young, we didn't get to resolve all of our issues before she was gone." My throat closed, and I swallowed the lump that formed. "The therapist said I should have had it out with her before she died so we could resolve everything."

"Ah, so she thought you and your mother would benefit from closure?" With a frown, she tapped her pencil against her paper. "I'm not sure I agree. While I hope to help you gain closure through our sessions, I don't think it would have been appropriate to spend your mother's last days arguing about things that occurred as part of your shared past."

"That's what I said!" The churning in my stomach settled as a feeling of validation swept over me.

She leaned forward, causing a lock of auburn hair to slip out of her clip. "Sometimes, the person we actually need closure from is ourselves."

I didn't understand what she meant, but something about her words resonated deep within me. I settled into my chair and smiled for the first time since the dance. Maybe therapy wouldn't be so bad after all.

—⁓⁓—

The hour flew by faster than I anticipated, and I was disappointed when she announced our time was up. But I made an appointment to see her the following week. Rose would be so proud of me.

We mostly talked about my mom and how it felt to be back in Cedar Haven. I touched on the situation with Nate a little toward the end, and she encouraged me to give myself more time. She said I had just ended a serious relationship and the last thing I should do was jump headfirst into another one.

As I walked to my car, I pulled out my phone and turned it on. My heart leapt into my throat when I saw I had a voicemail. I listened, relief washing over me as Nate apologized for not getting back to me sooner. I dialed his number, and butterflies fluttered in my belly when he answered on the first ring. His voice was gruff and cold, but I focused on the fact he was even taking my calls.

"I need to talk to you about the other night," I began. "Any chance you can come over?" When he didn't respond, I hurried on. "Or I could go there or meet you somewhere. Please just give me a chance to explain."

His silence made my heart pound harder, then he heaved a sigh. "You don't need to explain anything, Lanie. I understood everything when

James showed up, and he's come a long way to see you. You should spend time with him."

"James is gone," I blurted out, smacking my forehead as all of my carefully worded arguments floated away. "We broke up Saturday, and he'll be heading back to California tomorrow."

The silence returned, but it seemed different, more shocked than angry. I didn't allow myself to hope it meant he would listen to me.

"Please, Nate," I said. "Just give me a half hour. I promise not to take up too much of your day."

Another sigh. "Now is not a really good time."

Perhaps I had misread the cardinal's visit. Maybe it had come to comfort me, knowing that I'd lost my shot at a second chance with Nate. My breath hitched in my throat, and before I could stop it, my eyes swam with tears.

"Are you... Are you crying?" Nate asked, his voice softer.

"No," I lied, but then I sniffled, giving myself away.

"It's not that I don't want to see you. It's just, um, how do you feel about cats?"

Well, that was unexpected. I frowned. "Cats? Um, half my family is allergic to them, but I don't mind them. Why?"

He huffed a laugh. "It's a long story, but I can show you when you get here if you want to come over."

A grin split my face, and I was so relieved he was willing to talk to me that I brushed off his strange question. "Thank you, Nate. I'll be there in a few!"

On the drive over, I rehearsed my speech, making sure I went over the points I wanted to make to help him understand how I felt about him. And I hoped that in the course of our heart-to-heart, he would finally tell me about making peace with my mom.

When I arrived at his house, Nate nudged open the door, and I peeked in at the large dog he held back. He motioned me in and shut the door behind me, keeping a firm grip on the dog's collar.

"Sorry about him," Nate said as he led me into the living room. "We don't get visitors often, and Lucky tends to go a little crazy with new people."

"I didn't know you had a dog." I leaned down to stroke Lucky's head. He licked my face and let out an excited bark. His tail thumped heavily on the floor. "What kind of dog is he?"

"A mutt." Nate ran an affectionate hand over Lucky's back. "He's a mix of sheltie, golden retriever, and lab."

I could definitely see the lab in the dark fur and the shape of his face. "Why did you ask me about cats if you have a dog?"

Nate's expression changed, and he released Lucky, taking my hand instead. "Follow me."

We went to the side of his house where the bedrooms were, and he opened a door. The room had a desk and a computer on one side. On the other was a bed, two bowls, and a cardboard box with litter in it. Curled up on the chair by the computer was the cutest little gray kitten I'd ever seen.

"Aww, who is this little guy?" I asked, slipping over and kneeling to let the kitten sniff me. He nuzzled his face into my hand, and I scratched his ears.

"That's Shadow. I found him last night after the dance."

I looked up at Nate. "No mama cat around?"

He shook his head. "Not that I could find. This one was half starved and freezing. I took him to the emergency vet last night, and they said he was fine, just cold and hungry. I picked up a few odds and ends to make him comfortable, but I planned to get more stuff today." He crouched beside me, running a hand over Shadow's fur.

I smiled. "I'm glad to see you never lost your love of animals. Though I wish you'd found a way to turn it into a career."

"I've been thinking about that lately," he said, keeping his gaze on the cat. "While it's probably too late to start a career as a veterinarian, and I wouldn't feel right selling the shop, I've thought about volunteering at the animal shelter."

"That's a great idea! And who knows? Maybe you could find a position part-time at the vet. They were always seeking assistants when I was growing up."

He ran a hand through his hair. "I don't know. It might not be conducive to keeping my hours at the shop."

I shrugged. "So cut back. You're the boss, after all. And I'm sure Jeff would love to be in charge more often, gain that experience."

"Maybe. Anyway," he said, clearly trying to change the subject, "I've been bottle-feeding Shadow every few hours since I found him. That's why I haven't texted you." His eyes met mine. "Well, that, and I wasn't sure what to say."

I nodded, focusing on stroking Shadow's fur while I worked up the nerve to give my speech. Nate stood and held out a hand to help me up. Each time we touched, that familiar flash of heat traveled up my arm.

He led me to the living room. A black couch lined the back wall, directly across from a television stand. Perched on the stand was a small flat-screen TV, almost as dusty as the one we'd just removed from my mom's house. I supposed he didn't have much time to watch it with his hours at the shop.

"Do you want something to drink?"

"Water would be nice," I said, my throat suddenly very dry.

While he went to the kitchen, I mentally rehearsed once more what I would say as I surveyed the rest of the room. I noted how bare the walls were and how dark the house seemed, even with rays of light peeking in the window on the side. Had he recently moved in? Nate had always been a minimalist, but that was extreme, even for him.

When he returned with the glasses, I took a long drink, buying myself some time. "Have you lived here long?"

"A few months," he said, scanning the room as if seeing it for the first time. "I know it's a bit spartan, but I don't need much."

"So I remember."

He frowned. "You said you wanted to talk."

"I do." A flush crept up my neck as I remembered saying those exact words to James the other night. I cleared my throat and steeled myself. "I'm sorry for not telling you about James sooner. The truth is, I wasn't sure there was any point in it. When I first came home, I planned to finalize the estate as soon as possible and then hightail it to California."

"And now?"

I met his gaze. His eyes were wary, but underneath, I thought I detected a hint of hope. I didn't allow myself to dwell on that, as there were a few things I wanted to explain before I got to where things currently stood.

"James and I had agreed that we would go apartment shopping together. But then, the day you and the guys came over to help us move furniture, he called to tell me he'd found the perfect place for us to live." I twisted my hands. "I don't know exactly why that hit me so hard, but it did." Then I launched into the same things I had told James about feeling like I had so little control over my life and how being part of the process of finding a place to live meant a lot to me.

"I understand," Nate said. "Did you tell him that?"

I shook my head. "Not at the time, but we talked about it after we left the dance." My throat closed, and I swallowed the lump that formed. "He asked me if I still had feelings for you."

Nate went still beside me, as if he was holding his breath, waiting for the answer. I forced myself to look at him, wanting him to see in my face, in my eyes, the truth of what I was about to say.

"I told him I still care for you."

While a light came into his eyes, he didn't comment on my revelation. "What did he say?"

"Well, he wasn't thrilled." I closed my eyes. "He planned to propose to me that night." Nate sucked in a breath, but I went on before he could speak. "Obviously, that didn't happen. But he did say something that's been weighing on my mind."

"What's that?"

I opened my eyes and looked at him. "He said that I shouldn't live someone else's dreams for me, and I can't help wondering if he meant my mom." I dropped my gaze to my lap. "She made it no secret how she felt about you, at least in high school. And she liked James, mainly because she believed he was my ticket out of Cedar Haven."

"Was that why you were with him? For her sake?"

I sighed and stood from the couch before pacing the floor. "I wish I could say no. It's not like I felt nothing for James, but..." I stopped pacing and stared out the window at the back of the room. "I don't know that I would have stayed with him as long had it not been for her encouragement."

He was silent as he digested all of that, and I pressed my lips together to keep from babbling to fill the quiet. I returned to the couch and collapsed against it, preparing for a long wait.

"Is that why you applied for Mrs. Carlisle's position? To have control?"

I shrugged. "Yes and no. Initially, James's revelation about the apartment was a driving force. But something Steven said stuck in my mind as well. He thought I could do more good in a small school like that than in the special school in LA." I took his hand, lacing our fingers. "But I had other reasons."

His face softened, and he squeezed my hand. "Did you mean what you said to James? About... me?"

A laugh bubbled out of my throat, clearly surprising us both. "I wouldn't have blown up my relationship if I hadn't meant it."

He gave me that heart-melting smile then. "And you and James are definitely over?"

I nodded. "He returned to the city, and he'll be flying back to California tomorrow."

One minute, I sat on the edge of the couch, facing him, and the next, he yanked me into his arms and held me close. Once I got over the shock, I laid my head on his chest and listened to his heartbeat, sighing contentedly.

Too soon, he pulled away. "I'm glad you told me, but I want to take this slow, Lanie." I opened my mouth, but he pressed a finger to my lips. "Don't misunderstand me. I still have feelings for you too." He tucked a lock of hair behind my ear. "But you just lost your mother, are in the process of selling your childhood home, and ended a long-term relationship the other night. Any one of those things would cause a lot of upheaval in life, but I can only imagine how hard it's been dealing with all three." He took my hand in his. "So I want to give you the time and space to sort through what you want. You've still got that job waiting for you in California, and you may choose to go."

"I think that's wise," I said, though part of me didn't love the idea.

"But maybe I can help you sort through some things," he said. "Besides your mother, what drew you to James, and what made you decide to move to California?"

"We met at school, freshman year of undergrad," I said, not sure he really wanted to hear any of that. "I was sitting in the cafeteria, having lunch by myself. All of my roommates had classes in the afternoon while mine were mostly in the morning. He was with his friends, and they came over to ask if they could sit with me." I laughed lightly. "Later, he told me he felt compelled to sit with me, like something was pulling him there."

"Fate?" I could see in Nate's eyes how much it pained him to ask.

"I don't know that I believe in fate," I replied. "Not in a universal sense." I couldn't keep the edge out of my voice, and Nate noticed.

"What do you mean?"

I shifted on the cushion and avoided his gaze. "You're going to think I'm crazy."

"I promise I won't."

Little did he know that was a promise he couldn't keep. With a sigh, I pushed myself off the back of the couch and turned to look at him. "Have you ever heard a legend about cardinals?"

He shook his head and gestured for me to go on.

"I went to see my neighbor, Cassandra, the other day," I began. "I've been seeing this cardinal often, particularly before seemingly innocuous events in my life that later prove to be important in some way. I saw it the morning my mom's car had the flat, the day we had lunch at Bea's, the day you came to help with the estate sale, the day of my interview, before the dance, and this morning."

His eyes widened further, but he didn't say anything. Unsure what to make of his reaction, I pressed on.

"Cassandra told me that cardinals are visitors from heaven, our loved ones who have passed away, coming back to check on us, often with a message. She suggested the cardinal might be my mother, and the days she chose to visit were to help convey her message." I glanced at him. "It's like she's pointing me to you. After what you told me this morning, I-I'm starting to believe it."

Every moment that Nate sat there staring at me caused my anxiety to increase. He thought I'd lost it, and I couldn't blame him. My chest grew tight, and I stood to leave, but he grabbed my wrist and pulled me back beside him. I perched on the edge of the cushion, still worried he would have me committed.

"I saw a cardinal this morning before you called," he finally shared.

"You did?" I demanded, raising my eyebrows.

"Briefly. Besides feeding Shadow, I haven't been sleeping well the past two nights," he admitted. "I didn't like how we left things. When I finally gave up and went to get coffee, there was a little cardinal on my back deck."

"What did it look like?" I could barely breathe. *If the cardinal was a messenger, then what message did it convey by visiting Nate?*

Nate's lips twitched as he fought back a grin. "Like a red bird."

I rolled my eyes. "I mean, was there anything about it that stuck out to you? The one I've seen has weird black dots by its beak, almost like freckles."

"I didn't get that close of a look," Nate said. "You saw it this morning too?"

I nodded. "It was the sign I was looking for to call you." We gazed at each other, both digesting the revelations, then I grinned. "My mom is still meddling, even from beyond the grave."

Nate threw back his head and laughed, which was music to my ears. I couldn't remember the last time I had heard him laugh like that, so joyous and carefree. Certainly not since I'd been home.

"Did you tell James about the cardinal?" he asked, and the light in his eyes dimmed.

I shook my head, turning away. "I didn't see the point. Besides, he wouldn't understand."

"Why do you think that?"

"James is... practical... rational. He would explain it away as being coincidental." While I'd once loved James for his directness, he could be harsh, even when he didn't mean to be.

"Well, I appreciate you sharing it with me," Nate said, and his face was sincere.

I grabbed his hand and gave it a squeeze, and I fell back against the couch. The conversation and all the anxiety leading up to it had drained me. Frankly, I could use a nap, but I didn't want to leave him, not yet.

"I don't know about you," Nate said, "but I'm going to need something stronger than water if I have any hope of staying awake for the rest of the day."

We went to the kitchen, and Nate put on a pot of coffee. His house was small but adequate for his needs. The kitchen had all the essentials, but I could tell that the microwave saw the most action. Some of the labels on the buttons were worn down from use. A small window overlooked his postage-stamp yard.

And there on the back deck stood my cardinal. It chirped at me before fluttering closer to the window, peering in at both of us.

"Look! Do you see? I told you I was being stalked by a cardinal!" I pointed.

"I saw, and you're not going to believe this, but I swear when it came this morning, that bird *winked* at me," Nate replied, handing me a mug of coffee.

"Oh, I believe it." I shook my head.

"I think your theory about it being your mother is sound. I can't imagine anyone else being this persistent."

I gazed at him thoughtfully. Making up my mind, I set down my mug and went toward him, biting back a smile at the apprehension on his face. As I wrapped my arms around his neck, I tilted my face toward his, licking my lips. Nate froze, and as I pressed against him, I could feel his heart pounding in his chest. I angled my head closer, but at the last moment, I turned my face away and gazed out the window.

The cardinal perched precariously on the windowsill, staring right at us through the glass. I started giggling, and Nate joined me, though his body sagged against mine, and I wasn't sure if it was from relief or disappointment. But then he leaned down and kissed the top of my head. I sighed and pressed my face to his chest, breathing in his distinct scent of Old Spice and Ivory soap.

"I missed this," I whispered.

His arms tightened around me. "Me too."

Chapter Eleven

THE NEXT MORNING, I woke to the sound of my phone buzzing beside me. Bleary-eyed, I picked it up and tapped the screen.

The house is under contract.

I blinked. Already? While John had said he'd expected we would get offers soon, I'd thought we'd have to wait a few weeks at least. I sat up in bed and stared at my empty room. Steven said the closing date was to be determined, but I assumed it would be sometime in March. Things were happening a lot faster than I'd anticipated, and it made my head spin.

That also meant I would be moving out soon. I hadn't seen much of my father since the estate sale. Perhaps it was time to fix things with him. I didn't know how long I would be stuck there, and I didn't want us to spend that time at each other's throats.

As tired as I was, I knew I wouldn't be able to fall back to sleep. I stumbled down the stairs and started my usual routine. While I'd cleaned before the open house, I decided to spend the day shampooing the carpets. With most of the furniture gone, it would be easier to do a thorough job.

A few hours later, my phone rang, interrupting one of my favorite songs. When I recognized the number, my eyes widened, and my irritation melted away. Taking a deep breath to compose myself, I answered in my most professional-sounding voice.

"Lanie McAllister speaking."

"Hello, Lanie. This is Principal Wilson. Is this a good time to talk?"

"Yes, this is a good time," I replied, trying to keep the apprehension out of my voice.

"Good. I'm calling about the special education position. We were very impressed with your credentials and would like to offer the job to you."

"Oh, wow! Thank you," I breathed.

"Now, I understand you already have a position you're considering, so I wanted to give you all the details and then give you time to make your decision. Does that sound fair?"

"That works for me."

"While you wouldn't officially be in charge of the students on your own until next year, we're hoping that if you accept the position, you'd start working with Mrs. Carlisle in April so she can train you. The county has granted us a special dispensation to pay for both of your salaries during your training."

I listened as the principal continued detailing the salary and the expectations, nodding along even though Mrs. Wilson couldn't see me. I asked about a start date and was told they would be flexible.

"Before you decide, I'd love to have you work with our students on the Presidents' Day play. Mrs. Carlisle has done a wonderful job with the kids each year, and it would give you an opportunity to see what working in our school would be like. It's completely optional, of course, but I encourage you to think about it."

"That sounds like a wonderful idea. When are rehearsals?"

"After school from three to five. I'll send you an email with the official offer letter and all the details."

"Great! Thank you so much," I said. As I hung up the phone, the first person I wanted to tell was Nate, but I stopped myself.

Was it fair to share the news with him when I hadn't made up my mind to accept? Wouldn't I just be getting his hopes up if I later decided to go to California? As much as I wanted to tell him, I decided to take some time to really consider the offer. Then, if I did decide to accept it, the news would be that much sweeter, as it meant I was staying.

My phone chimed again, and I hated how my heart leapt into my throat when I thought it was from Nate. Instead, my father's name popped up on the screen.

We need to talk. Dinner? 6?

With a sigh, I confirmed I would be there, already dreading the evening. We needed to hash things out, especially since I'd be living with him for the foreseeable future, but that didn't mean I was looking forward to the conversation. He texted me the address of a restaurant outside of town, and I returned to the cleaning with a churning stomach.

Hours later, the carpets were drying, and a knot formed in my belly as I prepared to meet my father. I picked out a simple dress and yanked my hair into a tight bun. A quick dash of lip gloss and mascara, and I was ready to go. After tossing my keys, wallet, and phone into my purse, I headed out and climbed into Mom's car. It ran a lot smoother since Nate's shop had done so much work on it. I knew it would fetch a good price when I sold it, but at the thought of that, I felt a hollowness in my chest. Little by little, I lost more pieces of my mother.

As I pulled into the parking lot of the restaurant, I searched for Dad's car. It sat near the entrance, and I smiled ruefully. He probably arrived early to find a good spot. Max McAllister was a predictable man. I parked in the best spot I could find and went inside. He sat at the bar, nursing a beer.

"Hi, Dad." I gave him an awkward hug.

He grunted what passed for a hello and led me over to the hostess stand. "My party is here, and we'd like to be seated."

"Wonderful," the hostess said. "Right this way." We followed her to a booth in the back of the restaurant. My chest constricted at the distance between us and the rest of the diners. Did he request that spot because he expected a heated conversation?

"Thank you," he said as we slid into our seats.

The hostess nodded and scurried away. I wished I could follow.

"How are you?" I asked, trying to lighten the mood.

He waved his hand. "No need for pleasantries. You know why we're here."

"To have a nice dinner?"

"Don't play dumb, Lanie. We both know that we need to finish our discussion about your choice to leave."

I took a deep breath. Neither Steven nor my father knew that I'd even interviewed for the local position, let alone that they'd made an offer. I'd kept it from Steven for the same reason I hadn't texted Nate that afternoon—I didn't want to get his hopes up. But my father would take it as a win, and I refused to give him that satisfaction, especially since I'd yet to make up my mind.

"I'm not sure what's left to discuss." I kept my tone light and my eyes on my menu. "We've both made our feelings very clear, but as it's my life, I get the final say."

He opened his mouth, probably to respond with some sarcastic retort, but I was saved by the server. She took our orders, though I had to admit, the idea of eating right then made me nauseated. I resisted the urge to glare when he ordered steak and potatoes. His doctor had given him strict orders to avoid red meat because his cholesterol was so high, but we had enough battles ahead of us without adding his health to the list.

"Have you given any more thought to the position at the middle school here?"

I blanched. "How did you know about that?"

"Steven told me. Apparently, Nate told him about it when he came by to help move the furniture." My father raised his eyebrows. "Are you going to answer my question?"

Buying time, I took a sip of water. My best bet was to tell him a half-truth. He wasn't the most social of people, and I doubted he would find out about the offer before I told him. However, I knew he'd probably already heard that I'd interviewed.

"I applied for the position."

"Good," he said, leaning back in his seat with a satisfied smile. "What are you going to tell them when they offer it to you?"

"First, we don't know if they will offer it to me. And second, I have that job in California that I've already accepted—"

"I'm sure if you explain the situation, they'll understand," he interrupted. "Besides, you don't even start until the summer. If you tell that other school you've found a job here, that will give them plenty of time to replace you."

"Dad, we've been over this." It didn't matter that I'd recently begun to second-guess my decision to go to California or that I'd broken up with James. If I decided to stay in Cedar Haven, it had to be because it was *my* choice, not because I'd been bullied into it by my father.

He leaned forward, his thick, dark eyebrows pulling down over his brown eyes. A fire burned in his eyes, and I knew he was working to keep his infamous temper in check.

I stared back at him, rising to the challenge and not blinking. A moment later, he surprised me by lowering his gaze and taking a long drink from his water.

"Heard James came to see you," he said, his voice nonchalant.

I kept my face neutral. "And?"

"Well, as he's not with you, I assume he left in a hurry."

He was trying to rattle me, but I refused to let him see how much he'd succeeded. If he knew James and I broke up, he would use it to further his goal of convincing me to stay, and I couldn't allow him that power.

"He's in DC on business." I shrugged but didn't meet his eye. "He had to return to the city, and he's flying back to LA today."

Our food arrived, and I forced myself to focus on my salad, even though my small appetite vanished as soon as he mentioned James. He harrumphed a thank-you to the server as she set down his plate.

"So, things are still good between you?"

I sighed and set my fork down, finally raising my eyes to his. "Why? Have you heard something different?" Better to ferret out what he knew to avoid being caught in a lie.

"Just that you and Nate seemed to be having a moment in the parking lot before James showed up."

If I still needed a reason to go to California, that was it. In LA, I'd be just another face in the crowd. Small towns were the bane of my existence.

But from the pieces of information he was giving me, I guessed that someone had seen Nate, James, and me in the parking lot. For the first time since that night, I was grateful to have left with James. Our breakup happened in private, and it gave me plausible deniability in that moment, when I needed it most.

"It was a misunderstanding." I forced a smile. "James came back with me to the house, and we talked. Everything's fine."

His eyes widened for a second before he recovered. "Is that so?"

"Of course," I lied.

"I don't believe you," he said, his voice deceptively calm.

"What does that mean?" My carefully crafted cool demeanor cracked.

"I've seen the way you and Nate are together. Steven's seen it. For goodness' sake, the whole town witnessed the love song you sang him the other night!" He pointed at me. "You're still in love with him, and James found out."

I snorted. "You need better sources for spies."

His unwavering stare made me want to squirm, but I kept my body still, hoping the interrogation would end soon and we could talk of other things, safer subjects.

"Have you talked to Nate since James left?"

I blinked. What an odd question. "Of course I've talked to him."

He gave me a strange look. "And what did you talk about?"

I frowned. "I apologized for not telling him about James sooner."

"And that's all?"

What was he getting at? "Should I have discussed something else with him?"

When he didn't respond, I stared at him, trying to read between the lines. What was he hiding? And what did it have to do with Nate? But before I could turn the tables and interrogate *him* for a change, he took a large bite of his steak.

His silence gave me an opportunity to calm the churning in my stomach. I drank my water and force-fed myself the salad, hoping to appear calm and collected.

But when he cleared his throat, I knew the dance we were doing was about to get more complicated, and I already struggled to follow the steps.

"I think you've made your decision, but you just don't want to admit it, even to yourself."

In that moment, all I wanted to do was prove him wrong. I'd grown weary of everyone meddling in my life. James's search for an apartment without me, my father's coercive mechanisms to get me to stay, and even my dead mother's interference in my love life from beyond the grave.

"Why will no one listen to me?" I slammed my fist on the table. "Need I remind you that this is *my* life, and I would appreciate you keeping your nose out of it."

"You're right," he said, undeterred. "It is your life. So why are you willing to throw it away?"

I gaped at him. What did he mean by that? Choosing to pursue a life in California wasn't throwing it away. Even if I didn't have James anymore, I had a job. I had a future. Why couldn't he see that?

My father sighed and shifted in his seat. "I understand if you're scared."

"Why would I be scared?"

"Your mother's meddling did a number on you, and even though she's gone, I think you're afraid of disappointing her in some way."

I dropped my gaze, fearing my face would give me away. I hadn't told anyone other than Nate about the cardinal or my suspicions about my mother trying to communicate with me.

"I've done everything Mom asked of me. Why wouldn't she be proud?"

"You say that, but I don't think you believe it."

My head shot up. I couldn't even begin to dissect the meaning of those words. "That doesn't make any sense."

He put down his utensils, pushed his plate forward slightly, and folded his hands behind it as he regarded me. The salad turned to stone in my stomach. He certainly lived up to his nickname of *The Intimidator*.

"Your mother has spent years cultivating the Lanie she wanted you to be, and now that she's gone, you're still trying to live up to her expectations. But without her guidance, you're like a ship without a harbor, and you're pushing back on anything that goes against her teachings. Nate is one of those things, and despite how much you care about him, you're afraid to pursue things and end up like your mother."

Sometimes, I forgot how observant my father could be. A man of few words, the present situation notwithstanding, he paid closer attention than most people realized.

"Mom didn't end up so bad," I murmured. "Despite your issues, you two made your peace in the end."

He nodded. "We did. And now it's your turn."

"But Mom and I were at peace." I frowned. "At least, I thought we were." I put my head in my hands.

"It's not your mother you need to make peace with," he said. "It's the version of Lanie your mother has convinced you to be." He shrugged as he scooped up his mashed potatoes onto his fork. "Only then will you be able to make a decision about your next steps."

"And if that Lanie wants to go to California too?"

"Then I'll book your flight myself," he challenged, a gleam in his eye.

I picked at the salad, digesting his words more than the food. Was he right? Had Mom somehow distorted my worldview to the point I didn't know who I was or what I wanted anymore? Our relationship had been strained, especially after my parents separated. Mom had leaned on me a lot, perhaps more than she should have during that time. My father's words painted everything in a different light. I resisted his version, not wanting to think ill of my mom, but deep down, I recognized the truth in what he'd said. In some ways, I'd believed Mom was living vicariously through me, and at the time, I hadn't minded. But now, I could see what havoc Mom's actions had wreaked in my life.

"The school wants me to help with their Presidents' Day play," I said, pushing my food away.

"You should do it," he replied, having no issues polishing off his meal. "It'll give you an idea of what the position here is like."

I nodded. It'd been a while since I last worked with kids, and I missed it. They saw the world so differently than adults did, and I believed some time with them was just what I needed to help me figure out what the "real" Lanie wanted.

***

A few days later, I stood on stage in the old high school theatre with Mrs. Carlisle. We planned to do a quick run-through before she and I spent one-on-one time with each child to prepare them for the performance. It brought back memories of my own theatre days.

The board of education had organized the event. Several teachers had been chosen to play the role of various presidents, and each class was assigned a president. The students would ask the president questions about his life and contributions to the country. For Mrs. Carlisle's class, the script was more of a suggestion, since some of the students struggled to memorize dialogue. But it had guidelines for the types of questions the children should ask.

"All right, class," Mrs. Carlisle called out. "We're going to begin. As you know, we were assigned Franklin D. Roosevelt, and Ms. McAllister has offered to fill in as our president for practice. Does anyone want to start us off with a question?"

A young boy named Seth raised his hand. "Wasn't Mr. Roosevelt in a wheelchair?"

"I do use a wheelchair, young man," I said in a faux deep voice. "Do you know why?"

Seth shook his head. The other children stared at me with rapt attention.

"Because I got really sick, and when I recovered, I was no longer able to walk." I leaned down and whispered, "But that didn't stop me from becoming president."

Another child, Beth, called out, "What are you most proud of?"

I pretended to think it over. "Let's see. There was the New Deal."

"What's that?" asked Robert, a boy with reddish-brown hair.

"Well, there were several parts to it, but one of the most famous parts that still helps people today was a program where money was provided to people who were too old or sick to work anymore."

"Do you miss being the president?" a sweet-faced girl with pigtails asked.

"Sometimes," I said. "But I served as president for well over a decade."

The children continued to ask questions until Mrs. Carlisle called them back to order. She and I split up the students to work in small groups on memory games. I sat with one group to help them get started.

"Ms. McAllister, I'm scared of being on the stage in front of all those people," Beth said. "What if I forget what I'm supposed to say?"

"Mrs. Carlisle and I will be there to help you," I promised. "But it might help if you pretend that it's just us talking, like we did a few moments ago." I looked at the rest of the group. "Is anyone else afraid of public speaking?"

There were several nods among the students. "I'll let you in on a secret. I'm not a fan, either, though I performed in several plays back in high school." I gave a conspiratorial smile. "But it's easier if you think of yourself as a character. Then it's not you messing up a line, it's the character's fault."

The children giggled, and my heart filled with warmth. I'd missed that. With all of the focus on finishing my master's and then coming home to handle Mom's affairs, I'd forgotten how nice it was to spend time with children. Regardless of where I ended up, I knew as long as I could teach, I would be happy.

I checked in on a few other groups before moving over to where Mrs. Carlisle stood.

"You're doing a wonderful job with them," she said.

"I'm really enjoying helping with the play."

"But you're still undecided on whether you want to take the position." Her words were stated matter-of-factly with no judgment, but my stomach sank anyway.

"I'm still considering it," I replied, though I imagined that excuse sounded as empty to her ears as it did in my head.

She sighed. "I understand, but I do hope you'll make a decision soon. I'd hate to leave in the spring without someone in place to take over."

I nodded but had no response to that. The idea of leaving the children to some stranger gutted me, but if I accepted the position in Cedar Haven, it would mean going back on my word not only to the school in California but also to my mother. The promises I'd made felt more like shackles that I wished I could free myself from. My father's voice echoed in my head. What Lanie did I want to be? What did the *real* Lanie want?

"Anyway," Mrs. Carlisle continued, and I was grateful for the subject change, "we need some help with the set changes the day of the play. If you could put the word out for volunteers, I'd greatly appreciate it."

"Sure, I can do that," I said. "I'll go make some calls."

With a smile, she turned and began making her rounds to the different groups of children. I stepped backstage, knowing exactly who to call first.

"Hey, Lanie, what's up?" Nate's cheerful greeting washed away the awkward conversation with Mrs. Carlisle.

"I have news to share and a favor to ask. Which would you like first?" I still hesitated to tell him about the offer, but I couldn't see a way around asking for his help without doing so. What other reason would I have to be working so closely on the play?

"Hmm, how about the news? That'll tell me whether I should say yes to the favor."

I laughed. "I was offered Mrs. Carlisle's job at the middle school."

The silence on the other end wasn't encouraging. I tapped my foot as I waited for him to respond. Had I made a mistake? He'd been the one to encourage me to apply, after all.

"Lanie, that's amazing, and I'm proud of you."

"But?" I asked, hearing it in his faked enthusiasm.

"Are you going to accept?"

I stifled a sigh. He didn't want to sound too happy in case I didn't stay. While I wished I could give him a more definitive answer, I wouldn't lie to him. "I haven't decided yet, but it does lead into the favor. The school asked me to help with the Presidents' Day play, and we need some volunteers to help with the set changes. Would you be willing to assist?"

"Of course," he said, and that time, there was no hesitation in his voice. "When do you need me?"

I gave him the details for the dress rehearsal and event, and he promised to be there. As I walked to the stage to help the children with their memory games, his question about whether I'd accepted weighed on my mind. I knew I would have to say goodbye to Nate for good if I stuck to my plan to move to California. We'd tried long distance before, and it hadn't worked. His life was in Cedar

Haven, and I would never ask him to give up what he'd built. But I also wouldn't allow myself to base such an important decision on a man, no matter how much he meant to me.

Chapter Twelve

SUNDAY AFTERNOON, I STOOD backstage with the children, preparing for the dress rehearsal. In addition to Nate, I had roped in several of my friends to help with the set pieces. Trudy and her husband had painted a replica of the White House on a mural, and Steven had worked with Nate to build different platforms on which our presidents would speak to the children.

I went up behind Nate and Steven as they were putting the finishing touches on a set of stairs. "This looks great! How about you both let me take you out tonight as a thank-you for all your hard work?"

They exchanged a glance, and Nate suddenly seemed very interested in hammering a nail. Steven wiped his hands on his pants and gave me an easy smile that didn't reach his eyes.

"Thanks, sis, but I've got plans."

"Oh." I bit my lip to hide my disappointment. "Wedding planning with Rose?"

He scratched the back of his neck. "Ah, something like that."

What a weird response. I turned to Nate. "What about you?"

Before he could respond, someone tugged on my shirt. "Miss McAllister?"

I looked down with a smile. "Yes, Robert?"

"Can you help me run through my questions again?"

With a quick glance at Nate, who refused to meet my eye, I nodded and led Robert to a quiet part of the stage. But Nate's behavior needled me.

What was up with him? Had I done something wrong?

I tried to ignore the uneasy feeling growing in my stomach as I helped Robert with the subject matter, giving him pointers on how to remember the questions he would ask. But I couldn't stop myself from staring across the room, where Nate and Steven were still hammering away at the stairs.

After I finished up with Robert, I headed over to Nate. He was alone that time, as Steven had moved on to work on the wheelchair for President Roosevelt. I cleared my throat, and he jumped, spinning around, eyes wide.

"Everything okay?"

He gave a quick nod. "Yep, totally fine."

I cocked my head, not convinced he was telling me the truth. "So, did you want to have dinner tonight?"

"Oh, um..." He cleared his throat. "I would, but I can't."

"Hot date?" I teased, though the idea made me queasy.

He rolled his eyes. "Of course not. I signed up to volunteer at the shelter."

I blinked. Why hadn't he told me that before? "That's great! I'm so happy for you. How long have you been going?"

"Not long. Tonight's my third shift." He smiled at me for the first time all day. "Thank you for encouraging me. I'm really enjoying it."

Third shift? I took a deep breath. While I'd been busy with rehearsals, that was big news. And as he'd said, I'd encouraged him. *So why am I only now learning about it?*

"Well, we should celebrate!" I forced a smile. "I don't mind a late dinner if you want to meet up afterward."

His face fell, and he stared at his hands. "That sounds nice, but I don't know how late I'll be."

"Ah, okay, then." I turned to go, my heart sinking. What wasn't he telling me?

"Wait, Lanie." He grabbed my arm. "I'm sorry tonight's not good, but if you're free for lunch after the play, we could go to Bea's."

Maybe I was being paranoid. He'd just started to volunteer, after all. Perhaps he'd planned to tell me about it after the play, when I had more time.

"That sounds good."

He pulled me in for a hug, and I relished the warmth of his arms around me. But too soon, he let go, and I walked out into the cool evening air, alone.

I had no reason to doubt Nate's word. And I was proud of him for rekindling his dream. Just like teaching was my passion, animals were his, and I hated that he'd lost sight of that when he took over his father's business. But something about his behavior had left me off-balance, and I couldn't quite put my finger on what it was.

The day of the performance, Nate and I stood together in the greenroom, watching the kids changing into their costumes and getting their makeup done. I slipped my hand in his and squeezed. His help with the props and set had meant more to me than I could express.

"This feels like old times," I said.

"I was just thinking the same thing," Nate replied with a warm smile.

When our eyes met, electricity hummed around us. Although we were surrounded by giggling children, it was as if we were the only two people in the room. My heartbeat quickened as his dark-brown eyes melted with heat. I reminded myself that we'd agreed to take things slow, but the urge to kiss him grew whenever he looked at me like that.

"Miss McAllister." Robert, one of my students, tugged on my shirt's hem. "I think it's our turn."

I glanced up to see the eighth-grade class coming off the stage, which was our cue. "Why, Robert, you're right! Let's go gather up the rest of our group."

I gave Nate's hand another squeeze before I formed a quick circle with my students. Nate shot me one of his heart-stopping smiles before heading off to help with the set change.

"All right, everyone, remember what we've practiced. Who is your president?"

Robert raised his hand. "Franklin D. Roosevelt."

"Very good, Robert! And what are we going to ask him?"

"About the New Deal and his wheelchair," Beth volunteered.

"Both good questions, but remember to raise your hand so Mr. Roosevelt can call on you." I put my hand in the middle of our circle, and the students piled their hands on top of mine. "One, two, three, break a leg!"

Robert stared at me in horror. "I don't want to break my legs."

Stifling a laugh, I knelt beside him. "I'm sorry, Robert. It's an expression often used in theatre to wish the actors luck. No actual legs will be broken."

He gave me a quick side-eye before turning and rushing to the stage with the rest of the students. I stood up, shaking my head and laughing. Nate returned and slid his arm around my shoulders.

"You're amazing with them," Nate commented.

"They're such sweet kids." I faced him, and when our eyes met, a spark shot straight through me. He angled his head closer to mine, and my eyelids drifted shut as I closed the distance.

The sounds of the curtain rising and the audience applauding made us both jump. Nate blinked before giving me a sheepish smile and stepping away.

In that moment, I knew what I wanted, what the *real* Lanie needed. *This life, these children, this man, this—no,* my*—town.* Though my chest ached, knowing I would be going back on my promise to my mother, I knew the alternative would break my heart beyond repair. Somehow, I doubted my mother would be angry or surprised to find out I'd broken my word to her.

As I watched the play, in the back of my mind, I considered how to tell Nate I'd made my choice. We were going out to lunch after the play was over. Based on our history, Bea's seemed a fitting location to tell him the good news.

My students did an amazing job, and when they exited the stage with excitement on their little faces, I gave each of them a hug. Nate and I stayed backstage until the last class had performed their scene, then we joined my class onstage for their bow.

After everything was broken down and packed away, we headed to Nate's car. As soon as he unlocked the door, I slid into the passenger seat. He entered chuckling.

"What's so funny?"

"It's nothing," he said, but an amused smile pulled on his lips.

"Tell me!"

He turned in his seat. "It's just... When I picked you up that day on Main Street, you were so tentative around me. But now, you jump into my car like it's where you belong." I bit my lip, and he hurried on. "Not that that's a bad thing. On the contrary, I like that you feel comfortable with me again." His brown eyes softened as he took my hand. "I missed it. I missed you."

My heart melted, and I cupped his cheek with my other hand. He leaned into it, shutting his eyes, and I took advantage of the moment. Leaning forward, I brushed my lips against his.

When I pulled away, his eyes were wide and dark. I swallowed, hoping I hadn't just done something to jeopardize whatever was growing between us before it had a chance to fully bloom.

"I'm sorry," I said, pulling away from him.

"Don't be." He grabbed my shoulder to stop me. "I've been wanting to do that for some time, but I worried you weren't ready."

I grinned and moved close to him again. "So, does that mean we can continue where I left off?"

He huffed a laugh. "Let's not make out in the school parking lot." Then his face sobered. "I still think we should take things slow."

"As long as 'slow' doesn't mean glacial, I'm good with that."

That earned me another laugh as he twisted in his seat and buckled his seat belt. Then he drove us to Bea's. We were silent on the drive there. I was too excited and nervous, replaying the kiss in my mind while at the same time trying to rehearse what I would say.

When we arrived, I chose a booth toward the back of the restaurant. Our conversation didn't need an audience, though the whole town would learn of my choice soon enough.

As soon as we were alone, I slid my hands across the table. Nate eagerly grasped them in his.

"Thank you for today," I said, looking up at him from beneath my lashes.

"It was my pleasure," he replied, his voice growing husky. "I always knew you'd make a great teacher, but I guess I didn't realize how well suited you are for the role until today."

I smiled. "The kids make it easy. They're such a sweet bunch."

"Have you given any more thought to the job offer here?"

"I have, actually." I was brimming with so much excitement, I practically bounced out of my seat. "I'm accepting it!"

His mouth fell open. "You are?" He swallowed and shook his head as if he wasn't sure he'd heard me correctly. "You're staying?"

"I still need to call both schools and tell them my decision, but yes, I'm staying." I grinned, expecting him to congratulate me or say how happy he was with my choice, but he shifted in his seat, and my uneasy feeling from the night before returned. "Aren't you happy?"

"Of course I'm happy," he said, but it came out flat.

"You don't sound like it." He didn't look it either. I tried to catch his eye, but he avoided me, choosing instead to focus on a straw wrapper. What did that mean? Had he changed his mind? Did he not want me to stay? And then my stomach dropped. Was it because I kissed him?

"I-I'm just in shock." He laughed, but it was strained. "What made you decide to stay?"

I cocked my head, studying him. "A lot of things." My excitement deflated, and I stared at my menu with a frown. "Working with the kids has meant a lot to me. My family is here, and I want to be near them." I stopped myself from saying he was part of the reason because it seemed like that would be the last thing he would want to hear right then. And that hurt.

"How did your dad take it?"

I shrugged. "He doesn't know." *This is too much.* I lifted my head and stared at Nate until he looked at me. "You're the first person I've told."

His face softened, but his fist still gripped the edge of the table. "Are you sure you'll be happy here?"

I lost my thin hold on my composure. "Nate, what's going on? I thought you'd be thrilled to hear I'd not only finally made a decision but that I'd chosen to stay. After all, you're the one who told me about this position." I shook my head, trying to wrap my mind around what had happened between then and now. "I understood why you held back when it wasn't clear I would take the job, but here I am, telling you that I'm staying, and it's like you don't want that anymore."

"I just know that part of your indecision stemmed from your mom, and I don't want you to regret staying like she did," he blurted out. His face went red, and he clenched his jaw.

I narrowed my eyes as everything clicked into place. So it wasn't about the job or my decision to stay. *No,* this *is about the secret he's keeping.*

"Enough is enough, Nate." I stared him down. "Spit it out."

He fidgeted with his napkin, and I expected him to change the subject or insist he wasn't hiding anything. But then he gave a defeated nod and sighed. "You know how I told you your mother and I made our peace?"

"I vaguely recall," I said, a hint of sarcasm in my tone. *Like I would ever forget that.*

"Well"—Nate shifted in his seat—"I-I went to see her, your mother, before she died."

"You did?" I racked my brain for any memory of him being at my home, but nothing came to mind. "When?"

"She planned it for when she knew you'd be gone," he continued, staring at his hands. "She wanted to talk to me alone."

My heartbeat picked up its pace, but I worked to keep my expression neutral. "Why? What did she say?"

"She apologized."

"Apologized?" I stilled. I could think of a laundry list of things for which she could apologize. "For what?"

Finally, Nate raised his eyes to meet mine. "For breaking us up."

Whatever I had expected him to say, it wasn't that. I moved my lips, but no words formed, and no sounds came out. My mind reeled from the news. Mom felt responsible for breaking us up? Why? Sure, she had started dropping hints before I left for college about what I would miss out on if I stayed with him, then her hints became more direct the closer we got to my leaving date. And while, yes, she'd certainly never kept her dislike of Nate a secret, I would never have dreamed of blaming *her* for our breakup. I blamed the distance; it was too much for us. I blamed our youth because we were too young to make that kind of commitment. There was even a part of me that still suspected Nate had found someone else, despite his denials then and now. But my mother? I couldn't wrap my head around what he was saying.

Nate searched my face and sighed. "Melody told me things she did to try to convince you to break up with me. Pushing you to have new experiences in college, trying to stop you from making the same mistake she did in marrying your father so young."

I didn't know what to say. None of that made any sense. Nate rushed to fill the silence.

"The weekend she went to visit you, she took a lot of photos. Of you, the campus, but several of the photos of you were with various guys from your college." His brown eyes filled with an emotion I couldn't place. "When she came home, she not only showed me the photos, but she also told me I needed to let you go." His voice broke, and he cleared his throat. "She said that I was holding you back." He reached for me, but I pulled my hand away. "I don't know if she hoped I would think you were cheating on me or if she wanted to prove that you were better off without me, but whatever her motivation, it worked." He looked down, his shoulders drooping. "It's why I stopped responding to your texts and calls. I thought I was doing what you wanted, and when you came home and we argued, it just confirmed what she showed me. That you *were* better off without me." His voice lowered, and there was a wistful note in it. "After she told me all that, she made me promise to tell you. She hoped it might lead us back to each other, without any further interference from her."

Like death would stop her. An errant giggle bubbled up in my throat, and Nate frowned at me. Clearly, he thought I wasn't handling the news well, but the idea that Mom would allow a little thing like her own death to stop her interfering in the lives of those she loved was hilarious. Only Melody McAllister could continue to meddle in my love life from the great beyond. The small giggle morphed into a wide grin, and before I could stop myself, hysterical laughter burst out.

Nate's frown deepened as his eyes darted around the room, like he was debating whether he needed to find reinforcements to have me committed. Somehow, being placed under a seventy-two-hour hold didn't sound like such a bad idea at the moment.

"I'm sorry," I said as I regained control. "It was just... When you said, 'without any further interference,' I found that amusing because she's clearly still interfering by having you be the bearer of this news." I struggled to process what he'd told me, but I felt overwhelmed with all the information. It was just too much. So, my mind homed in on the one thing it thought I could handle. "I still don't understand when you would have had this conversation. I never saw you."

"I told you, she wanted me to meet her when you weren't home," Nate replied. "The nurse set it up." He must have sensed my disbelief because he leaned back and crossed his arms. "After everything I just told you, why would I lie about *that*?"

Before I could respond, the server arrived with our food. I wasn't sure what to believe as I tried to logic my way out of myths, legends, and first loves. I ate a french fry, but it tasted like ash in my mouth. Nothing about the conversation made sense.

I decided to approach it from a different angle. "If she wanted you to tell me, why did you wait so long?"

Nate stared at me as a plethora of emotions crossed his face as if an internal battle raged inside him. A few times, he opened his mouth but quickly closed it again.

"You were already in so much pain. And I thought, well..." He stopped and squared his shoulders as if steeling himself. "At first, I figured things were over between us. As far as I could tell, you had moved on. You planned a new life on the other side of the country, and then, when I learned you had a boyfriend, I didn't see the point." His eyes bored into mine with an unfathomable emotion. "But then, after that song you sang at karaoke, and when you broke up with James..." He shook his head. "I didn't want it to sound like I was telling you these things to manipulate you into staying. I wanted you to choose to stay because you wanted it, not because I wanted you to or because your mother had had a change of heart before she died."

"You're right. It does seem more than a little suspect." I lifted my hand, ticking off items on my fingers as I spoke. "First, you tell me about a job here, and you encourage me to apply even after I tell you I have a job waiting for me in California. Then, we spend all this time together, preparing for the estate sale, fixing my mom's car, and then this afternoon, after the play, we kissed, which would have been the perfect moment to tell me. But you never said a word." I shook my head, trying to clear it. My disbelief was fading as anger took its place.

"I wasn't going to say anything. I thought it would remain something that happened between Melody and me, but then Max told me at dinner last night that he knew—"

What the— "You had *dinner* with my *dad*?" I demanded, a fire building in my belly. Of *course* my father was involved. The one person who had consistently berated me for choosing California over Cedar Haven wouldn't be able to resist any chance to convince me to stay. My skin prickled with rage. His strange line of questioning the other night suddenly made perfect sense. *And what did you and Nate talk about?* Because he knew what Mom and Nate had discussed.

Nate blanched, and it was clear by the expression on his face he hadn't meant to tell me that. "Steven asked me to meet him and Max."

Steven too? I closed my eyes, trying to control my temper. Did *no one* in my family trust me to make my own decisions? Part of me wanted to go to California just to spite them all.

"Is that why you said no to dinner with me? Because you had plans with them?"

At his nod, the thin leash I had on my rage evaporated.

"To what? Conspire behind my back about keeping me here?"

Mixed in with my anger was a sharp pain, twisting in my gut. While I'd expected my father not to play fair, the idea that Nate was in on it cut me to my core. And then he'd lied to me about it. He'd refused to have dinner with me because he would rather collude with my family. Bile rose in my throat.

He dropped his gaze but not before I saw the guilt in his eyes. So, that was what this was all about. A stupid scheme to try to convince me to stay. I hated myself for how well it had worked. I was such an idiot, thinking that I'd figured out what the so-called "real Lanie" wanted. But no, it'd all been a conniving charade so my father could get what he wanted. I shoved my food away and stood, grabbing my coat.

"Wait, Lanie, don't leave," Nate protested, standing as well. "Please let me explain."

"I've heard enough!" I threw some money on the table and glared at him. "Don't follow me." Without waiting for a response, I turned and fled before he could see the tears gathering in my eyes.

Chapter Thirteen

I DIDN'T WANT TO go home. I couldn't bear to sit in that house after what Nate had told me. I wasn't sure which upset me more, my mother's alleged confession or Nate's clandestine meeting with my family. Either way, I needed some distance from anything that would remind me I was a McAllister.

Which was why it made no sense at all when I found myself pulling into the parking lot of the cemetery a few minutes later. I hadn't been there since the funeral. It hurt too much.

As I stood at the edge of the graveyard, that night didn't feel like the right time either. My emotions overwhelmed me, and I didn't know what I hoped to accomplish by going there. Would I confront my mother or at least what was left of her? Was that my plan? Or had I gone there for answers, ones I had little chance of ever receiving? If Nate's story was true, and he had not only seen my mom behind my back but had heard her confession with his own ears, then had everything I'd believed about my mom been a lie?

Fresh tears pricked the backs of my eyelids, and I bowed my head. I could admit there was some truth to Nate's story. I remembered the parents' weekend he referenced. Mom had been thrilled to see me making so many new friends, particularly ones of the male persuasion. I wouldn't have put it past Mom to do exactly what Nate described. And it explained his distance for the last month or so of the semester. It was why I'd thought he'd found someone new but just didn't have the courage to tell me. So it didn't surprise me when we broke up after I returned home. He'd sworn up and down that he hadn't cheated on me, and deep down, I'd always known he was telling the truth. But to learn that it might have all been Mom's doing cut deep.

My hands curled into fists at my side. Mom and I had never had an easy relationship, but that? That was by far the worst thing she had ever done to me. To sabotage my relationship was bad enough, but to not even have the decency to tell me herself? To entrust someone else to share the news? Especially someone who, up until recently, I'd never expected to have in my life again.

Tears blurred my vision as I stomped through the cemetery. I couldn't say whether they were tears of pain or rage. Perhaps it was some of both. But I knew the way. I'd chosen Mom's final resting place myself, and my sure feet carried me directly to the spot.

Though I'd picked out the headstone, I hadn't seen it in person. Seeing her name etched into the cold marble gutted me. In a way, it made it more real. The dates were carved deep into the stone, confirming to the world and to me that she was really and truly gone.

But even that pain couldn't douse my rage. "How could you?" I spat out. "How could you lie to me, for all these years, and then let me find out this way?"

The graveyard was silent. Not even birdsong filtered through the cold winter air. No helpful flash of a familiar red to brighten up the bleak, gray stones or provide me with the answers I so desperately needed. One question echoed in my head, over and over: *Why?* Why didn't she tell me? Why did she involve Nate? And most of all, why couldn't she see how much pain she'd caused by breaking my heart in the first place?

I'd cried for months after that fight with Nate. The only saving grace was going back to Seattle and drowning myself in school. Apparently, I'd never learned a better way to channel my grief, as I'd done the exact same thing when she'd died.

"I was here, for *months*, tending to your every need. You had ample opportunity to tell me this yourself. But you didn't. You *couldn't*." I started shaking. "You're a coward, Melody McAllister."

As soon as the words left my mouth, I slapped my hand over it. I hadn't meant to say that. And yet, I spoke truth. She'd said nothing the entire time I cared for her, and then she left Nate to do what she couldn't and pick up the pieces. I dropped my hand, placing it over my heart as it broke all over again.

"I didn't deserve to find out like this," I whispered. "You should have told me. You should have—" My voice choked off with a sob. I dashed an impatient hand across my tear-stained cheeks and spun away from the grave as I ran to the car. No. I would not break down. Not there, not then. She didn't deserve my tears.

I grabbed my phone and sent an angry group text to Steven and Dad, including Rose for good measure. Somehow, I doubted my future sister-in-law had been involved in the conspiracy dinner. Rose wouldn't have stood for such manipulation tactics, no matter how much she loved my brother. If I had hopes of an ally, my best bet was Rose.

Text sent, I put the car in gear and drove home, determined to discover for myself what was true. I no longer doubted Nate's words, but I needed more. I deserved more than a secondhand message from my dead mother.

When I arrived, I went straight to the file box I'd found. Steven had said it was probably filled with old bills, but I hoped it would hold the answers I sought. Something to explain my mother's actions. I was desperate for any clue that would help me understand why my mother had done that. After rolling up my sleeves, I lifted the lid off the box.

Inside were hanging files. Most were labeled for various bills: Mortgage, Electricity, and the like. But one was labeled Letters. I grabbed that one and opened it. Most of the letters were from my father, friends from a camp my mother attended as a child, or Christmas newsletters from family. There were even a few love notes from old boyfriends Mom would occasionally reminisce about but nothing that appeared recent.

Frustrated, I returned to the box. One folder wasn't labeled. As I opened it, my heart stuttered, and a chill ran up my spine. There were several crisp white envelopes, mostly addressed in Mom's scrawl, but a few were written in a neater hand. Each envelope was addressed to different members of my family. One for me, for Steven, for Dad, for Rose, and... for Nate? I hesitated over the letter to Nate, curiosity getting the better of me. His letter wasn't sealed, as if Mom knew I would find it impossible to resist reading its contents.

My hands shook as I removed a small piece of paper from the envelope and unfolded it.

Dear Nate,

Keep your promise. Take care of her.

Melody

The words were so simple and direct, but they said so much. Tears sprang to my eyes as I read the words over and over, as if they would suddenly change. I yanked out the letter addressed to me and ripped the envelope open. My mother's final words to me took up just one page. She must have written it in her final days. How had she managed to find the energy to do all of that without me knowing?

Dear Lanie,

Of all the letters I've written, yours is the one I struggled with the most. I want to start with two things. I love you, and I'm sorry. I hope Nate has spoken to you by now, but if he hasn't, please give him the chance to explain.

I know you're probably angry with me, and you have every right to be. I should have told you myself. Better still, I never should have interfered in the first place. Unfortunately, I'm afraid you've now learned a difficult lesson and one I'd hoped I'd be able to teach you in time. Parents, like most people, aren't infallible. We often get it wrong.

I've made many mistakes in my life, but none I've regretted as much as this. It was made out of misplaced bitterness, and if I could, I would take it all back.

The simple apology cut through the last remnants of my rage like a knife. The rest of the letter was filled with hopes for my future and how much she wished she could be there to see it. She encouraged me to follow my heart, wherever it led, and to "hold on to your dreams and dream big." Before her signature, Mom wrote: *You have my blessing, whatever you decide.*

I didn't know how long I sat there, clutching my mother's last words to my chest and sobbing.

I couldn't move and could barely breathe. It was as if she had died all over again, the pain was so fresh.

Only one question remained for me to answer. My mother had released me from my promise, but maybe I'd been right all along. Maybe the memories I'd made in Cedar Haven were too painful to bear.

⁓ℓℓ⁓

Two days later, Steven and my father came over to move me into my father's house. I'd barely spoken to either of them since I'd learned about their secret meeting with Nate. As Dad and Steven packed my things into their respective cars, I pushed my anger deep inside of me. The day would be bittersweet enough without throwing in an argument.

While the closing wasn't for another month, it was the last day a McAllister would live in that house, and it felt appropriate for it to be the day we truly said goodbye. Despite the lingering resentment toward my family, I appreciated that we were all together that day.

But things were awkward. Even Rose gave Steven the cold shoulder. She'd been supportive of me and told both Steven and my dad to back off. It was nice to have someone in my corner, especially as I'd felt utterly alone since that dramatic scene with Nate. While I hadn't reached out to him, he wasn't exactly banging down my door either. I chose to ignore the ache that reverberated in my chest whenever I thought about him.

Besides, I had enough on my plate as it was. Everything was happening so fast; it made my head spin. I couldn't believe how much we'd accomplished in the month and a half since I'd been home.

Once the cars were all packed and ready to trek across town, I stood alone in the driveway, facing the house. Steven and Dad came up on either side of me and slid their arms around me. The three of us gazed at what was once our family home and took a collective breath, remembering all the good memories we had there and the woman who had made it a home.

Then everyone turned and climbed into their cars and drove away, leaving me alone once more. A deep, overwhelming wave of sadness came over me, and I bowed my head under its weight. All the work to get the house ready was over. What would I do with all my free time?

I turned on my heel and walked to the car, my steps heavy and slow. I drove on autopilot to my dad's, and once there, I unpacked my car like a machine. Nobody seemed to notice the change in my demeanor. Well, nobody except Rose.

"Are you okay?" she asked as she carried a box of clothes up to my new room.

"I'm fine," I said, but my voice sounded robotic even to me. I tried to force a smile, but it was like I couldn't feel my face. Everything was numb.

Rose's eyebrows knitted together, but she didn't press the issue. Once all the boxes were unloaded, she and Steven left, and my father settled in to watch television.

I climbed the stairs to my new room and shut the door. Everything about it felt wrong. The sun was too bright, the walls were too bare, and the floor wasn't carpeted. I shut the blinds and closed the curtains. I knew I should unpack, but I couldn't find the energy. Instead, I moved all the boxes off my bed, crawled under the covers, and blocked out the world.

There was a soft knock at my door, and I burrowed farther under the covers, trying to muffle the sound. I'd long lost track of the days, but I couldn't bring myself to care. The only time I left my bed was when the persistent gnawing in my stomach told me that I needed to eat something. But even then, I could stomach only a few crackers before the nausea would take over. While up, I would force myself to shower, which really meant standing under the water until it turned cold. I'd worn all my comfy pajamas, though I thought someone had come in at some point to take my laundry. The details were a little fuzzy.

The knock came again, sharper. I opened one eye. The room was dark and unfamiliar with vague shapes standing out in the darkness. I knew I should be doing something, but I couldn't remember what. Whenever I tried too hard to figure it out, tears would leak from my eyes, and sobs would rack my body. So, I didn't try. Besides, all I wanted to do was sleep. I was so tired. But it didn't seem to matter how long I slept. Whenever I woke up, I still felt exhausted. Would I ever feel rested again?

"Lanie!" a deep voice shouted from the other side of the door. "Open this door, right now."

"Five more minutes," I moaned as I flipped onto my side and pulled a pillow over my ears. After a few more muffled shouts and pounds on the door, whoever it was gave up and stomped away. I drifted into a dreamless sleep, my favorite kind as of late.

Sometime later, my phone buzzed. I lifted my arm from under the covers and felt around my nightstand until my fingers brushed the familiar object. I picked it up and slipped my arm back under the covers. The bright screen blinded me, and I winced as I tried to make out the message.

A text from Nate. I groaned, shoving my arm out and dropping the phone back onto the nightstand. I didn't want to talk to him. He'd upset me, though I didn't allow myself to dwell on what exactly he'd done. Despite my lack of response, he refused to take the hint and kept texting. I rolled over, but sleep didn't come easily that time. My brain wouldn't shut off, as if it wanted me to remember.

Glaring at my phone, I threw off the covers. Why did I look at it? I'd successfully avoided it most of the time, picking it up only when the buzzing got incessant. With an irritated growl, I climbed out of bed and turned the phone off before shoving it into a box. There. I wouldn't be disturbed again.

Since I was already awake, I wandered downstairs to the kitchen. It must have been the middle of the night because the house was dark. I tiptoed around the creaky spots on the floor, which I'd memorized during other late-night forages for food. I opened the cabinet doors slowly to avoid the slightest whine of the hinges. A box of toaster pastries sat near the front. That sounded more appetizing than crackers. I gritted my teeth when the metallic wrapping rustled in my hands as I tore the package. After putting the pastries on a paper towel, I crept back up the stairs to my room and quietly shut the door.

I made it through one pastry before I lost my appetite, and I wished I'd thought to get some fresh water. The glass by my bed had been there for a while, possibly days, and tasted stale. But I gulped it down anyway. Then I slid back under the covers and fell into a restless sleep.

The bed shifted, and I startled awake. A gentle hand, warm, soft, and familiar, caressed my hair. I smiled, still half-asleep, and reached up to grab the hand but instead touched my own cheek. Outside my window, a bird chirped. An image of a red cardinal with black freckles near its beak flashed through my mind, but before I could make sense of it, sleep found me again.

"Lanie." A gentle, familiar voice whispered my name. A hand shook my shoulder. "Lanie, it's time to wake up."

I opened my eyes and rolled over, taking in the angular features of my future sister-in-law's face. Rose was smiling, but it didn't reach her eyes. Worry lines creased her forehead.

"Rose," I croaked. I cleared my throat. "What are you doing here?"

"I came to convince you to get out of this bed." When I went to roll over again, Rose grabbed my shoulder and shook it with more force. "No, Lanie. Not this time. Get up. Now!"

Shocked, I stared up at her. "What's your problem?"

"You've been in this bed for a week. Whatever is wrong, whatever has happened, you need to snap out of it."

"You wouldn't understand," I moaned as I buried my face in the pillow.

"Then you're going to have to make me understand." Rose yanked the covers off the bed, and I curled into a ball to escape the sudden cold air. "You're going to get out of this bed, you're going to take a shower—a *real* one with *actual* soap—and then you're going to go downstairs. Your brother and father are waiting for you."

After briefly considering mutiny, I dragged myself out of bed. I wasn't sure if it was the thought of a hot shower to escape the cold after Rose had so rudely ripped away my blankets or if it was my fear of what Rose might do next that drove me to obey. But the moment I was in the shower, I regretted not fighting back. For some reason, the water always helped me to think, and that was the last thing I wanted to do.

When I returned to my room, the curtains had been pushed back, and sunlight was streaming in. Birds chirped outside the window, and I could feel winter losing its grip on Cedar Haven. The promise of warmer days and fresh flowers brought a soft smile to my face. There were still piles of boxes stacked on the floor, and the simple furnishings my father had set up were a stark reminder of the life I had left behind. Dad had moved a few times since he and Mom divorced, and his latest house was much smaller than the one I'd shared with him my last semester of high school.

Voices drifted up from below, and I steeled myself to face the firing squad, a.k.a. my family. My behavior over the last... days? Weeks? I had no idea, but however long I'd spent shut in my room had led to the lovely intervention I was walking into. I took a deep breath and descended the stairs.

"Lanie," Rose cooed as she stood to embrace me as if she hadn't just dragged me out of bed. "It's so good to see you vertical."

Her words caught me off guard, and I laughed in spite of myself. The sound of my laughter quieted the rest of the room as everyone stared at me.

"Why don't you sit here?" Steven pulled a chair out for me. The kitchen was small, with a round table in the center surrounded by five wooden chairs. A little window overlooking the backyard was over the sink. The walls were bare except for a cow calendar Steven had given Dad as a Christmas present. My father didn't do much decorating. He preferred simplicity to style.

I glanced around at the familiar faces of my family. Steven's hazel eyes were clouded with concern, while Dad's thick eyebrows were pulled down in a perpetual frown. Rose kept a smile on her face, though it looked a little strained.

"How are you feeling?" Dad asked, leaning back in his chair.

"Better," I said, my voice still hoarse from disuse. "I didn't mean to worry you." I dropped my gaze to the table. "It's just... a lot happened over a short period of time." My breath hitched in my throat as I fought back tears. "The house selling, Nate's secret, breaking up with James..."

"You broke up with James?" Steven's eyes widened. With a quick glance at Rose, who conveniently looked away, he grabbed my arm. "Why didn't you tell us?"

"Like I said, everything happened so fast." After taking a deep breath, I told the whole story.

How James had shown up unexpectedly at the Valentine's dance and I'd subsequently broken up with him. How I'd received the job offer and decided to accept it, but then when I met with Nate for lunch, he told me about Mom and spilled the beans on the clandestine dinner. I glared at Steven and Dad, who, for their part, had the decency to at least look guilty. The more I talked, the more the ache in my chest eased, and my shoulders lifted as if a weight had been removed.

"Once the house sold, I suddenly found myself with a lot of free time. I couldn't go back to California yet because we still have the probate hearings, but there wasn't much for me to do here either. And I had a lot to process." With my head in my hands, I stared at the table. "Mom not only broke up my relationship, but then she also didn't even have the decency to tell me."

For the first time since our awful lunch, my heart went out to Nate. Clearly, we needed to talk. It wasn't his fault he'd been dragged into my mother's drama, though the fact that he'd gone along with her hurt more than I was ready to admit.

My head shot up. "How is Nate?"

They exchanged glances. Finally, Steven spoke. "He's fine. But he's not what's important right now."

"What about the house? Is there anything I need to do to prepare for the sale?"

Steven shook his head. "Everything is on schedule." He exchanged another look with my father. "But there is a matter you need to settle soon."

"You said you received an offer from the local school," Dad said. "But you haven't given them an answer yet."

My teeth worried my lower lip. "I-I haven't made up my mind yet."

"Given what's been going on the last several days, I think it's best if you take some time away from here," my father continued, his eyebrows pulling together in a deeper frown. "We've been looking at flight options, but your breakup with James complicates things." His fingers drummed on the table. "I don't suppose you have somewhere you can stay?"

My pulse hammered in my throat. He wanted me to leave? After conniving to get me to stay, he suddenly couldn't get rid of me fast enough? But I couldn't leave right then, not with everything still so up in the air. How could I do that to Nate? Just leave without a word? I closed my eyes and took a calming breath, forcing myself to focus on the present.

"I had planned to book an Airbnb until James and I found a place to stay," I finally said. "But I don't want to go." I glanced at Steven in hopes he would jump in and say he needed me for the estate, but he refused to meet my eye.

"Steven needs me. Don't you, Steven?" I pressed, trying to force him to engage.

"What I need is for you to get better," Steven said, his voice strained. When he finally looked at me, the pain in his eyes was like a punch to the gut. "And if that means you need to live on the other side of the country, then so be it."

I stared at the table. Since I'd returned, I'd told them I couldn't handle living in Cedar Haven with all the painful memories, and it looked like my family had finally gotten that message just when I wished I could take it back.

When I lifted my head, ready to declare I wasn't going anywhere, all I saw in their faces were worry and fear. My behavior over the last week had scared them, and they were willing to do whatever they could to help me.

Maybe they had a point. The memories I'd avoided had finally caught up with me, and I couldn't afford to spend the rest of my life hiding under the covers. Besides, that wasn't what Mom would have wanted. Regardless of whether I lived her dreams or my own, the point was, I needed to *live*.

"What about probate court?" I asked meekly.

"I can handle the hearings," Steven said, waving a dismissive hand. "And anything I need from you can be done remotely at this point."

My heart squeezed as I thought fast. I needed to buy myself some time.

"I have a therapy appointment tomorrow," I said, squaring my shoulders and looking them each in the eye. "How about I go to that and talk things over with her? That way, I don't make any rash decisions I may regret later."

Steven and Dad looked ready to protest, but Rose nodded. "It'll be good to have an unbiased perspective on the situation."

After exchanging glances, my father and brother nodded. I breathed a sigh of relief, though I knew it would be short-lived. The therapy appointment would grant me a reprieve from the intervention, but I'd have to figure out the rest.

My stomach growled, and I glanced at the refrigerator. "Um, is there anything to eat? I'm starving."

Chapter Fourteen

After my family finished their intervention, I needed to get out of that house. I'd never been more grateful to have my mother's car. Keys in hand, I headed to the grocery store, hoping to find some things to cook for dinner, since I planned to eat regularly again.

I'd barely stepped into the door when Nate appeared in front of me. Startled, I stumbled back a step, and he caught my arm. The spark of heat that I'd felt every time we'd touched was absent, leaving only an unfamiliar iciness in my veins. I yanked my arm back.

He shoved his hands into his pockets, and his eyes roved over me as if searching for signs of pain. But his exploration would be fruitless. My pain was tucked away deep inside.

"Lanie." His voice was soft. "I've been so worried."

"I'm fine." I took another step away from him, and his face fell.

He ran a hand through his hair and stared at the floor. When he raised his gaze back to me, it was filled with questions I didn't want to answer.

"Look," I said, trying to sound forceful. "I know we need to talk, but—"

"You don't need to do anything except take care of you, Lanie."

The sincerity in his dark-brown eyes caused my insides to melt a little, and I hated myself for it. Part of me wanted to escape his intense stare, but I had my own questions. Maybe it was better to talk then, to rip off the bandage and fully allow myself to bleed out before I put myself back together again.

I steeled myself. "Let's go sit in my car." Without waiting for a response, I spun on my heel and headed into the parking lot. The only confirmation I had that he followed me was the sound of his footsteps.

When we reached the car, I unlocked the doors and slid into the driver's seat. The role reversal wasn't lost on me. I couldn't remember the last time I'd driven him somewhere.

"Lanie, I—"

I held up a hand. "No, you've said enough." I turned on him, my lips pressed into a hard line. "My turn."

I hadn't practiced what I would say. Truthfully, I wasn't feeling fully coherent, having spent most of my week hiding in bed. *Just speak from the heart.*

And so I did. "I'm not angry with you for not telling me what my mother did." He visibly relaxed beside me. If I had been in a better mood, I might have laughed at his naivete. "But what I can't forgive…" I stopped and took a breath. "What I don't understand is why you took her at her word. She might have lit the match, but you stoked the fire." I raised my eyes to meet his and saw my own pain reflected there.

The words poured out of me faster than I could process them. "Why didn't you talk to me after she showed you those pictures, after she told you that you were holding me back? She'd tried so many times before, Nate. We even joked about it the other night. The yellow police tape, the tacos, all her subtle and not-so-subtle attempts to break us up." I shook my head. "And none of it worked. At least, not until I left."

His eyes welled up with tears before he dropped his head into his hands. I waited for him to speak, and when he didn't, I pressed on.

"You could have asked me, Nate. You could have point-blank asked me if I was cheating on you, if

I had moved on." I threw up my hands. "Hell, *I* asked *you*. That last fight we had, I begged you to tell me who she was. Who had stolen your heart away from me. And you swore there wasn't anyone else. But you never asked me the same." I swallowed past the lump in my throat. "Why was it so easy for you to believe my mother? Why didn't you trust me?"

"I never thought you were cheating on me," he said quietly.

I stared at him as tears streamed down my cheeks. At least that was something, but it didn't explain why he'd stopped calling me. It didn't provide me with an understandable reason for why he just let things fizzle out for months only to explode when we finally saw each other again. All it gave me was more questions.

"Then why? Why didn't you talk to me?"

"Because she was right!" His dark eyes flew to my face, and the rage and pain I saw there took my breath away. "I *was* holding you back, Lanie. You were always meant for bigger and better things than Cedar Haven, and I couldn't bear to be the thing standing in your way." He clenched his hands into fists. "Even now, even after telling you about the position here, even after you told me you were going to accept, I can't bear to think that you're throwing away your life for me."

"I'm not," I blurted out. I hadn't meant to say it, but I recognized the truth in my words. Nate might have told me about the job and given me *a* reason to stay, but it wasn't my only one. I'd fallen in love with those kids, and I hated the thought of leaving them with a stranger. But I also wanted to rebuild my relationship with Steven and spend more time with Rose. I wanted to reconnect with old friends and make a place for myself there, in my hometown.

"In some ways," he continued as if I hadn't spoken, "I think I told you about your mom when I did because I wanted to convince you that you were right all along. That you deserved better than this town. She didn't want you to settle, and I worried that if I didn't tell you, that's exactly what you'd be doing."

I crossed my arms and glared at him. "It doesn't matter what she wanted. What matters is what I want. And I wanted you. I've always wanted you."

When he met my eyes again, they were so filled with hope I couldn't stand it, but I wasn't done. "Which is why learning that you listened to my mother instead of talking to me hurts so much. Her betrayal was bad enough on its own, but coupled with yours—"

His mouth dropped open. "You think I betrayed you?"

"How else would you describe it?"

His throat moved as he swallowed. "I guess I never really thought of it that way."

I turned and stared out the windshield, gathering my thoughts. "Do you know how many nights I sobbed myself to sleep when you wouldn't answer my calls or texts? Do you have any idea what your silence did to me?" I closed my eyes as the memories of my freshman year washed over me. "It was hard enough being in a new city, meeting new people. The pictures my mother showed you were a farce. I met most of those people in classes and never saw them again after that first semester. But I put on a show for her." I opened my eyes and looked over at him. "Had I known what she would do with my performance, I never would have bothered."

He opened his mouth as if to respond, but I cut him off. I was tired of that conversation. I needed to get my groceries and get home.

"My family thinks I should go to California now," I said, unable to keep the bitterness from my voice.

His breath hitched. "You're leaving?"

"I haven't decided yet." I risked a glance at him, which was a mistake because the devastation I found there shattered my heart. I grabbed my purse and tucked my keys inside. "I need some time."

He grabbed my arm. "I'm sorry, Lanie." His voice was hoarse. "I didn't know."

I smiled sadly as I shook him off and climbed out of the car. "Because you never asked."

* * *

"That's quite a story," Dr. Brooks said when I finished telling her all that had happened since my last session.

I nodded and fell back against the couch, my energy drained. Reliving the last week had taken a lot out of me. But I also felt like a weight had been lifted off me.

"So, what are you going to do?" she asked, cocking her head. She was perched on her office chair again and had furiously jotted down notes while I talked. "Are you going to stay here, or will you go back to the West Coast?"

I bit my lip. Wasn't that her job? Okay, well, maybe she couldn't *tell* me what to do, but couldn't she give me a hint? Some guidance? My decision-making skills weren't exactly stellar, if the last seven days were any indication.

"I don't know." I widened my eyes, hoping she would see the plea in them.

"What do you want to do?"

Stifling a sigh, I dropped my gaze and fidgeted with a string on the cushion. That question was quickly becoming my least favorite. As if it were so easy to say what *I* wanted after spending so long chasing after what *my mother* wanted.

"I don't know that either," I began. Perhaps if I gave Dr. Brooks something to work with, she could steer me in the right direction. "I thought I wanted to go to California. I thought I wanted to marry James and teach at a special school." I stopped and took a deep breath. "But after everything I've learned about my mother, I don't know where she ends and I begin."

"That's understandable."

I glanced at her, hoping she would say more. When she didn't, I ground my teeth and glared at the floor. What was the point of coming for a session if she wasn't going to help me?

"What do you think I should do?" I asked, figuring it couldn't hurt. The worst she might do was give me some psychobabble about how I needed to determine what I wanted for myself and that no one could do it for me. That wouldn't be helpful, but at least I would know that I was on my own.

"Follow your heart."

That caught my attention, and my head shot up. In some ways, it was worse than psychobabble. At least if she'd given me some line about how I was the only one who could figure out what I wanted, she might have assigned some homework to guide me in that process. But her response was so vague. And I doubted she had any worksheets that would aid me in something as intangible as following my heart.

"But how will I know that I'm doing that if I'm so entwined with what my mother wanted for me?"

She was silent, and I shifted under her scrutiny. Then she smiled. "Let's try an exercise."

That sounded more promising than her vague responses so far. I sat up straighter and gestured for her to continue.

"We're going to play a word-association game. When I say a word, I want you to say the first thing that comes to mind. Some of your answers may be skewed due to your mother's influence, but don't worry about that. That's something we can examine later once we have an overall picture."

I wasn't sure I liked that game anymore, but I was willing to try anything. "Okay, let's give it a go."

"Your first word is 'lurk.'"

"Stalker," I blurted out and frowned.

She shook her head. "Don't overthink it. There are no right or wrong answers here." Glancing down at her paper, she continued. "Piper."

"Pied."

After making a note on her clipboard, she read the next one. "Face."

"Consequences." My mouth dropped open. *Where did that come from?*

A sly smile slipped through her professional mask. "We're getting somewhere now. 'Home.'"

"Cedar Haven." I swallowed and closed my eyes, wishing I could go back in time and decide not to play the game. I didn't like where we were heading.

"Good. How about…"

I opened my eyes and found her staring at me with interest.

"Love."

"Nate." Tears filled my eyes, and I covered my face with my hands.

"I think you have your answer," she said quietly.

I did. Despite my mother's influence, despite her dreams for me, even in spite of what I'd recently learned about her, what I wanted, what the *real* me wanted, was to come home. Protests bubbled up inside of me, desperate to claw their way out of my mouth, but I clamped my lips shut. Those were words that echoed in my head, my mother's voice distorted to sound like my own. The words I'd spoken without conscious thought—those came from my heart.

"I have one last word for you, but I'm not sure if it's necessary."

I shrugged as I wiped my eyes. My emotions were already chaotic enough. "Lay it on me."

She grimaced. "Mother."

"Human," I choked out as tears slid down my cheeks. And I knew in that moment that I'd forgiven her. I forgave her for breaking up Nate and me in the first place, for not telling me about her involvement before she died, for making Nate keep that awful promise, and for so many other things that I couldn't voice. As she'd said in her letter, she'd made mistakes, but at the end of the day, she was human. And humans were imperfect creatures.

"My one regret," I said when I had better control of myself, "is that I never got to tell her in person that I forgave her."

Dr. Brooks handed me a box of tissues. "As I said during our first session, we often need closure from ourselves. But there's nothing stopping you from telling her now."

"Except that she's dead." I stared out the window at the new blossoms on the dogwood tree just outside the building. "And heaven is too far away."

"Maybe," she said, and her eyes swam with unshed tears. "I don't consider myself a religious or spiritual person, but even I believe there are signs if we know where to look. So go somewhere you feel closest to her and tell her everything." She lifted one shoulder. "Who knows? Maybe she'll send you a sign."

I thought of the cardinal. What I had originally thought was my mother trying to meddle in my love life suddenly seemed to represent so much more. The bird had kept an eye on me, and I'd found comfort in its regular appearance. Whether my mother intended to steer me toward Nate or to help me find a way to forgive and let go no longer mattered to me. What mattered was that I knew my choice, and I knew what I needed to do.

After I finished with therapy, I went back to my dad's house. I found the number for the school in California and dialed, my hands shaking. Part of me would prefer to do that in an email, and I would send a follow-up message to confirm, but they'd given me my first shot as a teacher. They deserved more than a two-line email.

"Montgomery School, Andrea speaking. How may I direct your call?"

"May I speak to Principal McBride, please?"

"Certainly. May I ask who's calling?"

"Lanie McAllister."

"One moment, please."

The phone rang a couple of times, then a deep voice answered. "Lanie, what a pleasure to hear from you. How are things going in Maryland?"

"Well, sir. The house is under contract. All that's left is to file the finalized estate with the court."

"That's wonderful news. I'm sure you're anxious to get back to the West Coast and settle in before you start."

"Actually, that's why I'm calling." I cleared my throat and squared my shoulders. "I've been offered a position at a local school here, and I've decided to accept it."

The silence on the other end did nothing to help my pounding heart. I felt awful to leave them in a bind, but I knew I was making the right decision.

"I see," he finally said then sighed. "I can't say I didn't see this coming."

I blinked, unsure how to respond to that. "I'm sorry?"

"You're not the first person who returned to their hometown and decided to stick around," he replied with a chuckle. "Much as I think you'd be a great addition to our faculty, I understand, and I hope whatever school you're going to knows what a treasure they're getting."

"Thank you. I really appreciate the opportunity you offered me."

"If you ever change your mind, please feel free to reach out to me directly. I'm sure we'd be able to find you a place here."

I thanked him again and ended the call. One down, one to go. Next, I called the local school. That conversation took a little longer as we discussed the logistics of my start date, having an initial meeting with Mrs. Carlisle before I started officially working with the children, and finalizing the salary offer. When I hung up, I felt lighter and free.

But I wasn't done. I planned to do as my therapist suggested and tell my mother everything, but first, I wanted to clear the air with Nate.

I tried him at the auto shop and at home, but my calls and texts went unanswered. I supposed I couldn't blame him for not responding to me after our last conversation.

Walking into the kitchen, I saw the notes Mom had written, sitting on the table. The one for Nate lay folded beside mine. It dawned on me that I'd never told him about the note. Would he even want to know? Maybe it was best if he didn't. After all, he'd fulfilled his promise to her.

My head snapped up. As I'd suspected, the cardinal was perched on the railing of my father's back deck, staring at me through the kitchen window. I gazed at it for a moment before my eyes drifted back to the paper in my hand. Perhaps that was a way to reach him. He might avoid me, but

I knew him well enough to know he wouldn't ignore a dead woman's last words.

I scribbled my own note to him on an envelope and stuffed the letter inside. After grabbing my coat, I slid my feet into my shoes and raced out to Mom's car. Dr. Brooks had told me to follow my heart, and I intended to do just that.

Chapter Fifteen

I SAT ON THE partially frozen ground, staring blankly at my mother's headstone. I didn't know how long I'd been there, having lost feeling in my limbs long ago. Overall, I felt hollow and barely noticed the cold. My tears had long since run out, though the cool streaks they left behind were turning into icicles against my cheeks.

After leaving Mom's note for Nate, I went there. Per my therapist's suggestion, I'd gone to the place I'd felt closer to her. Which probably explained why I'd avoided the cemetery for most of my time home.

When I first arrived, I could barely get the words out over my tears. But I told her everything, and I forgave her for it all. While I'd hoped the cardinal would join me, if for nothing else than a sign that my mother heard me, I remained completely and utterly alone. Once I'd said what I needed to, the significance of what I had lost fully sank in, and I finally allowed myself to sit with my grief. No more pushing it away by staying busy or hiding from it under the covers in a darkened room. I let it wash over and through me, feeling everything and not holding back.

A series of images of my future flashed through my mind. The empty seat at my wedding, where my mother should be. Me in a hospital room, surrounded by nurses, with a man standing next to me, holding one hand and encouraging me to push while my other hand was closed in a fist because there was no one else there to hold it. Children's birthdays, first days of school, promotions, anniversaries, and achievements—all things my mother would miss. Graduation was only the beginning. I had a lifetime of events to experience without my mother.

I bowed my head, amazed as tears leaked from my eyes. How I had any water left in my body, I didn't know. And I grieved not only the loss of my mother's life but also the loss of what might have been, how different my future would have looked had she lived.

A sound roused me from my reverie, and I blinked my blurry eyes, attempting to focus. Footsteps crunched over the gravel road that led through the cemetery, and I raised my head, searching for the source of the sound. A figure in a dark coat moved toward me, but I couldn't make out much more than that in the dim light of dusk.

"Lanie?" a deep voice called, and my heart skipped a beat.

"I-I'm here," I croaked.

His pace increased, and soon, he was kneeling by my side. "Are you okay?"

I nodded and stared at my hands, not trusting myself to speak. Though happy to see him, I wasn't prepared to have that conversation then and there.

"Your family is worried sick about you," Nate said as he took my hand. "Your hands are like ice! How long have you been out here?"

I shrugged. My phone was in the car, and I wasn't wearing a watch. Not that I would have checked the time anyway. I glanced at the sky and guessed it had been several hours, based on the gathering shadows.

"I stopped by your house this afternoon, but you weren't there. So I came here," I whispered, unable to find the energy to speak louder.

"Oh, Lanie," Nate cried out as he pulled me to him, wrapping his arms around my frozen ones. "We need to get you inside and warm." He tried to help me stand, but my legs wouldn't cooperate.

"What are you doing here?" I blurted out.

His dark eyebrows pulled down over his brown eyes. "Looking for you. Steven came by my house, asking if I'd seen you. It didn't take long for me to guess where you might be." He stood and lifted me into a standing position, but my legs wobbled, and I couldn't stand on my own. After a moment of assessment, he shrugged and swept my legs out from under me before cradling me against his chest.

Too tired to resist, I rested my head against his shoulder and wrapped my arms around his neck. He carried me to his car and fumbled with the door before he was able to open it and awkwardly set me down in the passenger seat.

"But my car," I protested, trying and failing to stand.

"We'll come back for it tomorrow," Nate promised, resting his hand briefly on my shoulder.

For a moment, I considered arguing with him, but I didn't have the energy. He shut the door and went to the driver's side.

"I need to let Steven know I found you, and then I can take you home," he said as he climbed in beside me.

"Can we go back to your place?" I asked. "If my family is looking for me, they're likely to descend in a worried, frantic mess, especially after how I've acted the last week." I swallowed. "I'd really rather not deal with that tonight."

"I'll take you wherever you want," Nate said with a sideways glance as he pulled out his phone. He dialed Steven and faced the window.

I only half listened to his conversation. He had turned the car on, and I basked in the heat flowing from the vents. I hadn't realized just how cold I was until he tried to help me stand. I held my frozen hands up to the warm air and worked to rub some feeling back into them.

"I told Steven I was going to take you to get something to eat," Nate said as he put his phone away and got the car in gear. "We can stop at a drive-through on the way."

I looked at him then, and all the words that I needed to say to him caught in my throat. Maybe I should have gone home. Dealing with my family couldn't be any worse than the uncomfortable conversation we were about to have.

As if he could sense my thoughts, Nate glanced at me. "Let's just focus on getting you warm and fed. Nothing needs to be decided tonight."

We drove through the town in silence, speaking only long enough for Nate to determine where to stop and what to order. When we reached his house, Nate climbed out first and rushed to help me. The warm car had helped significantly with thawing my limbs, and I was able to stand and walk on my own. I still accepted his offered arm, both to prevent myself from falling flat on my face and to have a reason to touch him. Despite his assurances that we didn't need to talk, I disagreed. And the sooner we had that conversation, the better.

Lucky greeted us at the door, his tail thumping against the wall. Nate helped me out of my coat and led me to the kitchen. When he flicked on the light, Shadow blinked up at me lazily from his bowl, and I bent to pat his gray head.

"Have you given any thought to pursuing your dreams beyond working at the shelter?" I asked.

Nate set our food on the table. "I have." He glanced at me before grabbing some napkins. "I've actually signed up to take a few courses in the fall for a veterinarian tech assistant."

"That's great news!" I sank into a seat on one side of his small table, so he took the chair across from me. "But what about the shop?"

He shrugged, unwrapping his burger. "I talked to Jeff about a promotion. He seemed enthusiastic about the idea, so I could cut back on my hours."

I smiled at him. Regardless of what happened between us, I wanted him to be happy.

He gave me a tentative smile in return then gestured to my untouched food. "Eat. I can hear your stomach growling."

I scowled at him but obeyed. It hadn't occurred to me how hungry I was until I'd devoured my burger and started on my fries. While he tried to be discreet, I could feel his eyes on me, like he thought I might collapse on the spot.

"You can stop looking at me as if I'm going to break," I said, raising an eyebrow.

Nate's wrinkled brow cleared as he gave me a broad grin. "I'm just checking for hypothermia."

I rolled my eyes. Though it was early March, it had been a relatively warm day, and I'd worn a coat. "It's not that cold out."

"You'd be surprised," Nate said, turning serious. "Lanie, what were you doing out there for so long?"

"I-I..." I began, dropping my gaze. "I was... processing."

"But why there?"

"I needed to tell my mother a few things," I admitted, my cheeks heating. Would he think it was stupid? Talking to a dead person?

"I understand," he said, and his face was sincere. "But why didn't you tell anyone where you were going?"

With a shrug, I fiddled with my food wrapper. "I wanted to be alone. And it gave me time to think."

"About?"

I let out a long breath. "My grief." At his puzzled expression, I raked my hands through my hair. "When my mom passed, I didn't really deal with it. Yes, I went to the viewing and the funeral, and I cried, but... I compartmentalized everything." I gestured toward the front door. "It helped to leave this town. At school, I was so busy trying to cram two semesters into one, I didn't have time to grieve. And then when I came home, between the estate, the house, the car, and you…" I cleared my throat. "I was able to distract myself from my loss. But today, I realized how much of my life she'll miss out on." My eyes watered, and I shook my head. "Like if I get married one day, she won't… she won't…"

"She won't be at your wedding." He slid his hand across the table. I slipped mine into it, giving him a grateful smile. He squeezed my hand, and for a moment, neither of us said anything.

"Honestly, knowing Melody, she'll be there." He chuckled. "And you'll know if she's unhappy with the decorations or venue because something will break or spoil."

I laughed. "You really know my mom!" My smile faded. "But it's not just about a wedding. It's… my whole life."

"I'm sorry, Lanie," he said, bowing his head. "I had no idea."

It reminded me of the last time I'd seen him, and my heart ached. I'd said some harsh things that

I regretted. Rehashing the past might have given me the answers to questions that had haunted me for years, but they didn't make me feel any better. If anything, I felt worse.

"You couldn't have known." I waved a dismissive hand. "It didn't really hit me until today." I leaned back in my chair and sighed. "Besides, I didn't tell anyone what I was doing or where I was going, and I turned off my phone."

Nate didn't respond. I wanted to ask him if he'd received the note. I wanted to learn what he thought of my mom's final words to him. But I couldn't bring myself to ask. The elephant between us had returned, and I felt its presence like a crushing weight on my chest.

I stood and crumpled my sandwich wrapper before tossing it into the empty fry container. He followed and pulled out a trash can in the bottom cabinet by the fridge. When I turned back to him, my breath caught in my throat at how close we were, but he took a step back.

My heart plummeted, and I started to move past him. Then I stopped and took his hand in mine, searching his face for answers to the question I couldn't voice. He stared back, his expression neutral, but a spark of heat lit his dark eyes, and I knew it was now or never.

"We need to talk."

Nate started shaking his head. "Not tonight, Lanie. You've been through enough. You need rest. I'll take you home."

"No," I said firmly. "We've been dancing around this for long enough." I pulled him into the living room, where we sat stiffly on his couch, facing each other.

He shifted beside me as if preparing for an argument. "What do you want to talk about?"

"Did you get the note?" I asked, ducking to catch his eye.

He nodded, keeping his gaze on the floor. "But I already knew she wanted me to keep my promise."

"I left it for you because of the other part," I said. "When she told you to take care of me."

"It'll be a little hard to do that when you're in California," he replied, attempting to lighten the mood, but I didn't laugh.

"I'm not going to California."

His head snapped up. "Why wouldn't you go?" His eyes searched mine. "Didn't you already turn down the job here?"

"No, I accepted it. And I let the school in California know I'm staying as well."

He stared at me. "When?"

"This afternoon, before I stopped by your house."

His throat moved as he swallowed. "But I assumed... I mean, after everything's that happened... Why would you want to stay?"

"I love the kids at the school, and I would miss them," I said, lowering my gaze. "This is my home, even if I thought I didn't want it to be for a while." Steeling myself for his reaction, I raised my eyes and met his gaze. "And then there's you."

"Me?" A spark of hope danced in his eyes, but he blinked it away.

"Nate." I frowned. "After everything we've been through these past few weeks, do you really not know how much you mean to me?"

"I know our time together has stirred up a lot of old feelings for you," Nate replied gruffly. "But I don't expect you to forgive me for what I did. As you said the other day, I didn't ask you what you wanted. I let your mother get to me."

"I was hurt and confused. You have no idea how much your actions during my first semester have haunted me all these years." I leaned forward, placing a hand on his arm. "It's not going to be easy, and I imagine we'll have many bumps along the way, but I want to make that journey with you."

"You do?"

"Of course I do. Nate, don't you understand how much I care for you?"

"But that's not the same as—"

I took his hand and traced delicate lines on his palm. I waited for him to continue, and when he didn't, I looked up at him.

"It's not the same as love?" I finally asked. "Is that what you wanted to say?"

Nate nodded. I slid closer to him, wrapping my arms around him and laying my head on his chest.

"I do love you, Nate." My voice was barely above a whisper. I listened to his heart pounding against my ear. "I don't think I ever stopped."

His arms tightened around me. Then he gently grasped my shoulders and moved me back just enough to look at me.

"I *know* I never stopped loving you," he said with conviction. My eyes welled up again but that time with happy tears, and I hugged him, never wanting to let go.

When I pulled back, his eyes met mine with a question, and he reached up and cupped my cheek. I leaned forward and brushed my lips against his. His hands slid into my hair and pulled me closer, deepening the kiss. If I'd had any lingering doubts about staying in Cedar Haven, they melted away.

We stayed up most of the night, reminiscing, talking, laughing, and eventually falling asleep together on the couch, in each other's arms. I woke the next morning before Nate and went to the kitchen in search of coffee.

After brewing myself a cup, I stepped toward the sliding glass door overlooking the back yard. The cardinal perched on a tree nearby, looking in at me.

"I could have used you yesterday," I accused, pointing at it. "Where were you then, hmm?"

The bird lifted its wings in what looked like a shrug and chirped. I shook my head and laughed. When I turned around, Nate stood in the doorway, watching me.

"I see your mom's come to visit," he said, moving into the room and wrapping his arms around my waist.

"So she has," I replied, leaning into him. "I guess this means she approves?"

"I hope so."

I turned to face him before sliding my arms around his neck and giving him a quick kiss. "I know so." When we glanced back out the window, the cardinal was gone.

Epilogue

Two Months Later

I stood with Nate in the high school parking lot, watching my students prepare for the Memorial Day parade. I'd been working with Mrs. Carlisle for a little over a month, and soon, the school year would be over, and I would spend the summer preparing for the start of my first year as a teacher. In the meantime, I was looking for a place to live. While staying with my dad had its perks, I was more than ready to move out on my own.

I'd asked Nate to help put together the float, and his mechanical skills had certainly come in handy in making sure all the moving parts worked correctly. The kids had opted to create a fireworks float with lights set up to look like fireworks bursting in the sky.

As the kids prepared to leave to join the parade route, I slipped my hand into Nate's and gave it a gentle squeeze. It seemed the most natural thing in the world. We'd spent so much time together that spring, working on the float, helping Steven and Rose plan their wedding, and just enjoying being back together. With the summer coming, I hoped we might do some traveling as well.

"This feels like old times," I said as I stepped forward to fix a string of lights that had fallen out of place.

"I was just thinking the same thing," Nate replied with a warm smile.

My eyes met his, and the familiar electricity hummed between us. We were surrounded by giggling children, but somehow, it was as if we were the only two people in the room.

"Miss McAllister," Robert said, pulling on my arm. "I think it's our turn to join the parade."

I glanced up to see Mrs. Carlisle waving at me from across the way. "Let's go gather up the rest of our group."

We formed a quick circle as Nate made one last check of the float. I gave my students a pep talk before sending them onto the float to take their places. When I stepped back over to him, he slid his arms around my shoulders.

"You really are an amazing teacher," he said.

As the float began to move, we walked hand in hand with a few of my students. I couldn't imagine being happier than I was at that moment, parading through my hometown with my high school sweetheart by my side.

The parade route was mercifully short, which was a relief in the late-May heat and humidity. Once all of the children were reunited with their parents, I collapsed against the float and let out a sigh.

"I love those kids, but I'm very glad today is over."

"I hope you're not too tired," Nate said as he walked over to me.

"Did we have plans?" I asked, racking my brain. I didn't recall anything specific.

"No, but I have a surprise for you."

I sat upright. A surprise? I loved surprises! "Ooh, where is it?" I searched the storage room.

Nate chuckled. "It's not here. You have to come with me."

"Where are we going?" I asked when I saw we weren't heading toward Nate's car.

"Just trust me," Nate insisted.

We walked up to the building, which only confused me further. He grinned and grabbed my hand again, pulling me toward the auditorium doors.

"Nate, what are you doing? We can't break in."

"We don't have to," he said slyly as he reached in his pocket and pulled out a key.

"What the—" I gasped. "How did you get that?"

"I have my ways." He unlocked the door and led me toward the front of the theatre.

My eyes widened as I took in the stage. It was lined with LED candles, and it looked like someone had sprinkled something over the floor. As we drew nearer, the sweet scent of roses filled my nostrils. In the dim light, he helped me up the stairs and moved to center stage.

"What's going on?" I looked around with wonder. Rose petals were scattered across the stage in the shape of a heart. "Who did all this?" When I turned to him, he wasn't there. "Nate—"

He kneeled before me.

"Oh," I said.

"I wanted to bring you here, to the place where it all started. Where *we* started. To ask you a question."

I stared at him in disbelief. *Is he really...? Is this actually...?* My heart pounded in my chest as butterflies burst into flight in my stomach.

He held fast to my hand while the other reached into his pocket and removed a small blue box. With careful dexterity, he opened the box and held it up. Inside was the most beautiful ring I had ever seen—a white gold claddagh ring, an Irish symbol with two hands holding a heart-shaped diamond topped with a crown.

"Lanie, I bought this ring the summer before our freshman year of college, and despite all that happened between us, I held on to it in the hope that one day, you might come back to me. Will you marry me?"

I nodded, unable to speak around the lump in my throat. He had bought that ring when we were first together and kept it the whole time?

"You have to say yes," he prompted, his lips quirking up in an amused smile.

"Yes," I finally managed to croak out. His smile widened, and he slid the ring onto my finger. I pulled his hand, and when he stood, I threw my arms around him.

"I can't believe you've had this for so long."

"You were worth the wait," he murmured as he kissed me.

We stood on the stage for what seemed like forever but would never be long enough for me. I couldn't stop smiling. Everything about the moment was perfect, from the ring to the location to Nate. I'd never been happier.

"We should probably get to your dad's house," Nate said, his voice reluctant. "I know some people who are dying to know your answer."

"You told them?" I asked.

"I asked your father's permission, and I assume he told Steven and Rose."

I nodded, and we returned to the entrance. "What about all that?" I gestured at the candles on the stage.

"I'll be back for those later," he replied with a twinkle in his eye.

As we walked outside, a flash of red caught my attention. "Look!"

The cardinal perched on Nate's car. In the dim light of the setting sun, it seemed to almost be smiling. Nate reached for my hand, and the cardinal spread its wings and bowed before taking flight. It circled over our heads once before soaring into the sky, beyond where we could see.

~ele~

Enjoyed this story? You can make a difference!

Honest reviews of my books help bring them to the attention of other readers.

If you've enjoyed this book, I would be very grateful if you would consider spending just five minutes leaving a review (it can be as long or as short as you like) on the book's Goodreads' page.

You can jump right to the page by using the code below.

About the Author

Katie Eagan Schenck writes sweet romance and women's fiction that warms the heart and gives all the feels. She has an MFA in creative writing from Queens University of Charlotte and her debut novel, A Home for Christmas, was released in October of 2022. When she's not writing she's either drafting regulations for the federal government, baking delicious treats, or binging

Hallmark movies. She lives in Maryland with her husband, daughter, and their three cats. Connect with Katie on her website at keschenckauthor.com, instagram: @keschenckauthor, or Facebook: @keschenck

Also By Katie Eagan Schenck

A Home for Christmas
A Marine has just one wish this Christmas: a home.
Available at all major retailers.

The Love Birds trilogy
When Cardinals Appear, *When Swans Dance*, and *When Doves Lament*
Available at all major retailers.

Acknowledgements

First and foremost, I'd like to thank my mother, who encouraged me to pursue my dream of writing from the tender age of eight. I want to thank my husband and daughter, who have provided me with so much love and support throughout the whole process. Thanks to my father, whose quiet observations have impacted many of the choices I've made, and to my step-mother who helped me through one of the hardest experiences of my life. And a huge debt of gratitude goes to my brother and sister, who never gave up on me, even when I felt like giving up on myself.

I want to thank the teachers who believed in me, from the second-grade teacher who first saw promise in my writing to two influential high school English teachers. Thanks to the MFA faculty and staff at Queens University of Charlotte, who gave me the support, but more importantly, the deadlines I needed to finish this book!

I'd be remiss not to thank Angela McRae at Red Adept Editing for her wonderful help with cleaning up the book; Kathleen Sweeney at Book Brush for the beautiful cover; and Bryn Donovan whose coaching gave me the courage to put this book out into the world.

Finally, thanks to all my friends who have offered feedback on my writing over the years, especially those of you who were unfortunate enough to read my angsty teenage poetry. They say it takes a village to raise a child, and I think it takes at least that, and so much more, to raise a writer.